BY MOOR AND FELL

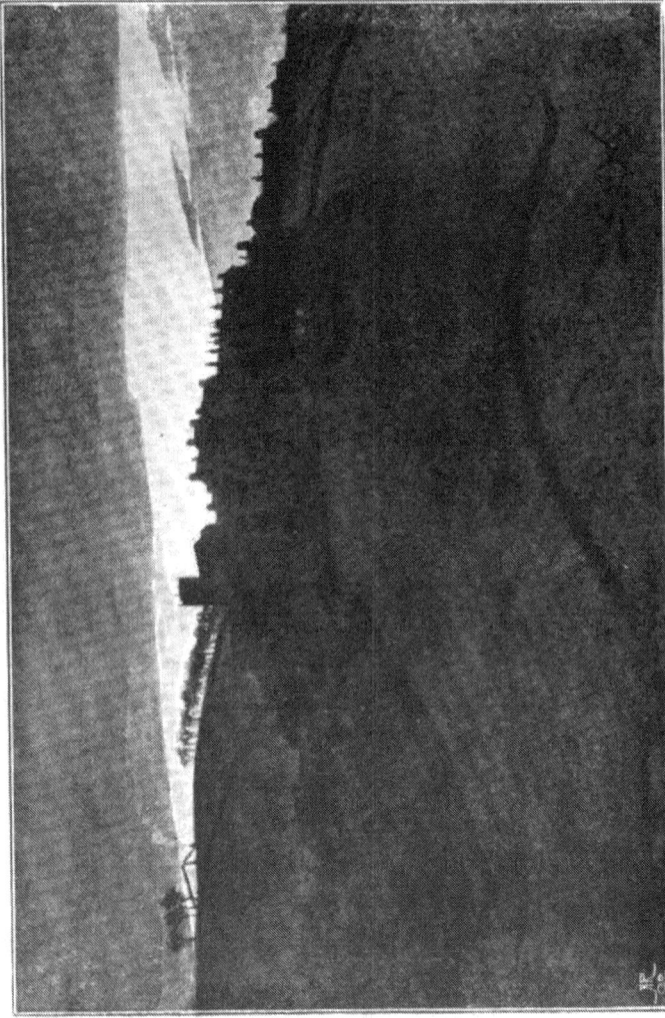

Haworth by the Moors.

AND LANDSCAPE

WEST YORKSHIRE

ILL S

BY MOOR AND FELL

LANDSCAPES AND LANG-SETTLE
LORE FROM WEST YORKSHIRE

BY

HALLIWELL SUTCLIFFE

Author of

"RICROFT OF WITHENS," "SHAMELESS WAYNE," ETC.

WITH SEVENTY-SEVEN
ILLUSTRATIONS BY
GEORGE HERING ✛ ✛

LONDON: T. FISHER UNWIN
PATERNOSTER SQUARE. MDCCCXCIX

CONTENTS

CONTENTS

CHAPTER I

HAWORTH

A VILLAGE unlike any other that has been, or that will be. A village whose charm ripens with long acquaintance, until, when one has known it long enough, its image dwarfs all others. A village which, like the folk who live in it, shows only to the eye of intimacy the charm and the distinction which underlie its rugged front.

Look at it from the opposite hill-slope, where the wide

sandstone road dips down between its double row of
walls into the valley of the Worth.   Close against a wild
spur of moor it lies, this Haworth, dark with age and
storms ; it seems to have clambered up the steep face of
the hill as far as its strength would allow, and then to
have clung there with might and main, unable to climb
higher, yet determined to yield no single inch of foothold gained.   Above the houses a few lean fields slope
up to the heather-line, and the square church tower
stands out black against the haze of moorland beyond.
Strong, grim, and self-reliant looks Haworth village, and
the grey sky, streaked with a sullen line of sunset red, fits
well its chill aloofness.

Or approach it from the road yonder which leads past
Manuels Heights and Flappit Spring, and Haworth shows
us a new face entirely ; it is no solid, close-packed
mass of houses now, but a long, straight-climbing street ;
the roofs seem to lean one upon the other ; the church
is half-resting on its neighbours, half-shouldering the
sky.   It is six of a clear June morning, say, and the
village has a curious quaintness, with the light haze
rounding off a little of its sterner aspect, and the blue sky
smiling at its gravity.   Haworth has changed ; it shows
no longer as a sturdy child of wind and storm, but
rather as a dim city of the clouds, which would melt
into the middle-blue if one attempted to set foot in it.

Or, last of all, stand at the bend of its one steep street
and look up toward the summit, where the signboard of

The Steep-streeted Village.

the "Black Bull" tavern swings out across the roadway. Like the Miller of the Dee is Haworth village, seen at close quarters—"I care for nobody, no, not I," it says from every line of its sturdy front. The street is narrow and rutty-hard of pavement; the houses run up and tilt at the sky itself; a thick-thewed cart-horse, half toward the top of the merciless climb, strives to make forward with its load, and down the street a lumbering stone-waggon comes jolting, slipping, swinging, while the brake creaks and sobs against the wheel in melancholy protest. Voice of the peewit over the heather, and creak of heavy-laden wains from quarry-land—these are the keynotes of Haworth village, the two sounds which, wherever heard, bring back to the heart of the heath-born man this land of peat and stone and scanty, thin-soiled fields.

Thoughts throng in on one while standing quiet in Haworth main street here, with the ghosts of a near past elbowing the workaday routine of life. Strangers come and go, thinking that the Brontës gave Haworth all its charm; but we who know it, whose fathers knew it before it was in touch with the outer world, have no sense of this sort; for before the Brontës crept into its life, to observe, and shiver a little, and reproduce, the village was hoary with storm and legend, instinct with the glamour which to-day is strong upon its children. Some part of this glamour the three sisters caught, and caught it deftly. They struggled against difficulty, hardship;

they came as "foreigners," and the villagers never
altogether lost suspicion of them on that count; there
was poverty within-doors and a harsh climate without
against which to battle. Yet even Charlotte, who had so
little understanding of the moors and the moor folk—
who could, indeed, prefer the soft purple of the August
heath to its deeper lore of grey winter and grim storm—
even she was drawn, in her own despite, perhaps, to
glean from the stern life about her those qualities of
straightforwardness, simplicity of passion, unswerving
faithfulness to the springs of human thought and action,
which have made her novels masterpieces of a rare and
satisfying kind.

And if Charlotte could gather inspiration from this
mother of the harsh front and generous heart, what is to
be said of Emily—the shy, self-centred girl who shrank
from her fellows, who nursed her lonely passion for the
moors until it brought to birth the most stupendous book
that ever startled, or shocked, or gladdened, a world that,
for the most part, could not understand its message? It
is Emily who stands as the greatest of the three, Emily
whose presence seems at times to overshadow Haworth;
yet the master is more than the disciple, and the village
stands, now as then, secure in older memories.

What is it that gives this moorland village the quality
which attracts at the first glance? Words cannot draw
its subtle lights and shades, its harsh, rough-careless
lines. Neither can the pencil give them altogether. Just

three places there are that impress on one the same atmosphere of singularity and charm. One is Clovelly, the second, Edinburgh, and the third is Haworth village, as seen from the middle of its street. Yet Haworth's charm eludes comparison ; there is none like it the world through ; there will never be another like it, for the race which built it is dying, up there among the silent moors.

Dying ? The thought creeps in and takes one unawares. Is it just the Haworth of to-day one has been picturing, or the Haworth of a bygone time ? A glance here and there shows a new house breaking the dark line of the street ; in the trough of the valley, out of sight, but scarcely out of mind, more than one factory pushes its lean chimney above lean blocks of modern cottages ; one does not know every face that passes one nowadays in the street, and even the natives move with a certain sense of hurry in their steps, with less of the old assured leisureliness that came of the knowledge of much honest work to be done and plenty of time in which to do it. The dialect is losing its smoothness, its Doric dignity, by contact with the debased speech of the towns, and we have to push out to the remoter villages to be sure of finding that rich, straight-set-up, tawny speech which seems to carry us back in a moment to the days of strong thews and downright blows. The Haworth we know blends insensibly with the Haworth that is, and only the stranger can say how much of its ancient, quaint simplicity is left.

Yet the " Black Bull " tavern is much the same. The same good Haworth name of Sugden stands above the doorway that has stood there time out of mind ; the cosy look of things indoors is warranty that modern make-shifts of comfort are not yet in date up here ; the plenty and wholesomeness of fare is reminiscent of the staunch appetites of old. There's no passing by this open door-

Haworth, from the Moor-edge.

way of the " Bull " ; its welcome is a friend's, and it were churlish to refuse its bidding to the snug back parlour which once was Branwell Brontë's especial haunt. The liquor is good here, but the company is likely to be better still if one finds a group of natives foregathered round the parlour table. They must be natives, though —must have been born in the parish, of parents whose fathers were born in the parish—otherwise one will miss the true flavour of the tales which, handed down from father to son, stand in place of the written history of Haworth.

There is Dick o' th' Hoyle Clough there to-day, let us say, and Tom o' Nat's o' Martha's, and a few others of the same kidney. Get the Branwell arm-chair if possible, for it is comfortable, and a full glass, and listen to the slow speech that comes from between slow-trailing puffs of smoke. Tale follows tale, each salted with dry York-shire wit and peppered with many a rough characteristic of olden days ; but Dick o' th' Hoyle Clough is the prime greybeard of them all. He is tall and spare, with not an ounce of fat on him and muscles that have astonished many an adversary time and time ; he may have done a little poaching in his day, but we are not concerned with what happened on the other side of the hedge ; he has been a "Scotchman," or travelling pedlar, has farmed a bit, has built a cottage or two, and knows the ways of shepherding or the price within half-a-crown of any beast you like to bring him ; above all, he has done much healthful leaning over gates, and has kept his bright grey eyes very open on a world which he has enjoyed to the full.

"Now, that brings to mind summat I'd forgotten this mony a year," says Dickie, comfortably settled with a fresh mug of home-brewed. "Ye'll call owd Jose Wark to mind ?"

You answer nothing if you are wise. One man may lead up to a Yorkshireman's story, but twenty cannot make him tell the same, unless they are willing to give him time in which to chew the cud of it.

"Eh, but he war a rum un, war Jose, an' proper," goes on Dick o' th' Hoyle Clough, after a long pause. "I mind him weel, though I war nobbut shoulder-high when he hed long sons of his own. A varry weel-set-up sort o' chap he war, so I've heard tell, i' th' days when Wellington war by way o' dressing owd Boney his jacket. Jose wanted to be wed, an' he'd getten a snug little farm ower agen Smithbank, an' th' lass war willing."

"They mostly is, is th' lasses," chuckles Dickie's right-hand neighbour—a burly, weather-reddened farmer, with a thick thatch of hair and twinkling, sloe-black eyes.

"Well, howsiver, he war bahn to be wed; an' just when all looked straight as a well-mown swathe o' grass, there comes a press-gang into Howarth Parish, an' they catched Jose lad as he war wending toward th' courting."

"Happen it saved him fro' summat war; happen lead bullets is easier to stand up agen nor a nattering wife," puts in the other, winking over the edge of his glass.

"That's as may be—an' tha should know, Ephraim, about th' way of a nattering wife," retorts Dickie grimly.

The laughter that greets this sally only serves to make Dick o' th' Clough more sober of face than ever, as his glance wanders round the company.

"Well, as I war saying," he goes on, "they catched

him, an' took him all th' way to Keighley, an' brought him
afore th' doctor-chap.   An' Jose, who hed carred varry
quiet-like on th' road to Keighley, war ta'en all on a
sudden wi' shiverings an' shakings, an' shakings an'
shiverings, till he fell i' a lump on th' floor ; an' it warn't
till they'd gi'en him a skinful o' rum that he framed to
stand on his shaky pins again.

" 'What ails thee, lad ? ' asks th' doctor.

" 'Nay, I know not,' says Jose.   'I wark,' says he—
' wark (*ache*) all ower—I cannot stand, nor lig, nor sit me
down, an' it's nobbut when I bend doubleways 'at I can
get a bit of ease.'

" Now th' doctor war a middling sharp chap, as doctors
an' sich go, an' ' Happen he's nobbut shamming,' says
he to a fellow i' fine feathers that stood close beside him.
Leastways, that's as Jose Wark telled me th' tale, for I
can't rightly say I war there myseln."

" Tha'd be a bonnie liar if tha did, ony way," murmurs
Ephraim.

" Well, Jose screwed hisseln into queerer knots nor
iver when he fund 'at th' doctor thowt he war shamming ;
an' he stutters out, all as gaumless as a new-hatched
chick, that he'd niver been th' same man sin' a load o'
hay fell fair atop on him a seven-week come Martinmas ;
an' th' doctor screws up his mouth at that, an' looks him
up an' dahn, an' jabbers to hisseln for a bit—an' then
he sends him packing.   Begow, but Jose niver stopped
running, sooin as he war out o' th' doctor's sight, till he'd

won safe inside th' 'Bull' here! An' my father's telled
me mony a time how he sat him down i' yond arm-chair
an' tried to fetch his breath—an' when th' breath came,
it war like blacksmith's bellows, nawther more nor less."

Dick o' th' Clough stops ; then, "By th' Heart," he
says, with a regretful shake of the head, "by th' Heart,
but they drank a sight o' stuff, an' proper, that neet. Th'
owd days hev passed away, I'm thinking, an' war hev
stepped into their shooin ; we're no drinkers, not to call
drinkers, i' these times."

"Nay, pike up, lad! Tha'rt varry fair at th' job yet,"
puts in Ephraim of the ruddy face, with a laugh that
shakes his whole round-bellied frame.

"A quart or two—I can tak my quart or so, I'm noan
denying," says Dick o' th' Clough modestly. "Well, ony
road, it like as it cured Jose lad of his warks for gooid an'
all, did that fair neet's go at th' drinking, far he war niver
known to complain o' pains an' warks again till he'd
getten weel on t' other side o' threescore. But th' name,
ye'll mark, stuck to him like a thistle-burr, an' Jose Wark
he war till th' end. Well, well, he war a rum un, war
Jose, choose who hears me say 't."

"Warn't it Jose Lad, an' all, what used to reckon to
bargain while he milked his cows?" asks a man from
the other side of the hearth.

"I should think it war! I've stopped mony a neet
when I've been Smithbank way at milking-time, an' set
my ears to th' mistal-door, an' heard Jose bargaining

away as if he'd getten all th' beasts i' Marshcotes to sell—
an' nobody theer to bargain wi', save th' owd cow he
war milking. Begow, but I mind heving a rare laugh
out o' Jose one day. He wod niver tak onybody's bid,
whativer he war selling ; so, knowing his way, I says to
him—it war a matter of a chitty-prat hen he'd getten
to sell—' Jose,' says I, ' what wilt tak for th' bird ?' ' I'll
tak a shilling an' twopence,' says he. ' Nay,' says I, ' I'll
gie thee fourteenpence,' I says. ' I willun't,' cries Jose ;
' I'll tak not a farthing less nor one an' twopence—not a
farthing less,' says he. An' sakes, he niver fund out 'at
I'd offered him what he axed—an' that war a sight more
nor th' owd chitty-prat war worth."

Dickie, after chuckling quietly at the reminiscence,
holds up his glass to the light and eyes it grudgingly.

" Th' beer is noan what it war, noan what it war," he
growls. "I mind th' time when th' ' Bull' watter ran
right through th' kirkyard—thick an' strong it war, afore
iver it touched th' malt. I tell ye, th' beer hed *body*
in't i' them days."

Dick o' th' Clough is a good hand at the gruesome, as
all his kind are. One leaves the back parlour with the
twang of that last jest on the tongue ; for it is as characteristic of the old Yorkshire wit as anything one could have
heard in Haworth village.

The churchyard which made the " Bull " ale what it
was lies close against the back wall of the tavern—the
very windows are there, as they were fifty years ago,

through which Branwell Brontë used to make good his
escape from the inn when friends entered at the front
in ill-timed search of him. Above is the Parsonage,
its sad grey front half hidden behind trees of recent
growth; and between the church and the "Bull" the
stocks once stood—a curious situation, suggesting that

the clients of parson or publican had frequent and
urgent need of them.

And what of the church? Only the tower is left of
the old structure, and of the new building there is nothing
to be said. It pleased the vicar, doubtless, under whose
auspices it was built; it has no solitary detail in keeping
with its surroundings. The mind goes back to the rough,
ungraceful lines of the old fabric, its plain honesty within,

its roomy family pews ; it was a moorland church, hard
of comfort, stout of wall, and the moor-winds were at
home with it.

There was an oddity about the pews, moreover ;
strangers were often puzzled by an inscription on the
door-plate to the effect that so-and-so held three and a-
half sittings in the pew, and so-and-so two and a-half
sittings. The usual assumption was that the halves stood
for children ; but in fact they meant that one holder of a
half-sitting could attend morning service, the other,
evensong.

The clerical element in Haworth life bulked large
aforetime. There was Grimshaw, rector at the time of
the Jacobite rebellion, a friend of Wesley, and quick to see
that the temper of the moor folk craved strong spiritual
meat, served " hot from the backstone " and naked of the
rags of ceremony. A brawny Christian, Grimshaw, whose
duty and pleasure alike it was to get down from the
three-decker while the hymn before the sermon was being
sung, to snatch up a hunting-crop which he kept ready in
the vestry, and to clear the "Black Bull" of all and sundry
who were drinking there. A man after the people's own
heart, muscular, unflinching, singularly heedless of class
distinctions ; a pastor who, Churchman as he was, helped
to make Methodism the dominant religion in Haworth
and in every neighbouring village of the moorside. Yet
Grimshaw had had his gay days—had been a mighty
drinker, a reveller, a squire of dames ; and the hunting-

crop with which in later years he pressed laggard sheep
into the fold had ridden with him in the wake of many a
fox and hare, with din of hounds between.   A health to
you, old parson, in a cup of the rarest wine that ever you
forswore !

And so back from the old church, with its busy Sabbath
life of praying parson and droning clerk and shifting of
farmers' stout-soled boots on the floors of oaken pews—
back to the churchyard, which is the same to-day in all
essentials as it was yesterday.   Looking upward from the
church porch, the stones, of many shapes and sizes, but
all of the one sober grey-black, seem to be jostling one
another in the effort to find room ; there is scarce a strip
of ground where one can tread without disturbing some
one's sleep.   Quiet, almost happy, look these green
shrouds of the dead, with the sunlight warm upon them
and the breeze soft-murmuring from the south.   Yet this
is but a Dead Man's Holiday in Haworth churchyard.
Close to the moor it lies, and the moor is not often gentle
as it is to-day ; there will be storms soon, and ravening
winds ; the rain will drive pitilessly down, down, till,
through the sodden earth, it gains the helpless folk who
slumber underneath ; hail will hiss between the wind's
teeth ; bitter cold it will be, above and below ground, and
not the living alone, but the dead, will surely tremble at
their loneliness.

As one strolls in and out among the graves, their
lettered headstones bring back a crowd of half-forgotten

stories. One could sit here for a day, with names of Shackleton and Horsfall, Sunderland and Heaton, to keep one company, and never weary of retraversing the paths of old remembrance. Here's this old fellow, who died at fourscore—he mortgaged his every yard of land to feed a love of horseflesh ; and the greybeard yonder, lying beside the sons and daughters of his

discreeter years, sleeps quiet upon the memory of how once on a time he used to poach his father's game for sport. Nay, but the road that Haworth gravestones point is long, and gloaming would surprise us by the way if once we trusted to their guidance.

Yet most of all, as we stand here, do we realise how great a legacy, in truth, the Brontës have left to Haworth. It is here that they seem to spring to life again and move, real out of a past that is full of pathos, from the wind-swept Parsonage above. Behind its walls the tragic years moved by, no less tragic in that their stage was reared among petty household cares and petty ailments of the flesh. We can see Emily helping to set the tea-table, her thoughts far off among the wide moor spaces; there would be some new trouble of Branwell's, it may be, touching money or family pride; and while she pondered over the mean tale of pounds and pence, wondering how to meet this last call on the family purse, her mind would move unconsciously to Heathcliff, whose faults were Branwell's glorified, whose character, slow working in her brain, was growing to master her by its sheer brute strength and passionate heedlessness. The indignities of debt and dishonour touched Heathcliff's image not a whit; he was a Titan, rough-riding over details, and while she limned him large on the mighty canvas of the heath, she felt a pity that was almost one of understanding for the brother who was a faint image of her hero. This scene in the Parsonage; and below, at the far side of the " Bull" kitchen, whose pots and pans and polished dresser we can just see through the low window, Branwell chinked hard-won silver into pewter pots, and told his cronies swaggering tales of drink and racket and con-quests over the frailer sex; or he stared grimly at the peats, and heard life ring hollow as a drum; or again he sat with head in hands, weeping with a poet's frenzy and less than a poet's excuse for tears.

Ay, the " Bull," and the Parsonage, and the quiet graveyard, are alive with the voices of a generation gone—are
full of a curious, wry romance, that has needed no likelier
food to grow upon than the life histories of three weak-
bodied sisters and one drunken, witty, despicable, half-
lovable lad, who just lacked genius, and paid his price
for the omission. And though the Brontë story stands
in the minds of the village folk as a disjointed episode,
scarce touching the ordered channel in which their lives
ran before the Brontës came and went, strangers in their
midst, yet it has left its mark indelibly, and not till the
free moor is gained can one fall into touch again with the
Haworth that was and is—the village self-centred in the
wilderness.

CHAPTER II

PEAT AND HEATHER

ONLY a few pasture fields and a short strip of lane separate Haworth churchyard from the heath. The gate at the lane-top is open to-day, and the gap is filled by a haze-flecked strip of sky, across which a grouse whirrs cumbrously toward the higher land. A few strides further, and we are on the peat. The sky seems nearer than its wont; purple of heather and green of bents stretch far as the grim, three-legged cranes that keep watch above the quarry-pits; away to the right old Stanbury village stands, compact and sturdy, on its bluff spur of hill; and from this to Lancashire there is nothing but mile on mile of sweeping heather-land. Out there, beyond the quarry-pits, are lonely reaches

where the notes of grouse and curlew, of moor-tit and
snipe, are oftener heard than the fretful voice of man ;
out there, across the purple of the heather, are solitary
farmsteads, where you will find the speech and manners
of an older day, where the women are fearless-proud
and the men have won stout hearts and sinewy bodies
from the sweat of meagre-profitable work. Like a step

into a stronger world, a world of old, is the first stride
across Haworth Moor, though as yet the busy hum of
the quarries disputes the underlying stillness ; the wind
whistles a careless stave on its pipes of heather, and its
breath is clean and sharp.

Harbour Spring lies westward out across the moor,
and now it sees more strangers in a day than once
approached it in a twelvemonth. Nay, once it scarce

saw a human face, save of shepherd, farm lad, or
wandering sportsman, from mid-winter to the falling of
the next year's leaf; and then a new friend slipped into
its life—an eager little friend, with steadfast and inquiring
eyes, who began to come often and more often to this
hollow of the moors, and learned, little by little, the
secrets that the waving rowan branches yonder tell to
the splashing waters of the fall below. And the new
comrade was Charlotte Brontë, and she and Harbour
Spring dwelt long together, unhonoured and at peace,
until fame crept shadowy from the silence of the outer
world and robbed them both of privacy.

But to-day there is no such figure by the streamside;
instead, a keeper stands, gun under arm, on the round
shoulder of the hill that tops the fall. A bluff, square
bulk of a man he is, and his eyes are fixed dourly on
the valley-track that leads from Haworth. Figure and
attitude are familiar as the moorscape itself, and one
knows, as well as can be, that our keeper has sighted
offending "furriners" on the road below.

A climb of a few score yards, and one is close beside
him. He turns with a start at sound of footfalls through
the bilberry clumps, and something puckers the corners
of his mouth—something that might, if mellowed by a
day or two of sun, grow into a smile of welcome. There
is a silent interchange of pouches; pipes are filled and lit;
and while we lie among the bracken and smoke together,
he drops by easy stages into gossip of fifty years ago.

"Ay, it war a different spot then, war Howarth parish," he says. " They're a weaker lot, to my fancy, these latter-day youngsters 'at think they mun be going to dee if they nobbut scratch their little finger ; an', as for poachers, there isn't th' odd un to be fund worth naming. Begow, but we hed mony a rare set-to i' th' owd days ! Poach ? They'd steal th' eggs fro' under a sitting hen, an' niver let her know on't ! Ay, there war some sport i' besting sich as yond. I reckon th' keeper war th' only chap i' th' moorside that didn't poach—th' gentry couldn't keep their hands off one another's game —an' as for a Squire 'at lived ower Airedale way—ye'll hev heard tell on him—they do say as he used to tak his own pheasants i' t' neet-time to hev a laugh out of his keepers."

He stops and points down the stream with sudden wrath, for the strangers have turned the bend of the path below and are gazing upward at the falls.

"Now, look ye ! " he breaks out. " Can ye tell me what hes brought yond so far across th' moor ? Why, nowt no more nor Charlotte Brunté—little Charlotte o' th' Parsonage, as weakly, undersized a piece o' goods as iver I clapped een on. *Her* write printed books ? I'll niver believe it. She got some cleverish sort o' chap to write 'em for her, an' then put her name to 'em for pride ; an' that's Gospel truth, for I've seen her myseln often, an' it war plain to ony man 'at it took a bigger nor her to mak a printed book."

My friend pulls meditatively at his pipe for awhile, then bursts out afresh. "An', what's more, I wish nawther her nor onybody else hed iver written these 'Jane Eyres' an' 'Shirleys,' as they call 'em. Sich folk as yond reckon to mak a rare to-do about th' lass; they mun run here, an' they mun run there, peeping an' prying, an' talky-talking—an' all because she hed a bit

The Brigg below the Fall.

of a fancy, like, to tak a morning walk to th' waterfall here. I've seen her myseln, bless ye, sitting on th' flat stone yonder an' scribbling i' her book. An' now folk come trampling down t' ling, frightening th' grouse, stepping into th' nests, likely, at breeding time. Nay, I cannot thoyle it, I cannot thoyle it!"

He refills his pipe, rams home the tobacco with a

horny forefinger, then glances down again at the offenders. "Nobbut last summer, I war crossing th' moor just aboon here," he resumes presently, "an' I leets on two lasses. One war ligging i' t' ling, wi' her lap spread wide, an' i' her knee a brood o' nestling grouse war cheeping up at her. I war that mad I could hev throttled her; but she peeped up soft-like at me, an' seemed to think it queer I should mak sich a to-do about it. They looked so bonnie, said she, an' she didn't know 'at there war ony harm i' taking 'em fro' th' nest, to play wi' 'em for a bit. So I gav' her th' rough side o' my tongue, an' proper."

"And then the lass began to cry," I put in, "and you went softish on the sudden?"

"Well, now, I niver could bide to see a wench i' tears; an' happen I war noan so sour as I mud weel hev been, for I telled myseln 'at th' Lord hed framed women, an' th' Lord knew best. But little Charlotte o' th' Parsonage hes brought me a sight o' worry, an' that's truth; an' if that's what comes o' making printed books, I'd boil my kettle ower th' lot on 'em, that I wod."

One leaves the keeper presently, feeling one's self richer for the new light cast upon an old topic. Passing up the stream that joins the waterfall-brook in the hollow, one is free of the wilder moor at last; there is no road here, and the track twists in and out among the boulders, or crawls up the shifting peat-banks when the bed of the stream offers no rock-foothold. Ahead, the waterway climbs to the level edge of moor ; behind, the quarry-cranes are no longer to be seen, nor any sign of habitation save a few farmhouses perched on the right slope of the valley.

Suppose we go back a moment, for a better look at these farmsteads which have crept so far away from men, which serve, not to lessen the loneliness of the scene, but

to increase it. There is Bully Trees yonder, named after the yellow bullace-fruit that used to grow so sturdily about the moor-farms ; to-day it wears a softened look, with the dropping sunlight on it and the trees full-leaved, and one would have to see it at a nearer view to read the storm's message graven on its stones. But the farm next to it, higher up the slope, has no covering save a

gnarled old thorn-bush or two; it looks up wry and
grim at the blue sky and the sun, as if suspecting irony,
and summer can do little with its churlishness. Like
the moor itself, they have a strange, personal air about
them, these farmsteads. At a first glance their loneliness
seems pitiful; then it grows clear that they are proud of
their isolation, of the sturdy front they show to winter
and rough weather; lastly, one understands that they
are in keeping, as if they had not been built by hands,
but had grown with the landscape and out of it, like the
thorn-bushes, the rocks, and the rough-coated acres of
the heath that shut them in.

And if this holds of the houses on the fringe of cultivation, what shall be said of Withens, which tops the
rough bed of the waterway, and looks out suddenly on
us as we scramble over peat and boulders? To north
and south, east and west, the moor has its will; the
winds creep sobbing in the wake of desolation; no man
could force a livelihood from so hard a land, one would
have said; yet here, in the depths of the wilds, some
Greatheart of the spade—dead long ago—has set the
record of his challenge. Green and fair the intaken acres
lie, tranquil in the stern grasp of the heath; stout and
grey-black the buildings square their shoulders to the
wind. And here again we seem on the sudden to touch
hands with Emily Brontë. She is coming, say, up the
path which we have lately taken, with Charlotte, note-
book under arm, beside her. At the foot of Harbour

Spring their ways characteristically divide—Emily is
hungering for the wider spaces, her sister stays at the
half-way house where nature cannot altogether say
good-bye to the softer arts of men. Charlotte will ripen
lesser conceptions under shadow of the waterfall; she
will be bold in her love of heath and running stream,
timid a little in her backward glance at cultivation and
the pleased air she turns toward the distant hum of
workaday fret and labour; she will bring exquisite work
to birth, but its background will be narrowed by the
valley trees and the waving of soft leafage, its foreground
will be dwarfed into harmony with the hesitations, the
stammers, the shrinkings of convention.

But Emily keeps upward—finds a gap in the wall that
circles Withens, and crosses the lean fields, and rouses
every dog about the farmstead by a peremptory knocking
on the door. We follow this shrinking girl, who scarce
dares pass the time of day with her equals, and find her
sitting at her ease on the kitchen lang-settle, with the
shining pewter behind her on the walls and overhead
the oatcake hanging from the creel. She has lost her
shyness with the first step across the threshold; she
talks, like the upland folk who have given her welcome,
slowly and with surety, and into her speech there steals
many a pithy proverb, many a touch of that graphic
simile which is part and parcel of the upland tongue.
Presently she will go to the far mistal, to have a look at
the roan cow or to see how it is faring with the wye

calves newly weaned. She will be insatiably curious as to all farm implements, more eager still to draw blunt tales of fight and savagery, or of patient, ceaseless toil, from the men of the farm. She will get into wordy conflict with the oldest farm hand, who swears by all that is damnatory in the Book and rates all women lightly —most of all such women as have sickly frames, and pinched, white faces, and only a pair of deep grey eyes to tell of the virile, godlike spirit that lies behind.

This is surely one picture from Emily's odd, two-sided life. They tell us that she wrote from within, seeing so little of her kind that experience could have given her nothing. Yet genius cannot unaided set down the speech of these upland farms, their ways of life, so naturally that one steps out of the printed page into kitchen, or laithe, or mistal fragrant with the steam of milk. Was Joseph a creature of her brain ? How comes it, then, that he is, from the first gesture, thought, speech, to the last, the Joseph whom you will find to-day in any of the lone-lying farms about the moors ? But the child of the Parsonage grew shy again when she returned to the less understandable companionship of the village, and she kept her own counsel ; and none could explain at a later day whence came her knowledge of a life touching which Charlotte herself was ignorant. They said, accordingly, that it was imagination, or fancy, or a trick of genius.

Emily will not stay, however, at the farmstead here. The

nearness of house-walls stifles her after awhile; we see her climb up and up, until her figure, slight against the sunset red, dips over the moor-crest and is lost. The wilderness has found its mate.

And so back to one's own day of meaner issues. The sun is hurrying to bed, and nightfall will be on us if we dally longer by the way. A sharp turn to the right, and the scene changes after a mile or so of heath, for we come

Scholar's Path.

to a deep valley, green with meadowland and trees; farms are sprinkled more freely on either side; a pleasant stream runs down it, and skirting its left brink is a level, grassy road.

There is a story about this road. The Scholar made it, that he might take his favourite walk along a smooth path such as would allow him to read his books by the way. Thomas o' Buckley the Scholar was always known

as, but few at this date remember him. Like a shadow
he lived at the little house down yonder; like a shadow
he came and went among his fellow-men—reading,
always reading, from his musty books. He had a
hermit's oddities. The clock in his kitchen was silent
for twenty years because its ticking disturbed his studies.
He used to forget the flight of time, and it is said of him
that a neighbour, passing his garden one Sabbath morn,
found the old man digging there; and in answer to a
pious remonstrance, thrice repeated, Thomas o' Buckley
raised dim eyes.

"Is it a Sunday?" he asked.

"Ay, for sure."

"Well, then, I must put my spade by. I forget that
the days run on; sometimes they seem to stand, looking
over my shoulder as I read," he answered.

A gentleman he was, as well as a scholar, if tradition
deals fairly by him; he sought no company, found
none; he built his road, he read his books, and so crept
quietly into his shroud, leaving behind him a vague,
illusive sense of mystery such as sweetens the talk of a
countryside. Well, there is little in the tale, when all is
said; yet the thought of that frail old scholar, hiding
his past humanity among his mildewed folios, is one that
lingers with and haunts one, like the faint scent of
lavender plucked yester-year.

The valley widens and turns at the end of Scholar's
Path; the further side, steep and rocky, shows now

4

as a bold gash in the cheek of the moor. Once
there were eagles here, but now they have left the
glancing hawks in undisputed sovereignty. A light cart
is drawn up at the roadside, and a couple of men are
busy carrying bee-hives into the crannies of the rock-
face opposite. There is a responsive kindliness about
bee-keepers always—an alertness, too, picked up, it may
be, from the clever hive-folk which work for them. One
learns that they are very late with summering their bees,
for the heather is already passing its pride of bloom ;
that the honey of Haworth Parish is "hard to beat,"
since the bees have the run of field and garden flowers
during early summer, of heather when the bloom-time
comes ; that there is no flower, of wild thyme, rose, or
honeysuckle, which gives so rare a flavour to honey as
these red-purple bells of heather ; that once on a time
the rocks would have been planted thick with hives, but
that fewer bees are kept by farm folk and by cottagers
than formerly. Then follow tales of prodigious honey
harvests in the past, before the world grew old; of
swarms in buried Mays that were worth a load of hay
apiece; of curious situations chosen by the Queen Bee at
swarming-time.

With the slow voices of the rustics, as they tell their
tales, mingle the pleasant droning music of the hives,
the whisper of the quiet wind, the pebbly ripple of the
waters ; but that way sleep lies, and the sun is going
down in earnest. We'll take leave of these followers of

a gentle craft, and strike round the sharp bend of the
stream, and cross it, and continue along the further bank.
We are on the first of the bogland now. There are patches
of vivid green that yield to pressure of the foot with a
spongy, gurgling subsidence. All full of little rills and
rivulets the moor is, and
there are wider patches of
peat among the heather
clumps.   Half hidden
underground, and fringed
with fern and bog-weed,
lie the three wells which
go by the names of Robin
Hood, Little John, and Will Scarlett. One may stop to
ask how they came by their birth-names, to wonder
why a man should have troubled to fashion them in
this out-of-the-way spot; but neither speculation nor
questioning of the moor
folk brings one nearer to
an answer.   No house is
here, nor even a shep-
herd's hut ; yet the wells
have been built for a
definite use in some far-buried time. And the names?
The springs are so called in old maps, and could not
have been christened by any modern whose intercourse
with the outer world was wider than that of the upland
folk aforetime. Robin Hood one might understand, for

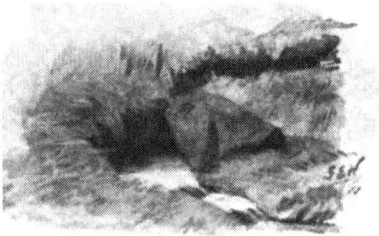

his name has long been current coin in the North ; but how came Little John and Will Scarlett so glibly to the moorland tongue ? Well, Sherwood Forest is not so far away as the crow flies, and Hathersage, where Little John's grave is—where, by the way, the lady of quality who gave Jane Eyre her name lies buried also—Hathersage must have been joined to Haworth by a well-nigh unbroken sweep of moor. There was a wide manory about Skipton then, and as fat deer in it as ever roamed through Sherwood ; Robin and his merry men found a change of scene convenient at times ; and their safest road to Skipton would lie straight over the moor here, and across the valley this side of Oakworth, and on into the dale of Aire. It may well have been that Lincoln green lightened, more than once, the soberer livery of the heather ; that plover and eagle screamed a fugitive defiance to the horn's challenge ; that the long-bow of yew, and the merry wanderers who fitted the wild-goose feather to the shaft, were honoured guests among the ruder fathers of the moor. Ay, and men of his own kidney would honest Robin find—hard-muscled fellows who could bend a bow with the best, who held lax views as to equality of rights in feathered game and furred ; for they were sportsmen ever in Haworth parish.

A turn to the westward here, and into the heart of
solitude. Less heather ; mile after mile of naked peat;
marshes, and round, black holes that are "filling"—which
are only half-liquid bog as yet, but which one day will
fill and widen and spread, till haply there will be another
bog-burst, such as fell like a thunder-clap on the moor
folk five-and-seventy years ago.

Small wonder if parson and people alike saw a visitation
of God in this catastrophe, so sudden, so unheard-of, so
awful in its brute, resistless strength. Looking now
across the grim land, it is hard to doubt that a conscious
soul lies under the dark, silent body—that the bog, as it
grew to a head with cynic quiet, was full of a wild, a
ravenous glee at thought of the time to come. Year's
rain had followed year's rain ; the liquid ooze pressed
more and more insistently against confinement, until,
after one last week of storm, it broke through all barriers
moved down into the valley, carried walls and rocks like
straws along its slimy current. And the people wondered
and were afraid.

Floods of clean, racing water they could understand—
thunder and tempest were no new experience to them—
but the bog moved slowly ; its solid, on-coming front
was black and sticky ; a man had time to count his sins
thrice over while the monster crept stealthily toward him.
It was at once a mystery, a very present terror, and a
portent. There are those about the moorside who
remember seeing the spectacle—awesome enough to

brand itself even upon childish brains—and they say that
it seemed as if the whole moor-top were turning over on
its side and rolling downward.

Reaching Worth Vale at last, the flood moved forward
into the waters of the Aire, blocking the archways of the
bridges or riving their pillars stone from stone ; and far
down toward the Humber the blocks of lighter surface-
peat could be seen floating like bales of wool above the
red-black waters. It has left its marks, too, this bog-
burst, on the land which nursed it to full strength, for the
streamway here is thick with boulders, little and big,
carried down by the moving wall of ooze and dropped
like pebbles in its path.

Patrick Brontë caught something of the horror that
was abroad, and turned it into the channel of prayer, and
preached straight to the mark on the Sabbath following,
while yet folk's hearts were chilled with awe. He warned
all men to look to the ordering of their lives, lest their
wickedness, increasing yet further, should provoke a
second and more dire calamity in punishment. Emily,
a child of five then, would doubtless be in the Rectory
pew, but her father's sermon would carry no meaning to
her ears. In after years, though, she would hear much
of the catastrophe ; it would be made to point many a
moral, doubtless, and Emily, true at such times to her
up-bringing, would bow her head submissive to the
wisdom of the Church. But afterwards she would go up
across the moor, her heart lightening as she went; men's

teaching would grow vague to her, and the moor's logic resume its wonted sway ; she would stand where we are standing now, and mark the wreckage, and glory in Nature's one emphatic claim for hearing. Even then folk were growing to the fixed insanity which rates man above the earth-mother who suckled him, and man's tawdry streets above the clean dwelling-places whose floors are teeming earth, whose roof is sky. And the child of the Parsonage, looking on the mutiny of peat and solid rock, would snatch a wild joy from the knowledge that this was, indeed, a visitation—a visitation of the Earth-God, who bides his own good leisure before teaching men that they must in the last day return to Nature.

The stream here has washed its way to the bed-rock, leaving nine-foot banks of peat on either hand. Here and there, as we move up the basin, a trunk of bog-oak lies in the water, or juts from out the crumbling bank. The moor splits up into countless gullies, all with the same drear look of barrenness. Brook after brook comes down to join the larger stream, but one and all are dumb as they slip, ghostly and dark, beneath the overhanging heather. And it is this last silence of the water which sets a seal on the deep, eerie hush of the forgotten land.

The full, unstinting sunset spreads before us, with nothing but Bouldsworth Hill to break its sweeping lines. From purple to lilac, from flaming crimson to the blush of a wild-rose pink, the piled clouds lie and slumber,

while the sun himself goes down to sleep. The gloaming
comes stealthily from out the dingles of the moor; the
face of the marshes grows sullen, black; the rushes on
the marge pipe in a hushed, afraid whisper. The breeze
wanders, sobbing, crying, wailing, across the darkening
foreground of ling and peat. And now, as the ear grows
tuned to the under-music, the streams are no longer
dumb, but sound far-off and faint as the clink of goblin-
hammers.

Emily's shadowy figure is at our side again—the figure
which last we saw outlined against the sky that hangs
lonely over Withens. Willy-nilly, the thought of
"Wuthering Heights" comes back to us, for it was here
that its creator bent soul and mind to the one effort of
her life; here that she strove, and sickened, and grew
strong again to catch the meaning of the moor; here
that Heathcliff, at such a gloaming-tide as this, was born
complete, a man—growing in the one sunset hour, it may
be, to full stature. Here, and here only, can any judgment
of the book find cogency; here only can its pages stand
out vivid and real from a real and awe-compelling background.

The farm folk, the minor characters of the drama, were
bottomed on more tangible experience; but Heathcliff
was compact of Nature's elements. The still, malign
cruelty of the bog; the masterful passion of wind and
racing thunder-wrack; the rare, deep tenderness of the
sun full-shining from a cloudless sky—all these went to

and fro, warp and weft, in the loom of the creating brain,
and formed a hero, flesh and blood. Emily Brontë may
not have known it ; she may have looked for no confir-
mation, from the world of men about her, that her
creation was more than fanciful. Yet the truth
remains that Heathcliff, framed from the wilderness, had,
in sober fact, more than one counterpart living on the
outskirts of the heath ; for if a man live lonely among
such scenes, his rough edges sharpen year by year, his
virtues stiffen, his vices grow to the large heedlessness of
Nature. There are tales—tales in plenty—current in
Haworth and in Oxenhope, which add a wildness to the
wind's note in the chimney-stack as one listens by the
hearth ; but they can rest—for we have Heathcliff.

He stands afar off from any other creation of our
language, alone, and naked, and jubilantly terrible. He
is an Ishmael, wresting a fierce zest of his own from a
life he rated cheaply. No rag of falsity clings to him, but
the brute and the god-man that lurk in all of us rise up
unconquerable and take their pleasure. He is the one
witness we have had that Pan has awakened at last, from
an English moorland—a new, lusty Pan, beside whom
his forerunner was a dreamer and a child.

Then Cathy grew out of the man's character, like Eve
from Adam's rib. She was what the sky is to the swart
moor, filling its crevices and taking minutely the contrary
shape. She was yielding and smooth where he was
roughly immovable ; she had the beauty of a rose or any

other milk-soft thing, while he would have been uncouth but for his grandeur ; when he brought passion—eager, tense, sweat-dripping passion — she offered affection, frightened for its own security. And she, in her weakness, lives unconquerable, as he lives in his strength. She snares our love, she tricks us into worship, against our saner reason.

If they had wedded, she and Heathcliff, what strange creature would have been born of them ? A rank fool, it may be—or something mighty. But no half-measures. Better as it was, perhaps. Heathcliff has left no heirs, and such as he stand firmer solitary.

The heath darkens fast. The plover's wail thrills through and through one. Swift out of the gloom one picture comes and stays with us—the picture of an upland house, with thorn branches wind-driven against the window of a little upstairs chamber.

" I want to be let in," the breeze is crying, as if in answer to a question. "Cathy—it is Cathy—let me in," it wails.

And we know that she is beating with her frail little hands—beating at Heathcliff's window—crying to be let in out of the pitiless cold. As long as the wind-beats last, her voice will sadden them ; as long as the moor is moor, and the peat lies bare to the sky, moor and peat and wind will not forget.

SEN.

The Older Ponden.

CHAPTER III

GREY PONDEN HOUSE

ONE has to go by the compass now, for road there is none, and the intervening sheep-tracks are useless guides. There is still a faint band of red low down to the north-west, and aiming a little to the right of this we start across in search of the upstanding pile of rocks known as Ponden Kirk. The moor's face is changed altogether ; ling and peat are of the like sombre hue ; only by keeping the glance far ahead can we catch the faint, sullen sheen which warns us that standing pools are waiting for the first false step. All is silence—a dense, limitless silence that weighs on one like a palpable hand. The gloom is prickly with a score of little sounds, unheard at other times; we are conscious of a strained sense, as of expectation mingled with disquiet; sky and heather seem one, and we stand, defenceless, on the outermost rind of creation. The land is full of ghosts—dumb ghosts, that will not talk to us, but move beside us with set lips and rustling garments.

Whirr! Tabak-tabak-tabak! A grouse gets up right at one's feet, with startling suddenness. It looms shadowy-big against the lightening eastern sky, and its harsh *tabak-tabak* comes ringing down the silence as it dips again into the heather and is lost. Such things are trivial by day; yet by night they keep the pulses beating long after the moor has regained its wonted quiet.

Fingers of vague light are creeping up the sky; a greyish haze steals over the blackness of the heath; the tangled sheep-walks show plainer. We take our bearings afresh, and find that we shall have to shift a point or two to the westward if we mean to strike Ponden Kirk. The moor grows dimly brighter until, at the end of another rough mile, we can see the pile of rocks rise swart into the haze. And then the moon, three days past her full, comes silvern white above the round, unbroken sky-line.

A strange relic of far-off days, this Ponden Kirk. A plaything now of lovers, who come, half laughing, to consult the oracle; if a maid can struggle through the narrowish opening in the rocks, she will be married before the year is out ; if not, she is like to go unwedded all her days. That is the accepted tradition throughout the country-side. The old significance of the pile is lost ; but it may well date back to that oldest of all religions, whose monuments have survived to our own day. Such shrines were always reared among the wastes, as if the larger freedom of moor and fell were needful for their

votaries ; usually they have been fashioned by primitive craft into a primitive, symbolic shape ; but always, whether shaped by man's hands or by Nature's, their ancient significance shows plain when gauged by the colour it has given to the traditions of the country folk. Lighter tales come and go ; but no tradition lives through forgetful centuries unless it be bottomed on some deep and vital instinct of humanity.

Well, it is lonely here, and the strife of tongues is far away; and this dark kirk of the wilderness, at which Pagan mothers once worshipped lustily, seems yet to have its message for the world.

Across the heath, on Crowhill yonder, stands another piled heap of stones, reared to the harsher god of storm. The moon is well up by this time, and little by little, as we blunder through the rope-like stems of heather, or cross the marshy tracts from tuft to yielding tuft of wiry grass, her clear light filters into every crevice of the heath. The sky is separate now; it no longer seems a part of the moor, but stretches far overhead like a sheltering roof. One sees all kinds of trivial details, unnoticed in full daylight—quaint shapes of rocks, curious marsh-mosses, even the webs of the fat-bodied moor spiders, which sag helplessly under the weight of shimmering dewdrops. A moor-fowl splashes out of the reeds yonder and disappears, its pathway breaking into golden sickles the reflected moon. The cairn stands just ahead, veiled in fleecy mist; the country folk call it Laddock Royle, Lancashire Lad, or Lad of Crowhill, and it marks the place where the body of a lad was found—killed by the storm in crossing from Lancashire to the sister-county. A sorrow of this sort seems personal in such a scene, as if the lad were kin to us; the summer night grows chilly on the sudden, and far to the far sky we see the white, unending plain of snow; the bitter wind again sweeps over from the north, driving the frozen topmost layers of the drifts in a grey cloud before it. There's a touch of squalor in the tale, moreover, to deepen its pathos; for Stanbury would not bury the alien, though he was found on their own moor; and Lancashire would not bury him, though he was a native of that county; and for awhile the mean dispute went on. Then

Rain on the Road of Stoups.

Trawdon, a Lancashire village, brought the keen eye of business to the matter, buried the lad at the expense of the parish, and thereafter claimed a goodly acreage of the moor which had brought him to his death. As business, it was a good stroke; and Stanbury Moor—according to the local gossip—is less to-day than it was before a Lancashire weaver lad was lost among the snow-drifts.

Behind us, on the bleak road that runs from Oxenhope to Hebden Bridge, there are monuments more impressive reared to the storm-spirit—a long line of "stoups," upright blocks of stone, whose whitewashed bodies and black crowns point the road to travellers whether dark of night or white of snow is to be combated. They are friendly guides to safety, these stoups; yet approach them at winter dusk, and they seem rather to be sullen mourners for the dead who were lost aforetime in snow or bog. Silent, morose, some squaring their shoulders to the wind, others bent forward with a sort of gloomy heedlessness, the stoups have each their separate character; but none has less than tragedy to offer to the passer-by.

We'll take no heed of winter though, for it is a summer's moon that lights us past the Lad of Crowhill, and down to the green fields that stretch this side of Ponden House. We pass a quarry-pit or two—caverns of dim romance they appear to-night, with the moonlight softening their roughnesses and the cool shadows lying like water at the bottom. The heath is full of such lone, deserted pits, since in old days the builder of a house on the moor-edge usually opened his own quarry somewhere near at hand, and even the cottages were built with prodigal expenditure of stone.

And Ponden House? Grey Ponden, that lies just below us, leaning quiet against the shoulder of the hill. It is a house the thought of which comes back to one,

unbidden, among alien scenes—comes like the smell of
hay, or the reek that steals through a half-opened mistal
door at milking-time. You shall see no such house
elsewhere ; nor is it easy to describe the individual charm
it has. From the deep-browed doorway to the horsing-
steps that stand on the far side of the courtyard, from
the gabled roof and sturdy walls of the house to the
roomy outbuildings behind—laithes and mistals and
stables—all is quaint, and old, and grey with the greyness
that comes of long living apart from the ways of men.
A strip of garden, flanked by a grey, rounded wall, runs
under the front windows, and there the primulas and
London-pride grow, the forget-me-nots and ladslove
and peonies, as if, forsooth, King Yesterday were not
dead, after all, and the world were still a place of dignity.
Turn for another look at the old place ; mark how the
trees, down-bending, intercede with the moor winds for
it ; see how strangely quiet and peaceful it is, for all
its victories over blustering weather ; let these things
form a clear picture in your mind—for you shall not see
their like again.

Old the house is, yet across the courtyard, fronting it,
stands the parent hall, built when the Heaton race was
young, and abandoned, as their fortunes grew, in favour
of a roomier dwelling. It adds to the dignity of the
scene, this older house that still keeps roof and walls
intact—that looks across at its successor with something
of a greybeard's mild beneficence who sees his eldest-

born carrying bravely on the sure traditions. There is a restful consciousness that the new has no place here, that even the old is reared upon a fabric more antique.

As it is with the house, so it was with the race who lived there, generation after generation. Fierceness, unruly temper, rough-riding over any hindrances that blocked the way of passion, these were the marks of one type of moor-bred man ; but there was another type, and one as clearly defined in its own quiet fashion. It was on the hillside oppo-site, I remember, that I stood one winter's day—a raw day, with sorrow in the wind, and a thin winding-sheet of snow on field and heath—and looked across the steep dip of the

valley, and saw a burial party wind slowly down the road. They were carrying John Heaton, of Ponden House, the last of a fine breed of yeomen, to the moorside graveyard ; and it seemed as if old days and manners went undersod along with him. Rugged and courteous of speech was John, a farmer first, and the owner of a good library afterwards ; shy of company a little, yet full of old-world hospitality when the need demanded ; sturdy, and up-

right, and fair-dealing. with a heart as clean as the winds
that rock old Ponden House to sleep at nights. Such
characters, like sound wine, are not mellowed in a
generation; there are few of the race to be found
nowadays, for they need free space in which to grow
—free space, and steady, life-long battles with lean acres,
and the sure consciousness that their fathers have handed
down a name well worth the keeping bright. The answer
of such as John Heaton to the outside world was complete; they wanted none of it—nor had it anything worth
while to teach them.

Well, they have buried John Heaton, and his day
already seems far off. Yet they are very near, these
olden times of a moorside that has lain away from the
beaten tracks; and folk who are scarce past middle age
can remember the time when the ladies of the neighbourhood rode pillion to Haworth Church each Sabbath
morning. John Heaton was a youngish man then, one
of five brothers who lived at Ponden House and who
were known among the maidens of the district as the
" five brethren"; bachelors all, they were shy for lack
of gentler company than their own ; and it was reckoned
something of a jest—an adventure almost—when these
maidens, spoiling for a frolic, knocked at the Ponden
door, and explained that they had come to take a dish
of tea with Mr. John, and Mr. Thomas, and the rest.
And the five brethren, at such times, forgot their shyness
as best they could, and bade their visitors welcome with

that courtesy which had the marrow of good manners in
it—which yet was no manner at all, but rather a large
sincerity that flattered all men by rating them over
highly.

There was an odd ghost at Ponden, if gossip is to be
believed, and to-day they will tell you minutely the path
taken by the phantom. Sometimes it came as a shadowy

greybeard, carrying a lantern; but oftener as a flaming
barrel which rolled down the fields, and past the house-
front, and along the curving highway, until it came to
rest in the "hive-holes"—a sheltered corner where the
Heatons used to keep their bees. The greybeard with
his lantern, however, was wont to take a different path;
there is a high-walled garden above Ponden House, and

he made for this after crossing the pasture-fields ; and
there is keen dispute as to whether he used to climb
the cherry-tree in the corner or the pear-tree that stood
over against the garden gate. Something was to be seen,
beyond question—some erratic shape, it may be, of will-
o'-the-wisp or bog-lanthorn—for our great-grandfathers
were wont to go to the bend of the Ponden Road and
watch the barrel come fiery down the hill—watch it,
apparently, as coolly as if it were no more than a cow
run wild after calving-time, or any other usual phenomenon of their lives.

The ghost was laid in due course. They will tell you,
minutely, how it was done. There was a man near Stanbury who understood the Black Art ; they sought his aid,
accordingly, against the spectre, and he waited on a certain
winter's afternoon until the ghost appeared—in the greybeard's form this time. He lighted a rush-candle, and read
the " Book of the Black Art" backwards, and held the
candle in the phantom's face. " Niver come nigh th' owd
house again till tha's seen this rushlight burn to th' end,"
said the ghost-layer, and put the candle, flame and all,
into his own mouth, and swallowed it.

And the ghost never did see the rushlight burn to an
end—as how could he, when it had passed down the
wise man's throat ? And so the phantom greybeard
fled like a hunted hare across the pasture fields, leaving
his lantern on the road ; and Ponden House has never
seen him since that day.

Just one last glance at the homestead—a thought of the cool living-rooms, with the rare china, the pewter, the carved oak that furnished them aforetime—a smile at the picture of demure maidens, sitting in the window-seat that gave them a view of the ladslove and the peonies, drinking tea (which was accounted a luxury then) out of fragile blue-and-white cups, glancing at one another slily when Mr. John lost his tongue or Mr. Thomas crossed and re-crossed one gaitered leg above the other in evident embarrassment. There will be a stir of bees, too, let us say, coming with the south wind through the open windows, and the lowing of cattle whose wide udders tell them it is near to milking-time. We could dawdle till daylight here, piecing together the quaint old stories that hang about the house thick as the lichens on its roof ; but it is time we left Grey Ponden to its moonlight and its memories.

Not far away lies the round back of Silver Hill, under which a vast treasure was said to have been buried during the '45 rebellion. The fields which climb this hill were well tilled aforetime through being constantly turned over in search of the treasure, and practical fathers may have been concerned, one fancies, to keep the legend alive in the minds of laggard sons.

Suppose we follow the ghost's path down the highroad, and past the hive-holes at the bottom, and up the further steep. To the left is Scartop hamlet, with its chapel standing gaunt and bare above the moon-flecked sweep of water that is fed by many a peat-stained upland stream.

" Scartop Charity "—the anniversary service connected with this same gaunt chapel—is still a notable function of the year. If the day be fine enough, the service is held out of doors ; a rough platform is erected in the mill-yard down below, and here the hillside lassies, gowned in white, range themselves on the raised tiers of seats ; the men-singers sit behind ; the fiddles, the

bass-viols, and the clarionets are in front ; to the right is the preacher's seat. Chairs, forms — any sitting accommodation that can be borrowed from chapel or from cottage — fill the remainder of the mill-yard. The congregation overflows the yard and sprinkles the hill-slope opposite with spots of colour, white and black. The fiddles and the clarionets strike up on the sudden ; the voices rise as one, and lift themselves, clear, strong, and sweet, to the march of a rousing

hymn tune. You will hear singing here at Scartop
Charity, singing such as can only be heard in the
music-loving west of Yorkshire ; for music is one of
the strongest traditions of Haworth parish and of Stanbury, and the girls' voices have a depth and richness that
only moorland air can give. You will hear a sermon,
too, hot, impassioned—a sermon that is hale and lusty
with the old, uncompromising dogma. They preach
with a will and they sing with a will at Scartop
Charity, and the service is good as a north-west wind,
full of tonic, tingling and alive.

The thought of Haworth music brings back its own
long train of recollections. What nights they used to
have, with fiddle, flute, and hautboy ! Arcadian nights,
of which the sweetness lingers yet, when men trudged
through rain and snow and keen north wind to meet at
this man's house or that for song and fiddle-play. Whole
families there were whose members each had skill with
some one instrument, and upland storms might shrill as
they would about the chimney-stacks—their voice passed
by unheeded, and time passed by unheeded, while father
and sons and trim-set lassies sat witched by their own
melodies. Sometimes, at the larger gatherings, they
would join all together in orchestral music ; and sometimes half of them would lay down flute and fiddle and
bass-viol, and practise Oratorio to the accompaniment
of the others—practise in no untutored fashion until they
were well-nigh perfect in their parts.

And Tom Parker, who lived wide of Haworth ? They said—the critics who came from the South to hear him— that he would have brought as fine a tenor voice to London as ever sang there if they could have snared him thither in his youth ; but Tom was a quiet man and a simple, and it was much that they persuaded him to sing in Bradford at the yearly Oratorios. Yet the moor folk of Haworth and of Oxenhope could always count on him for wedding-party, anniversary service, or Christmas junketing ; and men who now are greying remember how as little lads they crossed the moor to Parker's house, to bid him grace some rustic gathering with the voice which, at sixty, was mellow as a blackbird's on the first of May. Yet Tom never understood men's praise ; he sang as his brother blackbirds did, because the song was there and forced its own way out.

Rough folk they were up here, and staunch to hard- ness. But the hard soil rears the sweetest grass, and there is about this Haworth music a tenderness in the retrospect, a depth and melody, which colours all one's knowledge of the moor men. They could fight, and poach, and revel with the best—ay, but set a fiddle in their hands, and watch their faces soften and their bows go light about the strings ; and you would see the soft kernel hid underneath the rough outer shell.

Time wags, and we are still on the road from Ponden up to Stanbury. Across the valley lies Oldfield, half hidden by its trees ; a house that was tenanted once by

The Old Gentleman's Grave.

an eccentric, who put strange statues in his garden, and sought their company in preference to fellowship more human. He died in the fulness of time, this eccentric, and just before breath failed him once for all, he ordered his men-servants to roll a large stone down one of the fields which bordered the lower edge of his garden, to mark where the stone found a resting place, and there to bury him. They humoured the dead, as perchance they had been loath to humour the living, and they set the stone rolling across the grass-grey furrows of the pasture ; it stopped half down the slope, and there they buried him, in view of thousands upon thousands of the curious who had come to watch the ceremony ; and there his grave is to this day, walled off from the rest of the field, and fringed with little trees. The country folk call it " the old gentleman's grave "—so that our eccentric lives to-day by virtue of his whims, though we know as little of him as of that other ancient who was wont to read his books along the Scholar's Path.

It has changed hands with curious frequency, this house of Oldfield. Before the eccentric's day, a pack of harriers was kept here, and the neighbouring rise of " Harehills " recalls the time when hares swarmed thick on every upland field ; and recently, again, the place was held by as keen a sportsman as ever trod the moors—a past master of all the many grouse calls, a breeder of trout, and a right dexterous fisherman. It is

a queer, crooked, picturesque house, and every one says
it has a history—and none can tell you what the history
is. A tragic one, belike ; for histories are apt to run in
such grooves upon the moorside.

The moor is almost empty of game at this date ; but
it is curious how, among those who live round about
Oldfield here and Stanbury, the hunter's instinct has
survived, planted deep in their fibres by generations of
sporting fathers. They still have all the primitive lore
of fur and fins ; they are intimate with the habits of wild
animals, the ways of snaring them—all the hundred little
details which are known by the feel rather than by
teaching. And if such things are dear to the present
race, to whom game is chiefly a tradition, what of the
men of the older generation, who could start a hare in
every pasture, or wire a grouse at any of the thick-spread
feeding trails ? If they owned land, well and good ; if
not, they poached ; in either case they followed the same
honest sporting instinct. Nay, there was no case of will
or will not in the matter ; sport was a necessity to them,
as much as the food they ate, or the keen air they
breathed into their lungs, and the poacher in those fair
old days was own brother to the man he robbed.

The moon is strong on these sloping fields to-night—
such a moon as used to entice the hares to leave their
forms and sit, quiet lumps of brown that scarce showed
against the grey-green of the grass they cropped ; and
the scene brings back the thought of one disciple of a

craft which nowadays is much misunderstood. He is long since dead, but his memory is green as the parsley which flourished under his watchful care on many a grassy hill-slope. Parsley, indeed, was the only crop he ever sowed; whereby he exhibited a fine altruism, since it was not for his own sordid needs he reared it, but for the hares which show so marked an appreciation of the herb. Tough, wiry, with a grey eye that could see both sides of a wall at once, this old-time vagabond would have rejoiced the heart of the keeper who not long since was complaining that the younger sort of poacher was "a poor six-penn'orth o' copper."

The world treated him shabbily in his latter end; but he met starvation with the same alert eye and the old conviction that life was a rare frolic. He was reduced at last to selling oranges and what not, and the story goes that a playmate of former days, who had prospered and grown sleek, came across the orange vendor as he sat ragged beside his basket and invited custom that was slow to come.

"So you've sunk to this, Jack?" said the man of property, stopping to improve the occasion, and buttoning his pockets tight the while.

"Ay, I've come to this. It like as it war to be."

"Well, you had your chances, and you let them slip. No, I'll not encourage you—not a penny."

An angry gleam informed the poacher's right eye, and in his left the unquenchable humour lurked. "When

I want brass fro' thee, lad, I'll axe thee for 't," he responded.

" It is what I always said you'd come to, Jack. Look at me ; should I be where I am if I had followed such godless ways as yours ? "

" Nay, lad, tha'd hev hed reason to thank God A'mighty tha wert different-like—tha'd hev fund a lighter stick, an' all, to beat a limping dog wi'. Get thee back to thy hole-an'-corner ways, an' thy brass, an' crack o' godliness to them 'at sees more in 't nor me. Didst iver snare a grouse, lad ? "

The other shook his head, and turned to escape the whirlwind he had sown.

" Then tha's missed summat," went on the poacher, pursuing him with lifted voice. " Hark ye, lad, I've *lived* my life, an' it's been a gooid un—an' not if all th' brass i' Yorkshire war i' thy pockets wod I swop breeks wi' thee. I've lived, an' tha hesn't—tha's been ower flaired o' losing summat—an' I'll turn merrier toes to th' sky nor thee, lad, when it comes to deeing."

And he did—he went out of life as few of the wiser folk of this world can go out of it, with a sense that what was past had been worth while, that what was to come would be best met by an undaunted front. He had never had much to lose—and that is where true gaiety begins.

It is a mistake to begin talking about odd characters up here ; they lead one on so. Over there, on the far side of

Oakworth Moor, lived old Threelaps, a notable example of broken-heartedness. Threelaps was a usual fellow enough in his younger days ; but he was crossed in love, and he vowed that he would go to bed and never get up again, by way of showing his opinion of all women. He kept his love-vow—an unusual proceeding in itself—and stayed in bed for nine-and-forty years. Probably the seeds of the sluggard were sown in him at birth, and the lady served as a welcome excuse. At any rate, he did not leave his bed till the urgent claims of six-by-three demanded it ; and by that time he had grown so sloth-fully big that they had to lower his coffin from the window because the door was over-narrow to let it through.

A unique figure and a pathetic, old Threelaps ; other men have led forlorn hopes for the sake of unrequited love, but surely none has ever offered such sustained and passive homage to a contemptuous lady. Think of it ! No flare of trumpets, no rush, no perilous road to follow where it is only the first step that is difficult. To go to bed was easy—but to stay there for nine-and-forty years ! To lie and lie, years after one's anger had grown cool, and still to nurse the corpse of one's resentment, crushing the thought that, after all, one might be a fool for one's pains—yes, there was a touch of something near akin to genius in the man, and his memory lives at a day when many a worthier fellow has been forgotten.

Then, too, there is Teewit Hall, standing far up on the hill-crest yonder. It looks like a church, yet is not ; it looks nearly as time-worn as its neighbours, and is scarce a generation old. Gossip says that the square Norman tower, which flanks one end of the house, was built in order that its owner, a contractor, might look through his telescope and see whether his men were idling in the building-yard at Bradford. It is a dry stroke of humour, this, and no more, but the conceit is trim enough, and characteristic, moreover, of that northern shrewdness which keeps the business eye awake in noisy town or in the quiet retirement of the hills.

They do lead one on, these gossipy old wives' tales.

There was the cock-fighting Squire, now, who lived five miles the Lancashire side of Ponden—but he must wait awhile. The moon is wearing westward already, and the wind is none too warm for loitering.

The road, however, takes us straight through Stanbury village, and one must loiter here a little. Stanbury has no history, unless a vague legend that Cromwell once passed through it can be counted such. Cromwell was certainly at Skipton, not many miles away, during the Civil War, but we find no foundation for the story that he halted his troops at this village of Bury, cast an appreciative glance on its square-shouldered houses, and

cried, " Stand, Bury ! "   This, however, is the local
etymology of the name; while another version gives
Napoleon Bonaparte the credit of naming the village
—and Napoleon is pictured vividly in full, brow-beaten
flight across Haworth Moor, with Wellington in pursuit.

There's a fine quality in this wide disregard of English
history, a quality which is not understood except after

long intimacy with the people.   Their own stories they
know to the last detail : these rolling waves of heather-
land and bog, these tight-built houses, this over-arching
sweep of sky, make up their world, and all that lies beyond,
in the uncared-for unknown, is summed up crisply in the
native phrase of "the Low Country."   And so they are
inexact about the doings of Wellington, Cromwell, or
Napoleon, because the matter is unimportant either way;

but what Harry o' t' Nab gave for the speckled cow, and
how the Squire fought gamely in the beechwood bottom,
and the way the lass of Windy Farm slipped sideways
into wedlock—these are vital matters, clear-pictured and
repeated till they take the settled form of print.

It is the converse of the Imperial spirit, this; it is the
quality which has given—and must always give—tough-
sinewed fellows to fight Imperial battles without knowing
what the battles are about. They are no worse farmers for
it on Stanbury Moorside; they have a healthy, unassailable
outlook upon life, and a wit that can run under the guard
of any man who thinks to have the laugh of them. The
war of crops and weather, the constant fight to snatch a
livelihood from grudging land, have taught them deeper
lessons than are to be learned in the chattering marts of
men; they neither gloss over the cruelties of life nor rail
at them, and their sympathy, if its edge be rough at
times, is frank and unaffected, as their love is or their
hate. What could the Low Country give them that they
have not got?

One likes to think of Cromwell standing here, whatever truth there be in the legend. He would have
relished the sturdy, stiff-backed build of the houses that
line each side of the one street; he and they were fashioned
after the same model, and both reared themselves on a
hill-top above a world of which they had no fear. Well,
Cromwell came, or he did not—the village does not care
either way, for it needs no history. " Keep thyseln to

thyseln," old Stanbury village ! It's a moorside motto, and one that has kept you sweet and clean through many a racketty hubbub of the valley-places.

Heigho ! And the moon dipping behind the mistal-roof there that slopes downward to the street. It will be moon-dusk down Water Lane, but we'll cross it, for all that, and reach the "Bull" again, as we left it, by the moor

track that takes us through the churchyard ; and we will stop but once more on the way, to glance at the little farm above us yonder. It is unpretentious enough to look at ; but Jose Wark, the hero of the press-gang story, lived there, and milked his cows at even, and drove those imaginary bargains which salted toil for him. The story always comes back to one with its primitive freshness on seeing his farm ; one creeps in fancy to the door of the byre ; there is the steady splash-splash of milk into the frothing pail, and Jose Lad's running accompaniment of barter.

"What, gi'e me ten pund, wilt 'a ? Dost think I'm bahn to mak thee a gift o' th' beast ?" comes the murmur.

And still, as we dip to the foot of Water Lane and climb again to the open moor, we see the long, loose-built fellow seated astride his milking-stool. "Mak it ten-pund-ten," the soft refrain insists.

CHAPTER IV

SIMPLES, AND THE SOFT-FOOTED HOUND

WE cannot tarry to peep into every odd nook and corner of Haworth. The village is full of such nooks; the moors, too, are full of them, whichever way one turns. There is Emmott Hall, for instance, at a bend of the long main street—an old-world building of distinctive architecture, whose back is turned to the street, whose front, with characteristic wish for privacy, is toward the moor. It belonged aforetime to a Religious House, and its cellars, according to tradition, served as a monkish burial-ground in the days when the Romish Church held sway in England. It is hard to associate the Catholicism of Rome with Methodist

70

ideals; but the old faith lives still in the common speech, as it does to a more marked degree in the sister villages of Lancashire. Until very lately they were wont to swear " by th' Heart " in Haworth parish—the old folk still use the oath in times of peculiar need—and, although they would be the last to accept the fact, there can be no doubt that the phrase dates back to a forgotten ritual.

Emmott Hall.

To every house there is its one fitting atmosphere, and the time when Emmott Hall shows worthiest is on a winter's afternoon, with the sun dipping red behind the moor and the shadows thickening down the street. At this hour the back of the house is more impressive than its front, and the little courtyard opening on the road, with its grim, wide-mouthed gateway, has a curious signifi-

cance of its own. Like Oldfield, Withens, Ponden, we
feel that this old Hall has many a story hidden among its
shadows; but they are lost, and those to whom these
musty tales were family heirlooms have gone quietly out
into that Unknown which holds so many secrets, and
keeps them all. It was an important house, undoubtedly,
once on a time; people of consequence lived here, to
whom the village folk offered the hardy, unbending
respect which acknowledges difference of birth, yet meets
it with a subtle assumption of equality. Where have they
gone, these great ones in the land? What chanced to
them, that their names died out as utterly as if they had
never fretted through long years of storm and sun?
None knows; it is as though a sponge had been drawn
across the records of Haworth Old Hall, leaving its story
empty of such details as the fancy hungers for.

There is the Manor House, too, which stands at the
further side of Haworth; the greater part has been
rebuilt, but the narrow strip of the old fabric that still
remains is a good example of an architecture whose
secret we of to-day have lost. There was a ghost here
once. A seemly, usual ghost it was—no barrel rolling
fiery down the hill-slope, nor greybeard with a liking for
clambering up the mossy boles of orchard-trees, but the
phantom of a far-back mistress of the house who killed
herself in the upstairs room yonder. A quiet ghost, from
all accounts, which went about the house dumb-footed,
an unobtrusive and accepted guest.

The Manor is haunted likewise by a legend—a rough old tale, faithful in spirit to the darker aspect of a buried time, whether in detail it be true or false. They say that the lord of Haworth Manor, generations ago, was a gay liver, and that a neighbouring landowner played boon companion to him in all his revels. The pair of them met one night for a carousal, and the Haworth man's head for liquor proved, on this occasion at least, the weaker of the two. He passed from the convivial to the besotted stage, and his friend, getting paper and a quill, drew up a deed of gift of the manorial rights, which he persuaded the other to sign. The morning light brought repentance ; but neither threats nor appeals to old friend-ship could win back the deed of gift. That is one version of the story ; tradition does not give the bosom friend's side of the matter, and it may well be that the rights were not stolen, but given in payment of a debt of honour. As a legend, at any rate, the tale must remain, unless evidence of which we are ignorant now should ever be dragged from the musty storehouse of the past—an un-likely chance at this date, when those who could have a say in the matter are long since dead, and the descendants of the families implicated seem all to have disappeared from Haworth parish.

Ay, there have been rough doings, now that one begins to think of them. It is not long—fifty or sixty years, perhaps—since the last of the moorland feuds died out. A few miles wide of Haworth the two families lived—six

strapping sons of one house, four of the other. They
rarely met, at inn or fair, but some slight word was
twisted to a renewal of the old quarrel ; then blows were
hotly given and as swiftly returned ; and soon the battle
would be raging with a downrightness that smacked of
the days when harder weapons than the naked fists were
brought into play. One who watched many a fight
between the houses has confessed that it all but raised
his gorge sometimes ; it was grim earnest, and those on
each side, when at last they held off from one another,
were apt to be red-raw from brow to chin, and red-raw
wherever the flesh showed through their tattered clothes.
It was no casual anger that informed their blows, but the
true hate of feud ; and the onlookers thought more than
once that this or that big fellow had fought his last. But
not a bit of it—the next chance meeting would find him
refreshed, and eager for another bout. Brutal ? So far
as the brute's sturdiness goes, it was ; yet their wounds
needed only to be gained by sword-play to acquire the
dignity which we refuse to fisticuffs.

Other fights there were, whose memory, after the
fashion of Homeric combats, is kept alive in moorside
story—casual fights, with no bitterness of feud to back
them, and only a cracked jaw or so to emphasise the
peace-making that followed. There were staunch men in
the parish, though, who never deigned to use their fists,
regarding such sport as foolish child's play ; if attacked,
they ran in to close quarters and threw their adversary

over-shoulder before his first blow or his second was well driven home. They were wont to have the better of the argument, these wrestlers, and it was well if the battle were waged upon the soft peat of the moor ; for now and then they underrated the strength of their cross-buttock and the hardness of, say, a kitchen floor or the cobbles of a stable-yard.

Things slip into the shadows of one's mind, and come tumbling out with inconvenient speed when once that old wife, memory, is stirred. What of those nights, merry as the wind and wild as the hill-storms, when every careless "fly-by-sky" in the moorside foregathered to the drinking—rich men and poor men, poachers and gamesters, and those who in graver moments were pillars of the local commonwealth ? Nay, if you please ! They come down too near to our own day, and the tales have a sharpish twang with them, and those who have cased themselves in broadcloth do not always share one's own zest for forefathers who, if they had had the fortune to be born some centuries earlier, would have donned Lincoln green and pulled the yew-bow with the best.

We'll leave the Manor House, then, which awakes too many memories, and fare down the steep lane here to the hollow that shelters Springhead, a house which is young as houses go on the moorside, but singular in its remote, self-centred air of dignity. Two o'clock of a grey November afternoon is the hour for Springhead ; it asks no sharp contrasts of blood-red sky and inky shadow, but rather the even, lifeless unity of sky and field which comes when the year is tired and the very clouds are over-weary to let the raindrops through. The firs that stand on either side the garden walk are sober-green, and moan discon-solate; the trees, sloping southward in memory of many a dead

Manor House
Haworth

north wind, rustle in their nakedness, and are afraid; the bare house-front looks sadly out upon it all, and grieves without complaining. You would think there was never a primrose bloomed, nor a blackbird nested, about Springhead—unless, perchance, you came again while summer was tender with the uplands; and then you would wonder at the softness of the garden-grass, the mellow din of birds, the fragrance of old-fashioned flowers and herbs which snatch at the brief summer and make the most of it.

Yet the November grey is better. Standing at the road-foot here, with the dun fields climbing to the rounded sky-line, it is easy to understand Barguest, the ghostly Dog who holds first place among all the moorland superstitions. Barguest—they call him Guytrash sometimes—is of a piece with the drear look of the land, with the shrewd breeze that whimpers out of the silence and is gone again before its chill is realised. His coat is shaggy and dun-brown, this phantom dog's, his feet are shod with silence as he passes you, and in his wake an ice-cold wind advances.

Old faiths retire discomfited; but Barguest is dying hard, and fear of the Dog is a half-slumbering terror yet, inwoven in the brain and nerves of men whose fathers learned what panic waited on the Brown Beast's steps. Such a dread strikes deep, and manifests itself in many a curious guise; the honest, cheery dog of flesh-and-blood has been known to take on a borrowed significance from his ghostly cousin, and the malignity which folk attributed to his bite had in it, one suspects, something of a superstitious vividness, separate altogether from such physical danger as attended it.

Superstitions lead one far afield ; they fatten on loneliness and storm, and the marsh-candles which lighted unwary travellers to the bog-brinks have led men's fancies also into eerie places.

Strange cures for diseases they had, too, in an older day. Mouse-pie, for instance, would seem to be a drastic remedy for whooping-cough ; and grilled mouse, an alternative cure for the ailment, sounds not a whit more palatable. An egg buried underground in a jar until the shell disappeared, and then eaten, was a sure remedy for consumption, and a fresh trout laid on the foot was a well-tried cure for gout. Of this last there can be little question ; whatever the natural process is, it has been tried times without number, and times without number it has proved successful. A trout taken alive from the water was also deemed helpful in consumption ; the patient must put his lips to the mouth of the fish, and draw in its breath as it gasped for air—and if that did not cure him, nothing would. Consumption, it will be noticed, bulks large among the maladies needing out-of-the-way cures ; for the keen moor air, which ripens a strong man's health, is apt to deal hardly with the weaker sort, who need more sustenance, as an ally against wind and weather, than the oatcake, butter, and rough bread which form the staple diet of the hill folk.

Then there are camomile, and fever-few, and all the host of simples. A fragrant lore, the thought of which takes us back to the herb-doctors of the moorside, who could tell a fortune, or cure a fever, or heal cattle of the Evil Eye. Shrewd fellows, these, in worldly as in occult wisdom; their skill in foretelling the weather was eclipsed only by their power to read the innermost secrets of men's hearts; and parson and leech alike played second fiddle to them when a child or a cow, a troubled soul or a tangled love-affair, had to be righted. Jack Kay, however, whose influence as a wise man was paramount in Haworth parish seventy odd years ago, was of a different type; he counted it sinful to claim the power of fortune-telling, and he studied astrology with a reverence that was altogether religious. A quiet and gentle-mannered enthusiast, he laid no claim to super-human knowledge; what he had learned of star-lore, he was wont to say, any other man could learn by study and by long vigils on the hill-tops; but the moor folk, who measure no man by his own valuation, gave to Jack Kay such honour and respect as have left their mark on the history of Haworth moorside.

Curious customs have flourished in Haworth, along with its herb lore and its old-world remedies, and it is one of the few remaining villages where the feast of Rush-bearing is observed. The maidens of the parish no longer go in procession to the church, to strew rushes on the floor and lay their garlands on the chancel-rails; but the feast which used to follow the old religious ceremony still goes merrily on, between the hay and the corn har-vests, and still it bears its ancient name of Rushbearing.

Indeed, they seem to have been prone to junketings up here, for in Parson Grimshaw's time there was an annual race meeting at Haworth, extending over three days. History is silent—discreetly, perchance—as to the mettle of the race-horses; but we know that the company which crowded in to watch the sport was none of the choicest. Too much ale was drunk, and too many oaths expended to little purpose, for the fighting parson's taste; instinct, doubtless, bade him settle the matter by rough-and-ready blows, himself against the mob; but reflection must have shown him how hopeless such odds were, and he turned to prayer in his extremity. Withdrawing into a lonely place when the time for the races was approaching, he prayed with all his strength that rain might come down never-ceasingly so long as the revellings should last. Then he returned to his busy round of work—for there was no man in the parish who spared himself less than Grimshaw—and waited quietly for the answer to his prayer.

It has something of a Biblical simplicity and force, this tale; we can see the parson, with his man's strength and woman's faith, turning his glance toward the rain-quarter of the skies as he crossed the upland wastes to pray with, comfort, or rebuke, his scattered flock. There would be the quiver of faith justified when the eve of the races brought cloud-bank after cloud-bank up above the grey horizon. The folk were already gathering, many of them, in over-night anticipation of the frolic; and when day broke, they heard the drip of water—the drip that merged into a flow, and the flow that grew to a tearing flood, wind-pressed out of the teeming clouds. For three days it rained without cessation ; the racing-fields were under water ; the crowd, awed already by a phenomenon unusual enough to touch its superstition, was seized with veritable panic when Grimshaw, in his stubborn, defiant way, let all and sundry know that he had prayed for this. And since that answer of the waters to an old parson's faith there has never another race-meeting been held in Haworth parish.

There the tale stands, incredible or not. Grimshaw was over-honest to give a false cause to a fact which all men witnessed ; and he never doubted, to his last day, that he had been the instrument, through prayer, whereby an abomination had been rooted out from among his people. Well, are we wiser than friend Grimshaw, that we have need to doubt ?

The moor folk were always susceptible to weather-tokens, and Jack Kay, long after Grimshaw's time, uttered many a prophecy touching rain and snow, sleet and hail and wind, which gave him the same sort of hold over his neighbours' minds that the parson had acquired by prayer.

Scholarship, likewise, secured their respect, and one Abram Sunderland, who kept the village school at Stanbury, was a power in the land, enjoying something of Jack Kay's prestige ; for " book-learning " was a sort of

7

Black Art in itself, and the understanding of printed pages surely needed help from other-worldly powers. Abram, moreover, did not confine himself to the ornamental arts ; he could be practical on occasion, and his ability to reckon up the acreage of a field by mensuration was just the plain kind of quality which confirmed the villagers in their respect. Reading and writing were wonderful enough, yet they " buttered no bread"; but if such matters could teach a man to measure skew-walled fields —why, there was something in them.

Of the same kidney, but nearer to our own generation, was George Cockroft, who kept a private school in his little road-side house at Oxenhope. In character he was curiously akin to the best type of Scotch dominie : learning was no mere way of livelihood with him, but a passion ; teaching was not a thankless round of tasks, but a vital, heart-uplifting power, to be used reverently and to the topmost of one's strength. His enthusiasm bordered upon piety ; each of his scholars was at once a heavy responsibility and a keen delight ; he aimed to educate rather than to teach, and one ideal of right conduct and lofty thinking was, to his mind, worth a score of sums correctly added up. We need such men nowadays, to leaven the crass lump of what stands for education ; but their day is passing in Yorkshire. Bright lads had chances under Cockroft and his like, chances of rising to high places in the world ; they learned and broadened, while keeping their individual angles sharp—the angles by which, to-day as yesterday, men rive open a path to fortune.

It is not far to Oxenhope ; shall we cross to what was once our dominie's school-house, and peep in at the window ? We are going back half-a-century or so, and can therefore afford to choose our own time—a winter's evening, we'll say, with a swift wind from the north blustering through the door-crevices, and the flames of the two rush-candles, burning on the master's table, blown slantwise by the draught. The master is bending—tall, with a scholarly stoop of the shoulders — above his favourite pupil. Their shadows are preposterously big on wall and ceiling ; the slumbering handful of fire in the grate is not enough to keep the cold from running purple into starved fingers ; but neither has leisure to find the schoolroom chilly.

The lad has been home to tea after the usual school work of the day, and has returned, through snow wind-driven over the deepening drifts, to steal another hour or two at the books which one day are to prove good friends to him ; his father, doubtless, has grumbled, thinking he had better have foddered the cows or have helped with the sheep ingathered from the snow ; but instinct will out, whether it leads to pastures or to books, and the boy sees far ahead into that shadowy dream-world which promises more than lowing of kine and ripple of moor-water across mistal floors. The master has no dream-world ambitions, only a steady hope that the pupil will one day come to a riper knowledge than ever he himself has gained; he has realised, without jealousy, that soon the boy will outrun all he has to teach him. And so the evening wears on, until a fiercer blast of wind rattles peremptorily at the case-ment, startling master and pupil from their studies. The master casts a glance at the old clock standing this side the chimney-piece, smiles in a slow, pleased fashion at their joint forgetfulness, and hustles the lad out of doors; then, as an afterthought, he fetches a big lanthorn, grey where the tin shows through the grease-smudges, and lights the rush-candle within, and says he will set the youngster on his homeward road.

The candle is blotted out by the wind soon as they step across the threshold, and the master takes the pupil's arm—to keep the ghosts from him, he whispers. Not all their book-lore has robbed them of the childish faiths. Half-way they part, and the lad goes on, whistling to keep his terrors down, across a lone two miles of heath. It is pitch-dark, but he picks his way unerringly by aid of the sixth sense that comes with much night-walking; one day he will learn to thank this power of seeing in the dark, for it is a quality that helps more than a little when other sorts of darkness have to be combated.

"Well? What hest 'a to say for thyseln?" growls the father, as he opens the door to him.

"Nowt, father—I've been studying."

"Studying? An' to think tha comes o' godly parents

Haworth.

—christened, an' all; nay, get thee to bed, lad! I'm
feared tha'll be nobbut a raffle-coppin yet. Tha'rt
starving, likely; well, get a bit o' haverbread i' thy
belly, an' tha'll happen be noan th' war for th' wetting.
Ay, a raffle-coppin tha'll be, for sure."

But he proved no raffle-coppin, nor any other sort of
ne'er-do-weel. And if ever he sees this page—he must
be on the brink of old age by now—he will remember
the harsh winter nights that went to make him what he is
—will recall the look of the old school-house, and the
kindly, serious face which had a touch of drollery lurking
behind its studious furrows.

He had kindred spirits among the Scotch, this old-world
dominie, as we have said; but, indeed, the temper of all
the moorland folk is singularly in harmony with that of
their cousins further north. They have the same dry
wit, the same keen scent for a bargain and generous sense
of hospitality, the same grim acceptance of hardship;
each race works the better in face of hindrances, and
each has shown its power to climb head and shoulders
above the struggling press of men more delicately
nurtured. Even in speech we are curiously allied, and
the old Haworth tongue merges, through scarce perceptible gradations of North-country dialects, into the
hundred-and-one different forms of Lowland speech.
Scrupulous honesty, in each people, goes hand-in-hand
with their zest for barter; and their old love of poaching
—and of the twin-passion, border-raiding—was only the

interpretation according to primitive ideas of the law that the things which fly and the things that swim and the things that run on four legs are no man's property until they are captured.

The kinship between the two races is no accident ; it shows natural enough in the light of history, for it was only at a late period that intercourse with the southern counties was less than hazardous ; while the Scotch genius for finding ways out of their own country was developed at a very early date. And so the true division of the countries—the racial division—is measured, not by Tweed, but by the Humber, the wild marshes and forests surrounding which left the North-bred folk for centuries in happy isolation. It is this isolation, no less than his hardier upbringing, which has given the Yorkshireman his outlook on the Southerner, and to this day he regards him from the half-impatient, half-curious standpoint of one who visits a foreign country, and finds the people using a quaint speech and following unexpected habits. The strength of this feeling—which is rather one of armed neutrality, perhaps, than of antipathy—has been belittled ; but a stranger is a " furriner" still in Haworth parish, and the South-countryman seeking to conciliate the natives is apt to find them clothed in a chilly and impenetrable armour, which time and time has been mistaken for stupidity, but which is in reality a subtle form of wit.

Similar as they are to the Scotch, however, one distinc-

tion is clearly marked between the races. The Scottish
tendency to wander has been noted even in so out-of-the-
way a corner as Haworth, and a "Scotchman" has long
been the local phrase for any sort of roving pedlar whose
home is in the four quarters of the wind ; while the
Haworth men, on the other hand, have not at any period
of their history been wont to show their love of home by
leaving it. Perhaps their patriotism is of a tougher
growth ; it may be their land is less lean, or they bring
to the working of it a deeper love of tillage for its own
sake ; at any rate, they have shown in the past a stern and
admirable passion for the county of their birth. When
ambition or the fret of circumstance has driven them
from the steep-streeted village of the moors, they have
brought it honour in the forefront of many a battle, com-
mercial, or professional, or religious ; but the very strength
of their home-staying virtue has kept the sound-bottomed
glory of Haworth parish confined for the most part to the
hills that shut it in.

Only those who have watched the slow building up of
day upon toilsome day can realise the parish history—that
history which never finds its way into the records of
Empire, which yet is the bed-rock upon which the pomp
and majesty of State are reared. Families have grown to
honour here, and men have died with a sure life's work
behind them—humdrum stories, with never a touch of
melodrama across their pages, of cattle and sheep,
turnips and oats and meadow-grass—and the outer

world asks lightly, What has Haworth done ? Enough ; ay, and more than enough, to ensure its place in our hearts as the staunchest village in all the staunch West Riding.

Nor has agriculture claimed all its energies. A family could not always keep up the old traditions ; the land grew churlish, perhaps, after a succession of bad seasons ; so Nature was combated from another side, and the running streams were made to work for men's livelihood. The dingles sloping downward from the moors were rich in water ; mills—clean, wind-lapped places, with gardens trim-set round about their busy walls—appeared here and there by the stream-sides ; remoteness of situation mattered little so long as there was power to drive the water-wheels. The same dogged perseverance that had gone to tilling of the land was turned now into a trade-channel. Men prospered, and failed, and tried again. Prosperity dawned slowly over the moorside ; the happy interval of hand-combing came, when men could earn good wages by short days' work, when they were not herded amongst the smoking loom-racket of to-day, but worked in their own homes or in the large rooms known as "combing-shops." Mirthful days they were, full of rollick and the careless sense that fortune had opened both hands wide ; there was meat more often on the cottage tables than aforetime, and strong liquor could be paid for handsomely, since the mills offered a constant market for as many combings as the men might bring each week.

And all the while the masters were adding profits to
profits, working with their heads while the once-idle
streams did half their work for them.

These lonely mills are dismantled now, for the most
part, and their gaunt desolation adds not a little to the
sadness of the upland glens.   They take us back to
trade's childhood, and childhood has always its own
pathos.   The masters did not know yet the limitations

of wealth ; all was eagerness, and the shrewd round of
barter had in it a certain saving quality of fancy ; money
was more than the brute chink of gold to which it
narrowed afterwards—it was the material for fairy palaces
and dreams of high ambition.   Neither did the men—
those who brought combings to the mills and those
who wove them into cloth—foresee what turn this rose-
path of prosperity would take ; they had healthy work
and healthy play, and whether they played or worked

they had the heather-winds about them ; it was sunrise, fresh and dewy-bright, of a day that was to set in smoke-clouds.

Yet we are proud that the Worth Valley, in which Haworth stands, is accounted the richest of its size in England. The clean solitariness of the old mills has gone with the droning water-wheels, and the factories lie nowadays within easier reach of the trade-centres, whose smoke and din and reeking sweat have ousted the music of the moorland streams. Such as the plough is, however, the masters have put their hands to it steadfastly ; they have trodden an uphill road, and have surmounted it ; and our pride is rather in the achievement than in the means.

Shall we leave the smoke behind us, and steal to the moors again, for one last glance at the old order ? On the way we hear the rattle of a hand-loom from the upstairs chamber of the cottage yonder ; it is the last, or almost the last, remaining on the moorside, and we are tempted to go in at the open cottage-door and up the stair. A bed stands on one side the chamber, and the loom takes up a greedy share of the remaining space. Warp and weft move busily ; the cotton falls downward in ever-increasing length ; it is hard to understand that this tough old bit of machinery is hopelessly out of date. It can only produce cotton fabric of the best---it cannot measure time by the new standard.

We are going backward on the road of progress, and

feel the better for it. After the smoke, the clean, unhurried hand-loom strikes a welcome note. After the
hand-loom, again, we are glad to reach this quiet corner
of the moors, with wind among the heather, and the
time-heedless, restful sky down-arching to the slumberous
spaces of the hills. It is only a few rough fields, after all,
that we have come to see ; yet they have a story of their
own, well worth remembering. A man fought lonely
here against the heather—fought, through fair weather
and through foul, to wrest these fields from the moor's
retentive jaws. Steady, patient, uphill work, that scarce
looked to the reward of crops, but went from foot to foot
of the rescued land with a hard enthusiasm not lightly to
be understood. Land for the sake of what it will grow
one day is the first thought in the worker's mind when he
sets out to intake ; but land for its own sake--land for
sake of the hardship which its rescue entails—this grows
to be the master-passion. It is naked man come to grips
with naked Nature ; and Nature, who is greater than her
children, adds a cubit to man's stature also when she
stoops to wrestle with him.

What the Dutch learned of endurance and grim
patience, from their conflict with the thievish, stealthy
seas, this the upland folk have learned from Intake ; the
little plot of soil is meagre in each case—but the harvests
it has borne ! Harvests whose seed is toil, whose ripen-
ing weather is compact of storm and rain-winds that
whistle to the bone. Yet the Dutch have but the one side

of the moor-man's sturdiness ; they wage defensive war, with aim to keep the sea out only, not to win fresh territory from him at the spade-point ; they have a softer climate, and never a far-off line of hills to forbid them to be placid ; and so they lack that readiness to meet fight for its own sake, that alert, grim-humorous outlook upon life, which are the distinctive qualities of those whose forerunners have wrestled with the heather.

Think of it. Recall the individual steps of this one enterprise. First, the staking-in of the strip of virgin moor ; then, the slow-lengthening trench that seemed, when dug, but a scratch on the surface of what still remained ; the rain that soaked from without, and the sweat that soaked from within, as day followed day, and still the surly acreage to be redeemed seemed scarcely lessened ; the unbefriended labour ; the heavy, day-long silence that scorned one whisper of encouragement. The clang of swords is swifter, and touches a more obvious nerve ; but the battle-chant of strong men wrestling with the heather is strung to a finer pitch, and in it lies the ultimate expression of the heart of the North-country-man.

He finished his labour, this enthusiast, and died of it— died when his first-born crop of oats was greening. And now the heath is coming back; everywhere the tufts of ling show ragged through the grass ; in a few years it will be fruitless moor again. So Nature has doubly the last word—she killed her foe, and she is trampling on his labour. He should sleep sound enough after the moiling seasons; but does he? Or do the old dreams fret at times, and set him wandering, a wind-driven ghost, between these crumbling walls which mark the ruins of his handiwork? He may be content, despite the ruin. The work he did lives yet, and brain and sinew of the race are lustier for every well-turned spadeful of the peat.

The wind steals out of the twilight as we stand here, touching a deeper spring of sadness, perchance, than need be. The land is *going back*. Too many fields, hard-won as these, are going back. Are the moor-folk forgetting?

Bingley — main Street

CHAPTER V

THE moor still calls us, and the storied Haworth street. To leave them is to forsake good friends and true, from whom one goes with a touch of heartache and a sense that elsewhere one will meet no comrades like to them. Half our tales remain untold, and return insistent to the mind at this eleventh hour. And the moor? What further shall be said of it—this moor which wears a thousand faces to its beauty, yet offers fitting words for none? The valleys change with the seasons; but the heath varies hour by hour with each subtle alteration of the light, the wind, the clouds. Underfoot, and overhead, and away to the purpling vistas of the hills, this big world of the heath is never weary of its changes.

Let us stand one little moment longer, before we say farewell to it, at the dark edge of Haworth Moor. Again old thoughts come thronging back on one—old thoughts, and with them the sounds and scents of many yesterdays. The whistle of the North-Wester as it sweeps through the dried husks of last year's ling—the tongues of flame that start from the red mouth of the storm-sky—the thunder-crash that dies in stifled growls among the black moor-hollows—the reckless, sun-smitten glory of the August heather—the sob of rain-winds in November—the grey forlornness of the hill-mists—the ceaseless patter-patter-patter of the drops upon the red-rust of the bracken—all these rise from the buried years and live for us again as we look out across the heath. These, and the bitter-sweet scent of the marshes, the lush reek of mistals, the savour of sweet upland grass as it falls in grey-green swathes to the music of the moor men's scythes. Scents, more than any sound or sight, are apt to stir the heart of a man—a magic and a charm they have to awaken slumbering memories and half-forgotten dreams ; and, as we stand at the moor-edge here, it is the crisp of the marshland breath, soft-creeping from the heath, that brings dead Haworth back to us with swift and over-mastering distinctness. We have had the last backward glance we craved ; and it has grown harder still to say good-bye. Glamour of wind and rain and changeful sky

—glamour of story, of hates and loves that were reared in the wind-wild open—how can one leave this memory-haunted corner of the moors ?

But what would you ? Over the hill-crest there, snug-sheltered beneath the hinder edge of it, the valleys also call to us and claim their due ; and one of these valleys, though on the map it is marked plain Bingley, is known far and near by the bonnier title of the Throstle-Nest of England. There is one splendour of the moors, another of the dales ; the folk show differences of breed in each ; yet Bingley, after its own fashion, has characteristics well-nigh as marked as those of Haworth, and it is time that we made friends with it.

The year is at break of summer as we go down the Haworth street, cross the Worth River, and follow the road that leads to Hallas Brigg. No quality, perhaps, of our Yorkshire landscape is more surprising than the swiftness with which it changes, in a few short miles, from moor to shaven pasture lands, from treeless, black-walled sweeps of green to well-wooded valleys, where thrush and blackbird, robin and finch and linnet, drown the solitary complaining of curlew, grouse, or plover ; and no road in the shire gives us so good an impression of this quality as the track from Haworth to Hallas Brigg, from Hallas Brigg to Bingley. Bleak moor and bluff, storm-spattered houses go with us still ; turning, we see old Haworth swart against the hillside. Such trees as grow here have known the north wind and the west, and

carry the memory in every crooked protest of their limbs.
Overhead the peewits wheel, and up above us yonder,
on Manuels Heights, stands a lonely inn on a lonelier
moorland ridge. It seems that the world of bud and
blossom lies far out beyond the furthest edge of
sky.

Yet cross the road a little below Manuels Heights, and
dip over the bare hill-crest; climb the stile beyond the
farm yonder, and turn to the left across the lumpy strip of
grass-land, and so over the second stile this side of
Hallas Brigg. The scene has changed, completely as if
one had stood on the Fairy Carpet of legend and had
covered leagues in as many seconds. Beech and alder,
hazel and thorn and sycamore, are profligate with May-
time leafage. The undergrowth is hazy with the purple-
blue of hyacinths. An eager stream goes down between
fern-weighted banks into the pleasant valley-places.
Where is the moor? Where are the crooked, blunt-faced
trees, the houses that voice the majesty of desolation?
Gone--gone altogether. Through wood and coppice the
path idles on, through open glades where the lazy cattle
flick their sterns and the brown bees ply their craft. The
stream rounds to a shady pool under the foot-bridge here
--a place to linger by, lying face to the water and watching the trout hang motionless amid the cool green-and-
amber of the water-shadows. Have you ever tickled
trout? Well, no matter; it is scarcely a lawful occupation
for a summer's day; but the pool here was a favourite

resort once on a time for those who had delicate fingers
and no nice scruples as to the shibboleths of sport.

Above, the bleakness of the moorscape suggested effort,
and the stride lengthened as if one were making instinctively for some settled goal ; but these winding wood-
ways are paths of sheer idleness, and one walks them a
laggard with an easy conscience. The hawthorn buds are
breaking white, and wild-cherry bloom is fragrant at the
edge of wood and field ; cock pheasants—plump fellows,
airing their graces in view of the obsequious hen birds—
are filling their crops in every second pasture ; the song of
thrushes grows louder, merrier, until there seems no bush,
no tree, but holds its speckled minstrel. Marsh-mallows,
milkmaids pink-and-white, butter-cool sweeps of kingcups,
are gay against the lush green of fattening grass. We've
all the leisure in the world at our command, and yet not
time enough to stay at every hedgerow, every stream or
coppice-corner, which offers something worth the seeing.

There have been tales told in the keeper's cottage there,
which overlooks the broadening valley and the well-
timbered slopes that break in leaf-green foam against the
sky—tales of the old sporting times, when they hunted
the fox by day and the poacher by night, when the stars
shone down on many a rough-and-tumble contest that
ended now and then in tragedy. What if we call up the
shade of Keeper John, and set him, in unsubstantial
gaiters and shadowy coat of bottle-green, against the
gateway yonder ? For he can tell us the tale of how once

the Squire of Bingley was hoist with his own petard
—a tale, belonging to an older day, which has been
jostled almost out of mind by newer stories. Lead up
the talk craftily to the old Squire, until little by little
Keeper John is lured into the legend of Tom o' th' Cliff;
for even ghosts, if they be Yorkshiremen's, must be
humoured, and to angle for one special story is much like
tickling trout.

"It war this way," he will begin at length, taking a
filmy pipe from between his filmy lips. "Th' Squire, he
comes to me one neet, an' 'John,' says he, meaning
myseln, 'I'm not best pleased wi' Tom o' th' Cliff; I hear
he ligs abed while sharper chaps steal my game.'

"Now, this war true enough; for Tom o' th' Cliff war
th' keeper ower Howarth way, an' he hed a fine name for
idleness; but I'd allus hed a soft spot i' my heart for
Tom, an' so I says to th' Squire, 'Squire,' I says, 'they'll
say owt, an' I wodn't hearken, if I war ye, to tales of
ony keeper's idleness. Tak nowt on hearsay—that's
my rule.'

"Squire laughs at that, i' his round-bellied, mischeevous
way. 'I willun't, John,' says he; 'I'll cross to Howarth
this varry neet an' see for myseln,' he says; 'an' if I find
Tom o' th' Cliff abed, I'll whip him out on 't.'

"'What?' says I, for I war capped. 'Ye'll cross to
Howarth a bitter neet like this?'

"'Ay,' says he. 'I've hed a thrashing i' store for yond
shammocky lie-abed this twelvemonth past.'

" ' Ye've no hoss wi' ye,' I says, 'an' it's a fairish step to Tom's,' says I.

" ' I've a pair of sound legs, damme, an' they'll serve,' says he, blunt as th' wrang edge of a scythe.

" Well, I pulled a long face at that. He war a game un, war th' Squire, an' when he said owt he hed a trick o' meaning it. I tried all maks to lead his mind away fro' Tom o' th' Cliff, but nowt 'ud do but he mun hev his bit o' frolic."

Keeper John pauses, while the slow smile of reminiscence steals over his ghostly face.

" Well," he resumes, presently, " at after Squire hed set off into th' nipping wind—clear north it blew, an' cowd at that, for all it war nobbut a young November—when he'd set off for Howarth, I scratted my head fearful hard, an' I sat me dahn to do part thinking. I knew, weel as if I could see th' chap, that Tom o' th' Cliff 'ud be ligging between-blankets, an' I could no way thoyle to pictur' him snoring quiet as a babby, when all th' while Squire war walking ower to dress his jacket wi' t' thick end of a blackthorn stick. My own legs war getting stiff wi' wear an' tear, an' they war shorter o' knee-grease by th' half nor Squire's ; so it warn't mich use *my* seeking to best him ower to Howarth. Well, I thowt an' I thowt ; an' last of all a notion came to me—a notion that set me laughing summat th' same as Squire hed laughed a while back."

Another pause, and the echo of a long-dead burst of merriment from Keeper John.

"I lost no time, I tell ye, sooin as I'd getten square hod o' th' notion ; an' I off upstairs to th' room where my lad Joney war ligging asleep—rising fifteen th' lad war then—an', 'Joney,' says I, 'dost know where Tom o' th' Cliff lives ?'

"'Ay,' says he, sleepy-like.

"I hoicked him out on to th' floor at that. 'Then away tha goes as fast as thy spindle legs 'ull carry thee,' says I, 'an' tell him th' Squire 'ull be seeking him by an' by wi' a blackthorn stick. An' tak ower th' fields, for it's gainer by half a mile nor th' road Squire hes ta'en.'

"Well, my lad Joney, as it turned out at after, went like a grand un to Howarth, part running an' part walking, an' he hed a gooid start o' th' Squire at th' finish. An' he raised sich a din, did th' lad, outside Tom o' th' Cliff's, that Tom jumps out o' bed like as if 'twar Judgment, an' puts his head through th' window, an' axes what th' dangment war agate. Joney telled him, an' he thowt Tom would niver hev done wi' laughing. Then Tom o' th' Cliff, while he war putting on his breeches an' coit, punched his missis i' th' back, an' gat her out o' bed, an' made her come dahn to gi'e my lad a bite an' a sup for his pains ; an' then off he sets, fast as he could go, for th' road ower th' moor that Squire would hev to come by.

"Well, he carred i' t' ling, did Tom o' th' Cliff, an' bided, an' slipped his hand round an' about th' stick he'd brought wi' him. He hedn't been ligged there more nor a two-three minutes, when who should come along t'

path, treading nipperly, but Squire hisseln. Th' Squire
war balancing his own stick, too, an'—so Tom telled me
th' tale at after—he war talking to hisseln, summat this
fashion : ' Ye doan't trick a weasel, Tom o' th' Cliff !
Thowt Squire 'ud let ye sleep till Doomsday, an' niver
no more about it, did ye ? Well, we shall see—ay, we
shall see.' Tom let him talk—Squire coming nearer all
th' while—an' then he ups like a shot fro' t' ling and
cracks Squire bonnily fair a-top of his crown, an' knocks
him heels-over-head.

" ' So I've getten thee at last,' says Tom ; ' tha'll come
snaring my grouse again, wilt 'a ?' he says, an' fetches
Squire another crack, for luck.

" Well, Tom could scarce keep his face straight as he
watched th' Squire pick hisseln up, dazed-like ; but he
shammed gaumless, best he could, an' reckoned he'd
mista'en Squire for a poacher, an' war as full o' sorriness
as an egg is full o' meat. But Squire war noan th' man
to be ta'en in, an' he judged how matters war, though he
couldn't tell how Tom hed getten to know."

John the Keeper puffs at his filmy pipe awhile, then
proceeds, as if in answer to a question :—

" Did Squire bear malice, say ye ? Ye niver knew th'
owd Squire, that's plain to be seen. He war bested, an'
he owned to 't ; an' they say 'at Tom o' th' Cliff war th'
richer by a guinea nor he war afore he knocked his
master heels uppermost.

" ' Tom,' says Squire, at parting, ' niver tell nobody

that ye caught th' Squire snaring grouse. It 'ud look bad, Tom,' says he, ' when next I sit on th' bench.'

" ' I'll keep a still tongue, Squire, ye may depend on 't,' says Tom, grave as a pig.

" But th' next day it war all ower th' countryside how Squire hed gone to gi'e Tom o' th' Cliff a thrashing."

Well—as the keeper would say—it is time we were moving on, though our ghostly friend could tell us fifty such tales of the days when it was somewhat of a recreation to be knocked heels uppermost while seeing that one's servants did their duty.

Another story meets us by and by, on the highway that runs through Harden village to Bingley town—a grimmer tale than the last, which centres round the house on the left hand of the road there. The house—Hill End, its name is—shows as a trim farmstead now, but it still bears witness to the greater importance which once on a time attached to it. This was upwards of two centuries ago, when Samuel Sunderland lived there—a merchant who was reputed to be one of the wealthiest men of his day. Sunderland, a gentleman-miser of the old type, kept a store of guineas in a room at the back of the house, and took vast pride in adding to the store as occasion served. He seems, moreover, to have been well pleased that his neighbours should know the number of his hoarded guineas ; and certain ne'er-do-weels who lived at Collingham—relatives of Sunderland's, some say—determined to make off with the gold that was lying

so ready to their hands. They enlisted the services of
the Collingham blacksmith, accordingly, and induced
him to take off their horses' shoes and reverse them—
an easy job, which an expert smith could get through
in some fifteen minutes by the clock. Riding as fast
as their rough-shod beasts could travel, the thieves
reached Harden in the dead of night, with sacks for
the gold slung across their saddles and a little dog
following at their heels.

Why they brought the dog it is hard to guess, unless
they were anxious to feel that they had at least one honest
soul among them ; and in the sequel they paid dearly for
their whim—for, after securing booty to the tune of
several thousand guineas, they showed such desperate
eagerness to be off that they left the honest member of
their company behind, shut up in the room where they
had found the gold. Sunderland and the other men
of the house, roused by the tumult, were speedily aware
how matters stood ; they caught the dog which had been
left in lieu of guineas, broke one of its legs lest it should
out-distance their horses, and set it on the highroad.
The dog made straight for Collingham, and they followed ; and so, as is the way of this life, the forethought
which had bidden them conceal the trend of their depart-
ing hoof-marks was rendered futile by carelessness in
what seemed an unimportant matter.

The thieves, meanwhile, were likewise heading straight
for Collingham ; and so cumbered were they with their

spoil, that on the way they found themselves compelled
to throw down a part of it by the road-side, lest the
remainder, and their own necks with it, should be lost
if the dawn found them still riding on the public highway. They stopped at the Collingham inn to divide the
gold ; and the landlord, scenting something untoward in
their behaviour, crept upstairs, put his eye to a crack in
the ceiling, and saw what was going on beneath.

From this point the tale moves forward with a fine
dramatic irony. Picture the men—there were nine of
them in all, according to tradition—bending over the
table ; between their white faces the flame of the rushlight mounts smoky toward the smoke-grimed roof ; the
table-top is squalid with ale-droppings and bright with
piled-up gold. On a sudden the rushlight-flame is blown
aslant, and a stream of grease goes spattering over the
guineas. The thieves glance up affrighted ; they have
been too absorbed to hear the door open, and this shaft
of cold wind is their first intimation that they are watched.
In the doorway stands mine host, a fat and greedy smile
wrinkling the corners of his mouth.

"Come, lads, a quiet tongue has need of gilding," says
Boniface, with a glance behind to see that his way of
escape lies open in case of violence.

The men start to their feet, and eye each other
furtively.

"'Tis share and share alike in jobs of this kind," the
host proceeds. "Give me a tenth part of the guineas

yonder, or——" He points his sentence with a grim nod toward the village.

They give in at last, and have just finished their division of the gold when a little dog, making for home with the hue and cry behind him, limps into Collingham village. He passes the tavern just as his master is coming out of the door with his accomplices, welcomes them with innocent fervour, and throws them as neatly into the clutches of Samuel Sunderland and his friends as any Bow Street Runner could have done.

The thieves, with the landlord who had pocketed his share of the spoil, were tried in due course and condemned to death. Whereat one of the culprits, a burly, big-faced fellow, laughed outright with a merriment he could no way control. The judge, aghast at this levity in face of death, demanded the reason of his untoward mirth, and the Yorkshireman pointed at the shivering landlord.

" It's the landlord yonder," he cried. " He said he'd share and share alike, your Worship, and, by the Lord Harry, he means to keep his word."

There's more in this than just a dramatic finish to a tale of robbery; the ineradicable humour of the Yorkshireman is in it—the humour that needs a touch of bitter, a dash of stinging irony, to bring it to its finest flavour. More than two centuries ago this rogue, standing eye to eye with the gallows, found leisure for a burst of unaffected merriment ; and the same jest to-day would

provoke an equal jollity. There are times when ability
to laugh, not from bravado, but from good cause shown,
betokens the grittiest sort of courage ; and who is there
in Yorkshire but has a kindly thought for this rogue of
Collingham who died with a jest upon his lips ? Nay, the
jest has passed into a proverb, and " Ye'll tak your share,
like th' landlord o' Collingham " is a phrase well understood throughout the countryside.

We are in Harden village now, and perplexed a little to
choose from the countless old associations that linger
round the place. There was a skirmish here during the
Civil War, and a band of Cromwell's soldiers sleeps quiet
in the Squire's park above ; down in the hollow yonder
lies Harden Hall, where Fairfax stayed while directing
the movements of the Parliamentary troops in the neighbourhood—a black old pile, more like the grim moor-
dwellings than the prettier halls which stud the valley
lower down so thickly. The park itself is bold in
its sweeping lines of heath and tree-land : no sooner
have fat pastures given place to woods than the
woods in turn merge into a treeless waste of heath ;
grouse and pheasant lie down in peace together,
and the thrush has scarce done singing before the night-
jar—the lonely-hearted bird of dole—takes up the song
and tunes it to a harsher note.

There is a cave within the park-walls—a cave that has
given shelter in its time to many a hard-pressed fox. Only
those of slender build can win beyond its threshold, for a

Harden Brigg.

little way from the mouth two upright slabs of rock stand guard, leaving the narrowest of passages between them ; but within, if those who have won through this rock-gateway are to be credited, the passage widens, branches out north, east, and west, and finally leads to three separate, room-like cavities of the rock, lofty and broad, which seem to have inspired the country folk with a sense of the uncanny ; for the farmer and his wife who used to live, fifty years ago, above the cavern, had no manner of doubt that strange noises came from underground at night—voices, and the sound of a poker, wielded by human or by goblin hands, stirring a fire below.

No one seems to visit the cave nowadays ; it is in a secluded corner of the park, and all the tales of it come from the hillside elders who remember the days when they hunted over Harden Moor, and who recall the cave with peculiar vividness because so many attempts were made to drive out the quarry when it was run to earth here.   One Harden ancient—a man worth knowing, by the way—remembers seeing the name Richard de Ponte-fract cut deep into the rock-face of the cavern.   A pleasant footprint, this, of the times when Bingley was in the heyday of its youth, for Richard de Pontefract was vicar of the parish as far back as the thirteenth century.   The old-time parson, indeed, seemed always most in evidence when any sort of sport or adventure was on hand, from exploring a difficult cave to risking his neck in the wake of eager hounds.   Witness Grimshaw of Haworth, and a certain lusty vicar of Skipton, who, as we shall see, took part in one of the maddest escapades that ever lightened the sober round of history.

Ahead of us, walking with a square back and a downright gait which deny his five-and-seventy years, is that very ancient who was in our thoughts just now. We fall into step beside him, and he brings to mind another bit of local history—how they were not always convinced in Harden parish of the need for excise duties, and how the heather-clumps on the moor above the village hid many a private still in days gone by. Our friend talks quietly of the matter ; yet his eye has such a softness in it when he speaks of rye and fermentation, and he reasons so weightily in favour of the old order, that one comes to an accurate conclusion.

"Ay, for sure—free trade an' fair trade, it war," he murmurs, as he stops for a farewell word before turning him back to Harden.

" Free trade and fair trade," one echoes, full of that sympathy which the illicit picturesqueness of the old-time drink traffic never fails to claim.

Agreement with his views seems only to render him more argumentative ; for any man can be roused by opposition, but it needs a Dalesman to argue stolidly with one whose views are in accord.

" Let's argee it out a bit, now," he resumes, meeting one's eye alertly. " It's this way, ye see. Poaching is honest, an' there's none—save Squire, mebbe—as 'ud

9

think o' saying owt else. Well, now, we'll reason it out.
Poaching is honest, becos t' things that swim, an' t' things
that fly, are all men's right. An' isn't whisky one o' t'
things that flies? I should think it war, begow—I've known
it fly to th' head fair like a flock o' chattering starlings."

The logic is straightforward—and unanswerable. And
so they made their whisky, and sometimes they were
detected in their cheerful labour and were imprisoned for
the same; and they came out again undaunted, and found
a fresh corner for their still, and prospered for as long as
might be. For how could they, or their neighbours, look
on this sort of imprisonment as any disgrace? If they
distilled for their own profit, they did it also for the
poor man's benefit; and the poor, according to their own
wisdom—the wisdom, not of theory, but of hard practice
—have more need for solace than the rich, so that he who
gave them whisky cheap was worth a score such as
proffered advice that was even less expensive.

They seem a long way off, those days of private stills;
but men can remember yet how the spirit-vendors came
round from door to door of Bingley village, with a
serious, other-worldly cast of countenance and sheep's-
bladders full of whisky hidden underneath their coats.
There is nothing of the kind now, however; or we should
not, for fair play's sake, have stopped to chat of how
Harden, Eldwick, and many another unsophisticated
moorland village sent native spirits into the peaceful
valley-lands.

CHAPTER VI

HOW DOG STORMER PLAYED THE FOX

THE bonniest highway in the Dales, they say, is the road that runs from Harden down to Bingley; a road that is noteworthy also for two houses which lie scarce a stone's-throw from each other on either hand the way. St. Ives, hidden among the trees that crown the hill-crest yonder,

From Harden Down to Bingley.

recalls, each time one sees it, the old-world sportsman who lived and died there—that bluff, hard-hitting

Squire of Bingley whose memory, green among us
yet, takes us backward to the days when sport was the
one vital interest of the parish, and to hunt the fox was
accounted a merrier game than weaving fleeces into
cloth. The tales best remembered, and oftenest told by
the Aire-dale elders, are legends of the chase, and the old
kennels standing at the field-head there recall the mighty
hunt that happened all on a winter's day, when they
started a fox at Bingley, a mile down the valley, and
chased him hell-for-leather up the Vale of Aire, and
brought him to a reckoning in the middle of Skipton
town—ten miles as the crow flies, but somewhat further
as the fox-brush trails.

This same old Squire of Bingley, too, was the hero
of the story lately told us by John the Keeper, and it is
only one of many pithy tales which clamour for a hearing.
Firm in his hatreds, kindly and keen in friendship,
straight-running whether friend or foe were to be met,
"the old Squire" stands yet as a type of the true Yorkshire landowner. We knew him well in Haworth parish,
and if you ask the moor folk what they thought of him,
they'll answer guardedly, "He war a staunch un ! Ay,
he war a staunch un." And that, in moorland parlance,
sums up a character more deftly than half a hundred
phrases of the clipped modern speech could do.

The Squire, though, will meet us again by and by, and
meanwhile we'll turn down the broad, sandy road that
leads off the highway on our right and dips out of view

among the thick-leaved trees below. The contrast is of
the sharpest : St. Ives on the one hand, with its traditions
of the chase ; on the other, Woodbank, whose memories
are all of art.

There is nothing to show that a place of rare and
curious beauty lies at the end of this sanded road which
is leading us to Woodbank ; for the leafage hides roof
and chimney-stacks, and the breast of the hill denies us
a sight of the trim garden-ways that wind by lawn and
water through the sheltered hollow. Aldam Heaton lived
here once ; he remodelled the house on the fabric of an
older building, and fashioned the garden, and enriched
both house and garden with memories that bring back
to us an unaccustomed fragrance. His grandfather, by
the by, came from Haworth, and he was in all likelihood
a relative of those other Heatons who lived at Ponden—
a house to inspire the younger generation with fine
ideals.

Go down the sandy road, and in at the gate. The
house is untenanted, we'll say, and we are free to wander
in and out at will. There is an unusual, puzzling air
about the place ; the windows have lilies and roses
richly stained upon their glass ; the lawns slope smooth
to the stream, which widens here and there to mimic
lakes. A dovecot stands high on its rounded pole in
front of the summer-house ; and not long since, before
the arbour was furbished up afresh, a verse of the old
Hebrew Nature-worshipper's triumph-song, lusty after

long centuries, ran round the three walls in letters of antique device :—

"My beloved spake, and said unto me, Rise up, my love, my fair one, and come away. For, lo, the winter is past, the rain is over and gone : the flowers appear on the earth ; the time of the singing of birds is come, and the voice of the turtle is heard in our land."

Ay, and the garden sets the words to music on this May evening. The dying sun is tender with flowers half-closed in token of good-night ; the stream is quiet, and the lakes scarce stirred by the laggard wooing of the breeze. It is a place to lie back in, while one closes tired senses to the turmoil of the little world without. What is this air of youth perpetual, of serene and quietly philosophic age, which hangs like a kindly mantle over stream and dovecot, lawn and sleepy house ? One cannot tell— only, that the mind of him who wrought it all, under the Spring-God's hand, has laid on it a clearer impress of his brain and heart than any builder we have known, save the Heaton who reared grey Ponden House under shelter of the moors far up behind us yonder.

Rossetti stayed here. The influence of his school is apparent once we have the key to it, and it is easy to understand how Aldam Heaton came to be intimate with the master of a poetic brotherhood. Rossetti—that odd compound of the spiritual and the ultra-sensual—would find the one side of his nature in accurate harmony with this northern garden. He had better have dwelt longer here ; for, sheltered as it is and soft with a southern sort of richness, the moors lie close enough to keep its beauty sweet, and there is no room at all here for the mawkishness that comes of too long living with dulcet winds and lily-weighted airs. What the freakish gospel of the Pre-Raphaelites held of strength, that Woodbank shows in every mellow line ; the spineless side of it—the side that saps the strength and jaundices the blood—could neither win, nor keep, a place among these cleanly garden-breezes.

Well, Aldam Heaton took his gifts to London, and prospered there ; but he left Yorkshire the poorer for his going.

And so back to the highroad again, and down to Bingley, through woods that keep our thoughts in tune with the Rossettian house which we have left behind us in the hollow. It is easy, at cool May eventide, to understand how Bingley earned its name of "The Throstle-Nest of Old England." Overhead the trees touch fingers ; to right and left the hyacinths are blue as the sky that peeps through interlacing branches ; and through all, under all, above all, is the splendid clamour of the thrush. The spendthrift air of night has got into the birds' full throats ; they perform strange antics, they break off the ordered roundelay of soberer moments to whistle, trill, reverse their scale of notes—do all, in fine, that may be, to show their zeal in praise of benefits received. Our northern woods lack nightingales, folk tell you ; but the thrush fits them better—'tis a more honest bird, a merrier, with a wider range of song than ever the nightingale can compass. Does the thrush go sighing for what he has not all through a prime spring evening ? Not he ; like a sensible, good fellow, he dines well first, and afterwards is ready to give us poetry the poetry that bubbles from a cheerful heart and a body rightly nurtured.

All down the road, as far as the " Brown Cow " hostelry—the first house we pass in Bingley— the throstle-song goes with us, and we can still hear it after we have turned the corner and set foot on the bridge that spans the once-transparent Water of Aire. Give a glance at the long upstairs-room which flanks this side of the " Brown Cow." This was the magistrates' room in the old days, and it witnessed stormy scenes when Bingley was a hotbed of Chartist principles. It saw, amongst other matters, the Squire of Bingley face the rabble —no gentle rabble, either—and give them threat for threat, and browbeat them from passion into smouldering discontent. Riots had been general in the village ; the Squire had sent for a company of pensioners from Chelsea, to aid the local yeomanry in restoring law and order. They had arrested several of the ringleaders, and the magistrates, assembled in the upstairs room there, had sent them to take their trial at the York Assizes ; the

mob had rescued them as they were being led off, had
carried them to the forge that stood the other side
the bridge, where the blacksmith knocked their shackles
loose, and had paraded them in triumph through the
streets. Then they returned to the magistrates' room,
vowing vengeance on the Squire and on his brothers of
the Bench ; and the Squire—enjoying it all, no doubt, in
his grim way—squared his jaw, and roughened his voice,
and astounded them by that utter indifference to peril
which was his strongest quality.

A mob is always mean ; and this especial crowd
offered no exception to the rule, though the Chartists,
take them singly, could show as good men among them
as need be. When the Squire showed so plain a distaste
to nonsense, they turned on Thacker, the Clerk, whose
only offence was that he had been employed by the
magistrates in the transaction of their business. Seizing
the frail little man, with his wide choker and his narrow,
genteel body, they hung him over the parapet of the
bridge, half between land and water, and made him
recant all the law-abiding deeds which he had done in
the course of his nervously well-regulated life. "Wait a
tick-tack ! Wait a tick-tack!" pleaded Thacker, as they
dipped him nearer and nearer to the water in token that
his recantation did not speed fast enough. And ever after
he was known as "Tommy Tick-tack," until his baptismal
name was all but lost in this tradition of the amenities of
warfare. Some, who claim to have been bystanders at

the time, assert that Thacker was only threatened with

the water, not held above it; but the more dramatic tale has gained too great a hold on the popular fancy to be ousted by mere fact.

They were the cause of a ripe jest, these Chartists, though innocent of any hand in it. Alarm was widespread in the district; none knew what turn the excesses of the rioters might next take; no town in a state of siege could have been more ripe for panic. While matters were in this case, the Squire was sitting in his pew one Sabbath

morning—the same pew that stands there now, high up above the congregation—when suddenly, in the midst of the service, a man ran breathless in at the south door.

"The Chartists!" he cried. "The Chartists! They're massing on Harden Moor!"

Now the old Squire, for all his robust qualities, had an eye for spectacular effect, and he grasped the occasion promptly as affording just one of those romantic backgrounds in which his friend D'Israeli revelled. Leaning impressively over the pew-front, the Squire looked down on the devout yeomen who were seated underneath.

"To arms, my men! To arms!" he cried, with magnificent effect.

All was bustle. The men got to arms—seized their rusty blunderbusses, that is, or looked to the priming of pistols that were like to slay their owners at the first discharge. Amid the plaudits of the crowd and the half-stifled screams of ladies who feared they were riding to their death, the company set off for Harden Moor, their guide going on ahead with the Squire to show where the rioters were massing. Thoughts of the homes they might never see again were with the men, doubtless; they suffered the trepidations, the sheer frights, the martial glow, that wait on warfare; it was as real to them as if the French themselves were drawn up to give them battle.

And, true enough, a black mass of people showed ahead as they gained the moor. Their guide dropped modestly to the rear, and none noted that his face was convulsed as with an effort to keep some overmastering emotion in check. The Squire pressed forward jauntily, cheering his men to the attack. They cleared the intervening ground at a run, blunderbusses levelled, pistols cocked—and found a camp-meeting of Primitive Methodists, with a discreet minister of peace seated tranquilly atop of a waggon, eating his midday meal of cheese and bread.

They looked for the humourist then who had led them hither; but they found him not. And there was laughter in Bingley village that day until the sun went down.

The Bingley folk were ever fond of belittling a cause or a man's character by the simple plan of giving it a name too big for its merits; and so they called the Chartist movement here the Bingley War, because no blood was shed. Yet it was serious enough, for all that, and if there had been no men of Squire Ferrand's stamp to stem the tide when it was running at its ugliest, they would have remembered the riots in Bingley for graver reasons than for the jests afforded.

As we look back upon it now, it is hard to understand the pent-up discontent, the fury, that lay behind the movement; harder yet to realise that among those in sympathy with it were many hard-headed, serious men who had thought deeply in their time, and who saw no remedy but force for the disorders of the social body. For in Bingley they remember the humorous stories best, and this earnest rioting, with all its dreams of better

things to follow, grows ludicrous a little when measured
by the tale of how a band of patriots went to fight a
Methodist camp-meeting.

It suits the flavour of old Bingley, too, this rough-and-
tumble recklessness, which wore a grim front and hid
something of a laughing heart behind it ; and we move
again, with no perceptible transition, among the wool-
combers who peopled every cottage between the river-
bridge and the old church. Hard times they are said to
have been ; but, measured by happiness rather than by
comfort, they were fairer days than ever the working
man will see again. Hard times ? Nay, not in Haworth
parish, nor in Bingley here. Food might be coarse,
cottages scantily furnished—but what mattered it when
half the men's days were spent out of doors, when sport
and laughter and rough revelry brought back for awhile
a flavour of old Robin Hood to an age that was so soon
to settle into colourless sobriety ?

Nothing is easier than to piece together the village life
of forty years ago, before Bingley was a town, or thought
of being one. There is an old race and a new race here :
the new knows nothing of its traditions, but the old has
clung tenaciously to the atmosphere in which it was
reared, and to tales which its fathers told to brother-
greybeards when at even pipes were reeking round the
hearth-place. From the forge at the hill-top, where
the Longbottoms have plied a thrifty trade for generations out of mind, to the houses that cluster round the

Parish Church, all is much as it was, and we need only a bench at the street-corner and one of the true Bingley race beside us, to people each individual house and cottage with the boisterous life of yesterday. For no quality of the folk here is more strongly marked than

A Corner of Old Bingley.

their power of vivid narration ; they do not tell you a tale merely ; they point it so deftly with voice and gesture that you see the characters they describe and hear them speak.

There was Harry Lambert, who lived on Bailey Hill ; when he was not wool-combing, he was fishing or

playing the fiddle, and they say he did all three with
distinction. In the cottage yonder, opposite the church-
gates, there was a combing-shop for six, while its neighbour held pad-posts for four ; but the combing-shops
were empty on Sunday, Monday, and Tuesday of each
week, since no one thought of working while there was
time to be made for fishing, following the hounds, or
playing the rough jests which rendered Bingley no hospitable haven to chance travellers from without. On Saturday morning they had to take their combings to the mills,
and so on the Wednesday they would begin to settle down
to work ; Thursday would be busier still, and on Friday
the dawn would not seldom creep in at the windows of
the combing-shops and find the charcoal still burning in
the pot, the combs on the pad-posts still carrying their
fleeces, the men still dripping with the sweat riven out
of them by plying their heavy tools. The little lads of
the neighbourhood were wont to creep into the cottages
at nights and listen to the queer tales that followed the
day's work ; but they were hustled neck-and-crop into
the street on Fridays, for then there was no time for
anything but toil.

Then, too, a long bench used to stand just under the
wall that bounded the Terrace Walk on Bailey Hill ; and
here, when summer was kindlier out of doors than in,
the combers would sit at the down-going of the sun, and
send for Harry Lambert, and make him fiddle till the
stars came out to listen. What anglers' stories went the

round at such times; how many foxes were harried over remembered leagues; what practical jokes were ripened against some absent comrade, or jest repeated which touched the village gentry—a gentry that was, in its own way, as characteristic and peculiar as its humbler neighbours.

They were more like boys than men, these wool-combers—boys in their light-hearted carelessness. They lit huge fires on Guy Fawkes' Day; they laughed at nothing at all; they performed all sorts of laddish pranks in their old age, such as their grandsons are too staid to think of nowadays at twenty.

Bingley, indeed, was no place for "furriners." Witness the hawker of plaster images who came crying his wares over Millgate Bridge, past the combing-shop that stood this side the corn-mill.

"Begow, what's this lot?" cried one of the combers, dropping the wool which he was drawing through the sliver.

"A chap wi' a tray o' white-faced fooils on his head," said another, opening the window. "Danged if I doan't hev a go at yond plaster wench that's bobbing up an' dahn; she's nobbut loosish, I fancy."

An old boot, deftly aimed, caught the image behind the shoulders. Another missile followed, and another, until the window was thick with laughing faces, and **the** hawker's tray showed dimly through a rain of boots, iron bolts, and lumps of coal. Not a bit of harm in it—only the quick following of an impulse that never stopped to count the cost. Yet one feels that Bingley was decidedly no place for strangers.

Fishing, however, was the prime sport of all, and Aire River yielded brimful baskets of grayling and of trout. Why, for instance, was the building that used to stand close by Ailshird's Well called Fisherman's Cottage? Only because there lived in it a certain wool-comber, who brought more fish than wool to market. The fame of his prowess is still undimmed; the weight of his best catches lives, too—and grows.

Ailshird's Well, by the way, is a spring of ice-cold water, which time out of mind has possessed virtues for the curing of sprains and the cooking of vegetables; its name will one day be a puzzle to archæologists, who will trace it back to Norse, or Danish, or Icelandic origin; whereas it means no more than Alice Hird's Well, and its name-patron was a wise woman who once lived at Fisherman's Cottage.

Well, we cannot stay for ever with the wool-combers, their frolics and their sport. Yet look up the street to where the saddler's shop stands, and listen to the tale of Dog Stormer, who played the fox in his old age and beat the whole pack of youngsters. It was all on a hunting-day that Stormer lay outside the saddler's door yonder; he had been pensioned off after long and honourable service in the field, and he looked out lazily on a world with which he found naught so much amiss—harbouring

10

a pardonable thought or two, it may be, that he was the most important factor in the village life. While he lay thus, blinking contemptuous lids at meaner dogs who came for colloquy, there sounded a merry chorus from over the Millgate bridge. Stormer sat up at that, and turned his head towards a music that he remembered well, and sniffed a little as if the sweet rankness of the fox's brush were in the wind.

Round the corner swept the Squire's hounds, going to the hunt on the far side of the valley, their sterns turned skyward. Dog Stormer was on old ground again; he shook himself and advanced to meet these kindred spirits, with less of youth's frolic in his movements than aforetime, but with more of the assured dignity of age. The youngsters, however, mistook his overtures—whether wilfully or not, it can never now be known; the leaders made a dive at Stormer, and those behind followed hot-foot into the fray.

Stormer could not understand it for a moment. The pack was all but on him. Then, remembering the years that lay behind, he shot up the street with a speed begotten of old habit. The rest gave tongue and skeltered after. The huntsman, swearing his hardest, gave chase in turn. The combers came out of their cottages; the whole village was up and after hounds and huntsman, marvelling at the strange sport.

Old Stormer swerved when he gained the butcher's shop on the right hand of the street, and leaped the half-

door, and sped through the shop into the garden behind
—down the garden—over the wall—past Ailshird's Well,
and so into the road that runs by the riverside into the
corn-mill yard. After him came the hounds in full cry,
and after them the huntsman, breathless, wrathful, and
chagrined. Stormer was out of sight, however ; he had
doubled and found some place of safety best known to
himself, and the pack never came up with him again.
There was no second chase that day, for the huntsman
could do nothing with the demoralised youngsters, and
so perforce he took them back to kennel at St. Ives. And
later in the morning, they say, an old dog came strolling
carelessly along the street, and sat himself down again in
his accustomed place at the shop door, and laughed a
little to himself, in a quiet, elderly fashion, when the folk
flocked round to give him praise.

The tale of that hunt lives still, like Dick Turpin's ride
to York. Like the ride to York, too, its least detail is
remembered—what the butcher said, and where he was
standing, when Stormer cleared his half-door—the place
in the wall where Stormer leaped from the garden—the
set of the huntsman's cap and the terrible look on his face
as he chased his misguided pack. The story is a classic
by this time—and, unlike friend Turpin's feat, it is true
in every particular.

CHAPTER VII

CONCERNING THE SCHOOLMASTER'S MARE

WE will not leave Bingley yet awhile, for its history goes far back, and on the way it has gathered much of that fragrant dust which only age can bestow. An important place once, Bingley; it had a market so long ago as John's reign; and centuries before this, if one reading of the inscription on the Rune-stone found here is to be credited, a King of Northumbria considered the village of sufficient consequence to merit the gift of a baptismal font. The number of old halls, too, in the neighbourhood is noteworthy—The Grange, St. Ives, Marley Hall, Harden, Gawthorpe, Rishworth, Cottingley Halls, each with its own history, its own legends, its stately portrait-folk who surely lived and loved in an ampler air than we who are forgetting their very names.

Let us stroll to this quiet corner which has been left undisturbed by the innovations that have swept away much of the old town. The church, the school-house, and the old Grammar School—fast mouldering to decay— form three sides of a cool and pleasant square, sur- rounding a graveyard old and green and peopled with good company. The Rune-stone, most famous of its kind, and one that has set half the antiquaries of Europe by the ears, stood for many a year, inglorious and mute, behind the Grammar School, until it awoke to fame and at last secured a resting-place within the church hard by.

The tumble-down school across the kirkyard yonder is slipping out of sight and out of mind, like a decrepit grey- beard whose work is long since over ; yet boys have gone from it in times past, to make their mark in the world, and to remember at many an after gloaming-tide the homely, parochial fashion of their training—ay, they will recall the very gravestones, flat, square, and weather- stained, on which they chalked their rings for marbles, and the gaunt, up-standing monuments behind which they played at hide-and-seek when the lessons of the day were over. A school of the old type, it was, where rich men's sons rubbed shoulders with the poor and shared the teaching of a master who was sometimes a scholar and invariably a gentleman. " The old Squire " was educated here, among his humbler neighbours—an out-of-date practice, which identified landowners with their village as no other education could, and enabled them to move real among the interests of the community which furnished them with bread.

The long, many-windowed building here, which looks over the roadway and the graveyard at the crumbling school, has been for many a generation the head-master's house—the vicarage, too, for that matter, in the days when vicar and head-master were one and the same. A characteristic house, this, built in the days when it was reckoned an advantage and a distinction to look out upon the highroad and watch the busy idleness of village life ; its whole front runs with the street, protected only by a strip of green and a line of railings ; within, it is full of queer pantries and store-rooms and the like ; it has passages with doors set here and there across them for no apparent reason, and a stone-paved kitchen of old-world roominess. Behind the house a garden mounts in terraces until the topmost lawn is level with the chimney stacks—the most whimsical garden, it seems, that ever was conceived by roving fancy. Two flights of steps lead upward, one on the left hand, the other skirting the orchard, whose trees grow upon a sloping bank. The highest terrace runs the whole length of the garden, and here, too, are apple trees dotted unconcernedly about the lawn. The gnarled old fellow yonder is one rounded mass of bloom to-night—the crab-apple tree in the orchard is snow-white, dashed with pink—the pear trees by the wall are white and green—the place is alive with blossom-sweets and hum of bees, with persistent clamour of the thrush, and steady caw of rooks, and drone of heavy-moving beetles winging their way to bed. From the church tower, upstanding behind the garden trees, the curfew rings out its lazy summons, and the antique clamour of

the bell seems well in keeping with the garden's old-world air.

It is a garden that makes one long to know something more about it. It ought to have a love story for every apple tree, a legend for each spreading box-shrub, a tragedy for the great yew that overshadows the right-hand flight of steps. We entered the house from the level, and now we are on the top of Bailey Hill—who built this erratic place of ups and downs, where foxgloves flutter their spotted bells under wide hazel boughs, and fruit trees share the self-same soil with garden flowers ?

Tradition says—no flimsy tradition, indeed, but one deep-rooted—that a castle stood on Bailey Hill behind the garden here. Not a vestige of the building remains ; not a trace of those who lived there is left to us ; castle and guardians of its walls alike are blotted out as if they had never been. Yet this old garden has survived ; and all that seemed strange about it grows clear if we attribute its terraces, its steps, its trees of yew and box, to the builders of the castle. It was not built, then, above the house, but sloped downward from the castle to the hill-foot ; and what is now a sport of architecture was once a natural garden enough, like many another in the hilly North.

They begin to whisper that Bingley never had a castle, because no trace of it remains ; but tradition is stronger than the sceptics, and so long as Bingley keeps its memories the fathers will tell the children how fair a castle stood on Bailey Hill, over against the church. Some say that the church tower itself was raised with stones taken from the castle ruins ; others that the school-house owes the thickness of its walls to a like pillage ; others, again, assert that a curious stone trough, which lies in this same old garden here, could have come from nowhere but a substantial castle roof. No one knows, however ; for history is silent, and gossip contradictory.

It is better so. The uncertainty leaves us free to-night

to people the garden as we will. The sun is down, and the gloaming has brought a moister air with it, deepening the scent of valley lilies and of apple-bloom. Our castle folk begin to rustle through the stillness—there's a comedy of love going on beneath the orchard trees down yonder, and here on the shaven lawn a tragedy of hate is being played out to the tune of shrill-voiced rapiers ; under the great copper-beech behind us passion is catching fire at disdainful eyes, and a wooing that is not of comedy goes hotly forward. And now, again, my lord's jester is at our elbow, jingling his cap and bells and giving us the pith of a dry philosophy under cover of rank foolery. Well-a-day, there's no end to the company which we may entertain in this old garden-place !

Come through the garden and see another house, flanking the orchard and showing dimly in the twilight. Like its neighbour, it runs the whole length of the roadway, and outwardly its architecture is much the same. Within, however, it is unique ; built on the hill-side, it has a row of cottages beneath, and the upstairs windows of these cottages are on a level with the drive that leads to the house-door—a perplexing arrangement, as hard to plan in the first instance as now it is difficult to describe. In its palmy days this house ran from the stable at one end to the well-timbered garden at the other ; it was all on the same floor, and a crooked passage led inconsequently from kitchen to parlour, and from living-rooms to bed-chambers. A porch of green woodwork, thick with roses and honeysuckle, was approached by the flight of steps that led to the front door ; and within there was the flavour, subtle and no way to be imitated, which comes from old oak panels, and lavender, and beeswax rubbed into shining floors—that quiet daintiness which marked the presence of the old-world gentlewoman.

If measured by years, rather than by the change the years have wrought, no long time has passed since a certain maiden lady lived here—a maiden lady whose memory still brings the scent of rose-leaves with it. She lived within a stone's-throw of those rollicking, rough-handed wool-combers who made Bingley a pitfall to the stranger ; but the outer life passed by her, while she tended her flowers, and made her wines—of elder-berries, and currants black and red—and moved, with quiet and unsuspecting dignity, toward the grave that could scarce be more peaceful than the gentle order of her days had been.

This old maid did not merely dislike men ; she had a horror of them—the instinctive shrinking that some people have from cats. If a carpenter had to be called in, she would open doors and windows wide after he had gone, and "Mary," she would say to her favourite servant, "there is *an odour of man* about the house. We must keep the windows open, Mary, until the rooms are sweet again." Her tenants came twice a year to pay their rents ; and on these occasions the mistress of the house, moved by a self-sacrificing sense of hospitality, invited them to enter the forbidden precincts. Chairs were set in a formal line round the kitchen, and upon these the tenants sat for a chilly quarter of an hour, while they drank a glass of home-made wine, and ate their sponge-cake, and watched the little lady flutter disturbedly about the open door, as if fresh air were needful to her during the ordeal. Then, after they had finished their cakes and wine, their hostess would take a cambric handkerchief, place it in her tiny, well-bred palm, and hold it out for the reception of the moneys ; and after that her tenants would bow themselves through the creeper-covered door and down the well-kept drive.

Not on any account would the old lady touch men's hands, or money that had been in them ; when she went into the street she wore gloves that were an inch or so too long, and any gentleman who knew her ways—and who did not in Bingley ?—understood that etiquette forbade him to do more in the way of greeting than shake the limp glove-fingers. They remember yet how a new vicar came to the village who was ignorant of these characteristics, and they describe how the parson and his sensitive parishioner met for the first time in the street. The vicar wished to be cordial with an important and pleasant member of his flock ; he shook her warmly by the hand, not by the glove-fingers ; he approached her more nearly than any gentleman of the neighbourhood had dared to do this score years past. And the little lady, they say, went whiter and whiter, despair warring with politeness ; for every forward step of the vicar's she took two backward paces, until at last she was brought to bay against the railings that front the school-house—and then she turned half-face to her tormentor, and sidled back along the railings, and pleaded shopping as an excuse for cutting short all further colloquy.

Then, had she no friends, this little old lady who detested men ? To be sure she had—friends of the selfsame fashion, who formed a Round Table of old maids, and who met constantly to discuss the weighty topics of the parish. Indeed, as we look back upon their tea-parties, and morning calls, and evening walks among their garden flowers, Bingley shows in a fresh guise altogether, as the Village of Old Maids. Where have they gone, these gentle maiden ladies, with their lavender, and mittens, and rustling gowns of silk ? We meet none like them now—none with the same soft voices, the same well-bred avoidance of distasteful topics, the same quiet courage when courage is demanded. There is too little lavender grown nowadays in the world's gardens.

Further along the highroad, also, lived a certain bachelor--John Lawrence, let us call him—of the old school of manners, who had found life go merrily enough without assistance from the gentler sex. What he lacked in knowledge of women he gained in sound judgment of port and sherry ; and when he drank a glass of wine he

drank it with deliberation and respect. A rich vocabulary
he had, moreover, culled from an older generation ; and
he was one of the few men of his time who could use
tawny oaths without offence. Without offence ? Well,
not always. Who does not remember the story of how he
went to dine for the first time with a neighbour ? The
neighbour's wife had never heard a round oath delivered
with the stately precision of which this old bachelor was
a master ; and half through dinner, as ill-fortune had it,
the genial buck upset his wine-glass.

"Damme, I'm sorry," he cried, turning to his hostess.

"Mr. Lawrence !" she murmured, aghast.

"Why, yes, it was a damned clumsy thing to do—
damned clumsy——"

"Mr. Lawrence, I am shocked—I am *grieved.*"

He lost his head a little then, never guessing that his
innocent language, and not the accident itself, could be
in fault ; and he used all his power of speech in the effort
to exculpate himself ; and ever after he was convinced
that his hostess must be even more testy than the rest of
her ill-regulated sex, to make so much ado over a ruined
tablecloth.

And what of that other bachelor, Jackie Hulbert, who
lived across the valley in the ghost-ridden Hall of Priest-
thorpe ? A mighty hunter was "Squire" Hulbert, round
of body and jolly of face ; and the tales of his sporting
feats would fill a chapter in themselves. He was brother
to one of the ladies of the Round Tea-Table, and one

wonders how our little old maid rallied after chance
meetings with this plump fox-hunter, who distilled rich
health and jollity from every pore.

We have gone far afield, but our feet are still set in the
garden of the school-house. It has seen some queer head-
masters in its time, not the least absent-minded of whom
was the pedagogue who rode to Keighley one summer's
day and brought a long-to-be-remembered jest home with
him. The tale goes that, soon as his business was done in
the town, he went to bid the tavern-ostler saddle his horse
for the homeward journey; no ostler could be found,
however, and so the pedagogue, being in haste to return,
took down a saddle and bridle, played the groom himself,
and rode back to Bingley in great tranquillity of spirit.
On reaching home, he found his man John at the stable-
door, threw the reins to him, and bade him rub down the
horse.

John looked at the nag, and from the nag to his
master; a slow smile spread from the straw in the left
corner of his mouth to the wart in the middle of his
right cheek. "What is't ye want doing, maister?" he
asked.

"Rub him down, of course, rub him down," answered
the other, turning impatiently.

John felt the beast's legs, and stroked its muzzle; the
smile deepened on his face, and threatened to run outright
into a guffaw. "*Him*, did ye say?" he went on. "Well,
ivery man hes a right to an opinion, but if ye axe me, I

should say this hoss o' yourn isn't yourn at all—an', what's more, *he's a mare !*"

" A mare ? Dear, dear, I must have saddled the wrong one by mistake. John, you must ride him—her—back to Keighley at once—at once, do you understand."

John took the mare back ; but before nightfall the whole parish knew how the schoolmaster had turned horse-thief in his latter days.

A tale is like an old bell-wether—once it leads the way, a score of others follow it helter-skelter. Old Bingley lives again for us to-night ; one by one the many-angled folk who dwelt here come back and play their parts afresh, each with his own marked personality, each with some little characteristic story of his own. Oddest of them all, perhaps, was the village doctor who lived not a stone's-throw from the garden here. A clever leech he was upon occasion ; but whether he healed the sick, or left them to their own devices, depended entirely on the caprice of the moment. The gossips tell us yet how a woman knocked at his door at three of a snowy winter's morn, and brought the doctor's night-capped head to the window.

" What do you want ? " he asked.

" You must come to my mother, doctor. She's broken a blood-vessel."

" Deuce take her ! Why couldn't she wait till the morning ?"

" The blood is pumping out fair like a well-spring, doctor. She'll die, I'm thinking, if you don't hurry down."

The doctor thrust his head still further out of the window. " How old is she ? " he asked.

" Sixty-seven."

" Then tell her she's lived long enough. If she'd been fifty, I would have come—but sixty-seven ! Get away home, woman, and tell her to thank Heaven she has been spared so long."

The casement was shut with a snap, and the leech went back to bed. And that was how they healed the sick in Bingley.

How the rascals fared in Bingley.

CHAPTER VIII

OLD BINGLEY TALES

WE are still in the old garden behind the Bingley Church, and still old stories lead us on. But time is jogging; the moon is up above the hazel trees already, and midnight will surprise us if we tarry longer with the maiden ladies, the pedagogues and doctors and country gentlemen, of a generation past and done with. Yet the church-tower keeps us dreaming still, for it, too, has its memories. It held a famous peal of six bells –there are eight now—this square old tower with its grated belfry windows; and in its day it has seen as staunch a succession of ringers as any in the country. Good bells they

were, and their tones gathered sweetness from the rang-
ing hills and wooded slopes that caught the music, and
mellowed it, and sent it back and forth in soft, re-
echoing waves. Whatever they did in Bingley, they did
with a whole heart ; and if you ask the last-remaining
of the old ringers to step into the garden here—he lives
close behind its red-brick wall—you will hear such praise
of campanology as makes you suspect that hunting the fox
is light and unenthusiastic work compared with that intricate maze of up-rising and down-descending bell-ropes
which taxes muscle and brain to the topmost of their
strength. There are few enthusiasms so deep-seated as
the older-fashioned bell-ringer's; he can talk by the hour,
and never weary, of Crown Bobs and Royal Bobs, Snap-
pers and Taking Peals ; and if one fails to grasp the
details of technique, one realises that in its broader
aspect ringing is not only an art, but a sport that calls
forth every sporting trait of nerve and hard endurance.

This Bingley peal has a history unique in the annals
of its brethren ; for a hundred years it was rung by a
company of earnest fellows, son following father, who
worked with persistent courage to master every difficulty
that was presented by their art ; they composed arrange-
ments of their own ; and once—on the Shrove-Tuesday of
1826, it was—they rang upwards of eight thousand changes,
on thirty-five methods, without a mistake of any sort. The
feat occupied more than five hours, and it stands alone as
an exhibition of faultless and sustained change-ringing.

Old Henry Dickinson, a prime Bingley character, rang on that occasion ; he was young Henry Dickinson then, and six-and-forty years later we find him ringing second in a round of nearly two thousand changes by way of celebrating his eightieth birthday. The youngsters tire long before two thousand in our own day ; and few will credit that a greybeard of eighty could have an arm so full of sap, and a head so clear, as to perform the feat—a feat which is handed down, not by hearsay, but by history. Nay, more ; he had not rung enough when they finished their round ; and so, by way of further exercise, he and his five comrades rang nine-score changes of Bob Minor ; and then they went to feast, carrying wet brows and appetites outrageous.

As far back as 1793 they rang an historic peal to commemorate the coming of age of a local magnate, and again in 1849 there was a noteworthy performance, rendered singular by the fact that three pairs of fathers and sons took part in it, and yet again—but the story of Bingley bells is long, and in their time they were as well known to ringers as the Rune-stone underneath the belfry is known to antiquaries.

The older generation is always pessimistic about the younger, and not seldom with good cause. What does our veteran say of the new race of bell-ringers? What is sadly true of nearly every town and village in the West Riding.

" There are no such ringers now," he says, as we go

down the garden-steps together and in at the house door. "They haven't the brains, and they haven't the muscle, and they'd rather have it done by machinery."

Here and there the old spirit lingers, but it has grown old-fashioned, like enthusiasm, and the parochial spirit, and all the other cleanly things of yesterday. Progress has crushed out bell-ringing; and progress, when it takes, is apt to give so little in return.

Once indoors, the talk slips round from ringing to the ringers, and from them we get to a score of characters who used to flourish in the village. Jacob, the cabman, for instance, whose memory is fading—Jacob, with his whims, his honesty, his old-fashioned tenderness for the bottle. Once, so the story goes, he drove up beyond Harden to bring Mr. Lawrence from a dinner party; the night being shrewd, Jacob was well primed against the cold, and so it chanced that he fell asleep on the box as he was waiting for his fare. While nodding, head on breast, he dreamed that the front door was opened, that the guests came out, that some one stepped into his cab and shut the door behind him. Then Jacob awoke, with his vision strong upon him; he whipped up his nag, drove back at his best speed to Bingley, and drew up in grand style before John Lawrence's porch, ignorant of the fact that his fare was at the moment awaiting him beyond Harden, and wondering why his cab was so long in coming. He had a manner, had Jacob; and he flung his cab-door open to-night with the

sweeping bow which never came to its full dignity until
the small hours had ripened it.   Then he waited for his
fare to emerge ; and the man-servant, coming out on
to the gravel, also waited ; but no one stepped from the
cab.

" We're here, sir," said Jacob, with unsober gravity.

No answer from within.

" We're here, sir !" repeated Jacob.   But the rest was
silence, and so the old man, forgetting his dignity, began
to wax facetious.   He inquired if Mr. Lawrence wanted a
further drive for his health's sake; if he would like a little
trip over Rombalds Moor; or if he preferred to go to bed
in the cab, and would like the horse to be taken out forthwith.

Finally, Jacob put his head in at the window from
one side, the man-servant from the other ; and their eyes
met across the gloom.

" Well, I'm danged ! " murmured the cabman.

" The master's not inside at all—never has been, I'll be
bound," said the other.   " You're drunk, Jacob."

Jacob straightened himself.   " Was never known to be
drunk—fare's slipped out on the way so's he needn't pay
me—have the law of him," he muttered.   Then, a happy
thought occurring to him, " Begow, I shouldn't wonder
if he's fallen through the bottom ! " he cried.

But investigation showed that the cab was sound, and
Jacob at last went home sorely puzzled as to whether he
were the sport of fairies or of Mr. Lawrence's mean wish

to escape payment of the fare.   And ever afterwards he
maintained stoutly that he had been bewitched on his
way to Harden ; nay, he recalled the very corner of the
road—a lonesome corner, tree-shadowed—where the
fairies had danced round his horse's fore-feet and had
afterwards climbed up beside him on the box.   But the
obvious explanation, which all the town accepted, was
denied by Jacob with a persistence worthy of a better
cause.

Not that his suggestion touching the insecurity of his
cab was as freakish as it seems ; for history relates that
once on a time, when Jacob was driving a new vicar to
the parsonage, the bottom of his cab did actually collapse ;
and the vicar, in telling the story afterwards, agreed
entirely with the hero of the sedan-chair episode—that, if
it had not been for the honour and glory of the thing, he
might as well have walked.

Was there not Lamach Lee also, the merriest blade in
Bingley in his time ?   He still lives near the blacksmith's
forge, and the fun is quick in his shrewd grey eyes as he
tells you what share he took in the old Bingley revels.
A noteworthy feature of the place, these revels ; they
were known as "The Bletherheads," were discontinued
scarce twenty years ago, and afforded scope up to the last
for the old devil-may-care jollity which was at full flavour
in the hand-combing days.   A blether is Yorkshire for
a bladder, and a bletherhead is a man with a skull like
a bladder—empty.   And so the key-note of this yearly

festival was topsy-turvydom, and he who could show the maddest turn of foolery was dearest to the crowd. The actors, however, must be proved men of sense ; for the zest of the spectacle lay in seeing men who were ordinarily sane make elaborate want-wits of themselves. Undoubtedly the revels harked back, in spirit, to the old morris-dances, but they were conducted on a wider scale ; indeed, one can find mention of no village festivals which offered half the variety and prankishness of this Bingley Masque.

We'll watch the show, let us say, from the cobbled space here where the bull-ring used to be, and where bulls were baited less than seventy years ago. The laughter of the crowd, as we wait, comes down to us from the street-corner, announcing the arrival of the procession ; and soon the hurly-burly is in full progress underneath. First comes a band of many instruments— cornets, hautboys, flutes, bass-viols, any and every implement of wind or strings. They are good musicians, most of them ; but on this day they are pledged to discord, and any of the company who dares to play a note in tune with his neighbour is fined on the spot—the fine going to swell the fund for after-drinking. The screech is deafening ; it drowns the laughter, the shouts, the jests of the spectators.

A triumphal car follows—a waggon, likely, tricked up with foolish decorations—and on it are the Queen and Baby. The Queen is the ugliest man in Bingley, raimented in gorgeous apparel ; the Baby, too, is personated by a man, thick-set, with brawny arms that show to full advantage under their short sleeves of red. The Baby is laid in a ponderous cradle, and the Queen feeds him with a wooden spoon. Then come strange figures, mounted on horses still more strange—figures on foot— figures on donkey-back.

"Begow, it's a rum day that finds donkeys riding asses," mutters a wry-visaged neighbour, who sees "nowt but foolishness i' t' moil."

But he is hustled into silence, for folly is let out to grass to-day, and it rides rough-shod over sober wisdom. The din of tortured hautboys, flutes, and fiddles still roars triumphant up the street. No antics are too wild, no jests too broad, for the merry-makers. At each stage of the journey some fresh foolery, planned out beforehand, is acted for the applauding crowd, or some unrehearsed effect is compassed by the intrusion of a rotten egg, a carcase, or an over-ripe carrot into the train of merry-makers.

Last of all comes a man seated astride a form, riding it as if it were a hobby-horse—an indication clear enough as to the origin of this revel of the Bletherheäds.

The market-place and stocks used to stand just above the bull-ring here, and both have seen strange sights pass up and down the street—have seen scolds escorted to the ducking-stool, and men whipped at the cart-tail, and other drastic punishments of an age which was not wont to spare the rod. Above the market-place, again, stood Elm Tree Hill, with its group of shops, its tavern, its dusky, oddly-fashioned dwelling-houses.

There's a pathos about a vanished tavern ; one misses it, as one lacks any other hospitable friend whose steps have wandered graveward. When Waterloo was fought, the ancients of the village used to sit, with pipes and snuff, outside the door of this Old Elm Tree Inn, wagging white beards upon the matter and saying hard things of Frenchman Boney ; and they have left us, along with the tavern that seemed like to outlast them by a few odd centuries ; and the dim houses, too, with their ghostly air of other days, their gardens down-sloping to the river, their murmuring hives of bees, are vanished almost out of mind.

Yet the owner of one of these houses gave a proverb to the town, and not every man can boast as much. Why do they say in Bingley, *He has come all at once, like Christopher Hanson ?* Why, because Christopher Hanson, who lived and died on the Elm Tree Hill here, went forth to the wooing once ; a nervous man he was at the work, and when he reached the lady's door he knocked so loudly on the panels in his excitement that the door flew open, taking the swain at unawares and admitting him head-over-heels. The lady was working a wool-sampler by the hearth ; she seems to have been a self-possessed maiden, for when Christopher picked himself up from the floor and sheepishly began to dust his clothes, all that she said was, "So you've come all at once, Kester ; it is better than never coming at all." And that is the simple explanation of a proverb that is like to puzzle many a future generation.

A stalwart Methodist, this Kester Hanson—one of the old type which was to be found in its extreme form in Haworth and in Bingley. Indeed, it is a curious fact that jollity and Puritanism have gone hand-in-hand in the parish. Puritan to the backbone Bingley was, and yet staunch tenets could not quench its laughter. When the folk prayed, they prayed with desperate earnestness ; when they kept holiday, they kept it with a vigour that was boyish in its light-heartedness. It is the fashion nowadays to ridicule or to disbelieve the Revival stories of sixty, forty—nay, of twenty years ago. But ridicule has no concern with them, for they were tales of simple piety; and disbelief is folly, for if one were to attempt exaggeration in describing a Revival meeting, the plain record of the scene would still outdo one.

No language was too wild for the preacher, no simile too vivid ; his voice passed in a moment from frenzied denunciation to broken-hearted appeal, and he had no sooner given promise of heaven to the saved than he went on to paint the hell that waited for the damned. And he liked hell the better ; heaven was a pleasant, idle place of flowing streams and twittering harps, but he found range and depth for his fancy when he turned to picture the up-leaping flames, the venomed worms, the thirst perpetual, that were Satan's ministers. Emotional these Revivals were—but it was real emotion, such as racked men's hearts with a pain that was almost·physical, and left them, after the battle of faith had been fought and won, with a peace that passed all understanding, and a secure trust in salvation, which we of to-day find hard to realise. Strong men would cry like babies under the keen shaft of the preacher's eloquence ; cries of *Glory-glory, Hallelujah, Saved,* rang like trumpet-calls from every corner of the chapel ; and all the while the preacher thundered down his message — his face transfigured by the beauty that is born of all strong feeling.

That was the old Methodism ; like it or not, it compels our admiration ; ridicule it or not, we can point to no deeper and more pregnant upheaval of men's hearts than was witnessed by these swift, tumultuous Revivals. They were a return to man's ancient longing for something beyond the meat and bread of life, something that was not mapped out in straight, soul-deadening lines of the possible and the impossible ; and the same passion, the same breathless sense of the mystery of life, that comes to the green earth once a year at flood of spring, were the fountain-heads of the Methodist extravagances.

The sour wilfulness of the Puritan who stands as a type had no place, as we have said, with these Yorkshire Methodists ; they saw life whole, and accepted mirth as part of the vast scheme which so over-awed them in their moments of exaltation ; and now and then they could not keep rollick out of prayer, as is shown by the tale of what chanced once to the Vicar of Bingley.

A portly man and a dignified, this Dr. Hartley, who was vicar and schoolmaster both ; and he happened to come down the Elm Tree Hill one afternoon, past the old house behind us, while Kester Hanson was holding a prayer-meeting in the parlour that looked out upon the street. The vicar heard groans and shouts from the house, cries and pitiful entreaties ; he did not guess that they were wrestling with a ghostly adversary, and straightway conceived that foul play was going on within. Clearly he could not pass by, when perchance a man was being murdered, or a woman beaten, within ten paces of him ; so the good man opened the door and stepped in with a resolute air.

" Kester, Kester, what is this brawling in your house ? " he demanded sternly. For the room, low and scantily windowed, was almost dark, and the vicar could not realise what was going on until his eyes had grown accustomed to the gloom.

Kester Hanson spoke never a word ; and those with him spoke never a word ; but they got to their feet with one accord, and seized the portly Doctor of Divinity, and forced him on to his knees in the middle of the floor. Then they knelt in a ring about him, and prayed their hardest that this episcopal soul might be saved as a brand from the burning, and compelled the vicar to join them

in a like entreaty on pain of severe handling. And it
was said that not one of the company smiled, until later
in the day ; and then they did let a dry laugh escape them
while telling their cronies how they had converted the
vicar to a new faith.

Old tales are leading us on again, and we have not
touched yet on one of Bingley's most distinctive hobbies.

Aire River.

The country, after all, has wider and more varied interests
than the town, and all its interests strike deep—none
more so than the cottage gardener's. So, if you have
talked your fill of bee-keeping and fox-hunting, fishing
and change-ringing, you have only to turn into a work-
man's garden, and to bring something of his own enthusiasm with you, to open up a whole new territory.

Suppose we go through the town, and on to the allotment gardens which lie beyond its borders—fifty of them
in one fertile hollow that hugs the river's bank. Let us
stroll in at the first gate we come to, and fall a-talking
with the first gardener we meet ; one cannot well get
wrong. He has been working throughout the day, this
gardener, at foundry, or mill, or shop ; and now, after
despatching a hasty meal, he has come here to make the
most of the long summer's evening. He'll show you
his peas and marrows first, his gooseberries and what
not ; and then he'll take you to his greenhouse, and
point out Alan Richardsons, and "Glory-be-Johns,"
and a certain white rose which a year ago was unknown to
florists. Little by little he will open his heart to you, and
he will talk the poetry of Nature—he will be decided in
his conviction that "summat comes out o' t' soil that
betters a man"—he will confess, without shame, that the
rarest holiday he can picture is to come here at sunrise
and potter up and down among his plants till nightfall.
All this with a quiet and self-assured air, as if it were
no unusual matter nowadays to see the Godhead in green
things. He talks plain prose, our gardener, and does not
guess that it is poetry ; and in among his fruit and flowers
he gathers the reputation which none refuse him—that of
being the sanest good fellow in the parish.

Or go on the evening before Bingley's annual gooseberry show is to be held, and you will find every other
gardener packing the berries into square boxes—boxes

split up into little compartments after the fashion of cases for birds' eggs. That green berry yonder, big as a walnut, seems own brother to its neighbour ; but it is of a different species altogether, and it needs something of an apprenticeship, first to realise that the veinings differ, and then to class each variety according to its marks. Hairy berries and smooth berries—berries with long and slender figures, and others round as a Dutchman—the variety is bewildering. There is one among the number, doubtless—a quiet and unobtrusive berry, whose symmetry of shape conceals its real size—which you think unworthy of a place among its more showy brethren ; you rashly assert as much, and that one gooseberry, you learn, is the pick of the whole batch ; and then you turn to a subject which exposes fewer aspects to your many-sided ignorance.

There's romance of another sort about these allotment gardens, for they were opened in the first flush of the Young England Movement. "The old Squire" had sympathies with this Tory-Democrat creed, and Lord John Manners was a friend of his ; D'Israeli stayed with him in the palmy days when he wrote "Sybil," and framed dream-politics. All three were present at the opening of the allotments here, secure in their faith that no man could be discontented or a Radical if once he rented a slip of land.

Yes, there's a romance about it, looking backward. Young men all, these politicians, with young notions of setting the world straight in a day or two. D Israeli's lavish theories budding amidst the shrewd, common-sense atmosphere of Yorkshire. The trio meeting over the dinner-table, after the day's sport, to evolve fresh subtleties from their gospel that the rich were the poor man's friends. The son of toil was to have his cake and eat it ; the landlord was to have his cake and eat it ; what more was needed for the Millennium ? No disrespect, mind you ; the gentleman to be still a gentleman—a rather magnificent one, withal—while the humbler-born looked up to him, a brother, but a brother at a distance.

The plan was simplicity itself. Pity that a hard world would none of it. Yet it roused a generous enthusiasm in the breasts of three young men of family who might never have cared a rap what position, if any, was held by the working man ; and it was this enthusiasm that gave Bingley its allotment gardens—a boon which none but those who occupy them can estimate aright.

Well, the gospel is dead, and only the little speck of practical seed which it dropped in this corner by Bingley River serves to remind the townsfolk of it—that, and the famous cricket match which followed the opening of the allotments. The scores have been forgotten, but the match itself has been handed down with a hazy, mysterious glamour about it, either from the prowess or the stately grace displayed by the Young England gentlemen who took part in it. D'Israeli, surely, would cut a pretty figure at the wickets ; but one wonders if the prettiness scored runs, here as at Westminster.

Morley Hall

S.E.H.

CHAPTER IX

PLEASANT MARLEY

THEY call the village Eldwick; it lies over the hill-crest that shelters Bingley from the north-east wind, and its people, like its stories, have all a distinctive flavour of their own. The occupations of the villagers have varied widely in times past. They have been poets and painters, poachers and cock-fighters; yet one trait has distinguished them all—a certain character, namely, a certain pithy thoroughness in their last enterprises.

There's the cottage-house, for instance, lying down yonder by the beck ; that was built, and well built, by its present occupier in his intervals of leisure. Though he lived a couple of leagues away and laboured the night through in a factory furnace-room, he yet found time to walk to Eldwick day by day, to quarry his own stone and chisel it, to build the walls up little by little until at last he reached the happiest moment of his life—the moment that saw his dwelling roofed, windowed, and complete. He was his own architect, moreover, and cunningly contrived the building so that, when sitting by the kitchen hearth, he could look straight through the open bedroom door on to his favourite bit of landscape ; and his garden, hewn out of the rough hillside, rounds off as snug a cottage-property as you will find in all the parish.

No slight performance, if one retraces the pathway of the months that went, day upon toilsome day, to the rearing of this cottage by the stream—the six-mile walk before a stroke of real labour could be done—the difficulties, and disappointments, and war of churlish weather—the triumphant finish, that found not a trace of careless work from weather-tight roof to neatly-fitted doors and windows. As with intake, such love-labour strikes deep into the character, and this cottage-house, one fancies, has grown to be semi-human in the builder's mind ; its face is a friend's face to him, and the smoke, slow-curling from the chimney-stack, is the life-breath of this child of his old age.

Eldwick has seen rough days in its time, but it is clear from a school-prospectus which first saw the light here five-and-twenty years ago, that education was not neglected in the village. You may still find a copy of this quaintly-worded document in one or other of the cottages that cluster round the stream, and the subtle humour of it never falters from the first line to the last. The schoolmaster did not bear the name which we have given him, but for the rest his prospectus ran as follows :—

ELDWICK BECK SCHOOL,

NEAR BINGLEY,

1874.

Mr. T. Morton now ventures to commend his scholastic attainments to the inhabitants of the neighbourhood of Eldwick, feeling confident he has made himself master of a good, sound English education, after pursuing the above object many years—nevertheless returns his sincere thanks to those who have favoured him with their patronage, and yet earnestly solicits a favour of greater patronage, feeling assured that by strictness, perseverance, economy, and wonted ability he will give satisfaction to both sexes in tuition, and also to parents by imparting to their children a liberal Education, consisting of Reading, Writing, Grammar, Geography, Arithmetic in all its extensive branches and powers, also Mathematics and Drawing.

N.B.—Mr. Morton deems it highly necessary to remark that it is a matter of great materiality regarding the progress in any boy or girl being absent at school, as their progress entirely depends on their attendance, if the Teacher do his duty, and it is an undeniable fact that Learning cannot be acquired unless attention be paid, hence Mr. Morton only wishes to have attendance of boys and girls, to prove what he has stated above, but he begs to say that he wishes parents would liver their Children into his hands and charge, as he has already proved in several cases that indulging Children in laziness and not making them obey their duty have been their ruin—thinking this a sufficient remark, yet without verbosity or any vulgar assurance—he hopes this will be conclusive and worthy of the readers' attention, without embarrassment of unaccomplished achievements.

METHOD.

I.—A course of intelligent study is initiated and steadily pursued, having immediate reference to the requirements of his meanest pupils. II.—The exercises worked by his pupils are carefully corrected and honestly criticised, and every means are taken to secure rapid improvement. III.—The result of six years' experience are offered for consideration.

TERMS.

Learning the letters 2d. per week. Drawing, Mathematics.
Beginning to read 3d. Geography, &c., from 9d. to 1s. 6d.
    Do.   Writing and Arithmetic 4d. per week.
Small handwriters 5d.
Those learning Grammar 6d. per week. Payments Weekly.
  School hours from 9 to 12.15 a.m. and from 1.30 to 4.30 p.m. Children supplied with all necessary books, &c., at very reasonable Prices.

Good Tommy Morton ! It does not seem more than a year or two since he was with us, with all his exaggerations, his pompous speech, his talent, that came near to genius, for wrapping the simplest assertion in swaddling-bands of verbiage. The longest way round was ever the short cut home to this pedagogue when he had aught to say. If one met him in the fields and stopped to pass the time of day with him, he would turn a slow, benevolent eye to the heavens, would cough a little guardedly, and, " Yes, one might asseverate with certainty, sir, that the elements are propitious," he would respond. His ignorance was naïve, his knowledge pompous ; yet he was a kindly soul, and one whom we miss about the

Eldwick fields ; even his absurdities had a raciness of their own that was the equivalent of charm, and if he were unsure of certain matters of grammar and the like, yet he had a sound knowledge of Nature's alphabet and a keen ear for the unstudied speech of beasts and birds.

Then there was the roving ne'er-do-weel, whom we may call Ned o' Banktop. The cultured arts had become a sort of tradition in Eldwick ; it could claim a poet who was reckoned by good judges to be easily first among the band of dialect rhymesters ; Nicholson, the neglected poet of Airedale, had many a favourite haunt up here at Eldwick, and art for art's sake grew to be an accepted principle among the youngsters of the hamlet —a principle curiously at variance with the rough temper of the folk. Ned o' Banktop, however, was sworn to the creed of art for idleness' sake, and picture-painting with him was little more than a graceful mantle to a vagabondish life. He lived here and he lived there, picking up a livelihood as best he might ; many doubted his power with brush and colours, but none ever disputed his natural gift for romance. Ned shunned the truth by instinct, as other men avoid infection ; plain facts were crude, and he was never known to deal in them ; he might well have founded a family on the proceeds of some miraculous cure-all. He was too lazy, though, and his talent for fiction seems for the most part to have been sadly misdirected—as witness the story of how once he counted a sheltering roof well lost for romance.

A random tale, it is, which has a faint touch of Thoreau in it—Thoreau, that other vagabond whose fancy played always a score miles or two ahead of what he chanced to be doing at the moment. At the foot of the village is a neglected roadway, leading to a neglected mill and empty cottages ; and here it was that one of Ned o' Banktop's friends—a wanderer, like himself—took up his abode, without leave asked or granted. He repaired door and windows, put the slates in order, begged or borrowed a chair, a table, and a bed, and settled down in his new home with a comfortable sense of ownership, and a sly enjoyment of the knowledge that he paid neither rent nor rates. Ned o' Banktop heard of this, and the notion liked him well ; so he, too, begged or borrowed a chair, a table, and a bed, and his friend awoke one morning to find that he had a neighbour. The first-comer grew anxious a little ; for he did not know if Ned were paying rent to the owner of this dismantled property, and he feared lest there should be visits from the agent and a short shrift for all unauthorised squatters.

"Ned," he asked, on the second morning, "I'm noan just easy i' my mind about this job. Dost pay a rent, like, for thy bit of a house ? "

Ned o' Banktop had never paid a rent in his life, and that gave him his cue at once. "Why, for sure," he responded gravely. "Dost think I can live i' another man's house for nowt ? Doesn't *tha* pay rent ? " This with ingenuous surprise.

"Nay, I pay nowt to nobody."

"Well, I wodn't be i' thy shooin for a brace o' hares. T' agent 'ull be coming by an' by, an' if he finds thee here—begow, he'll show thee what t' inside of a prison-cell is like." And so on, with many a detail, woven of fancy, concerning the privations attendant upon prison life.

The first-comer made no reply ; but he went up alone to the hill-tops, and pondered ; and the more he pondered, the surer he grew that Ned o' Banktop had spoken a true word. He said nothing at all to Ned, however, and the days jogged on until the artist, sitting at ease in his shirt-sleeves and watching Nature's panorama from the door-way of his borrowed cottage, was surprised by a visit from the agent.

"Now, my man, what are you doing here ? " said the agent briskly.

Ned removed his pipe from one corner of his mouth and placed it in the other. "I'm studying lights for a pictur," he responded. "Look at yond bit o' wood, wi' t' blue-bells shimmering i' t' sun. Hest seen owt to beat that sin' first tha toddled on two pegs ? "

"You won't see it long, I fancy—from this point of view, at least," went on the other, grimly. "I am agent for this property, and I've come to tell you that out you go unless you pay the rent down on the nail."

Ned o' Banktop began to see light. "Oh, that's t' way on't, is it ? Now, who told ye I war here ? "

"Your neighbour," laughed the agent. "He walked ten miles the morning before last to tell me what I shouldn't otherwise have learned till Doomsday, and he put his arrears of rent down on the table, saying he hoped I wouldn't be hard on him, as he didn't know the law of it until you told him. So then I thought I'd just step up this way and see what *you* were doing."

"Ay, yond neighbour o' mine war allus a softy," said Ned, after a reflective pause, "allus a softy. I niver pay rent; it goes agen my conscience; so I'll hev to flit, I reckon. It's fair a pity, though; yond blue-bells like as they itch to be painted, an' there's no spot like this doorway for seeing 'em fro'. Well, well! It's queer to be born as soft as some folk is."

And so he flitted.

They seem to have been fond of squatting in Eldwick, and the farm up yonder, standing in a green patch won from the surrounding moor, bears witness to the talent of the village folk in this direction. The story goes that a man built himself a hut where the farm stands now, and enclosed a slice of land with a ricketty fence. He dwelt there undisturbed—overlooked, apparently, by all save his nearest neighbours—and kept a quiet tongue, and when the legal time had expired he claimed the land by virtue of long residence without rent paying.

It is a far stride from Eldwick village, with its living comedies and tragedies, to Marley hamlet, whose day is long since overpast; but the afternoon is wearing cool, and the breeze comes crisp from the westward, and we'll even take the longer way that leads us over the brigg beyond the waterside allotment-gardens. Pasture fields and a shallow, twinkling breadth of water to the right ; meadows and tillage-land, flanked by deep woods, on the left ; hawthorn hedges on either side the lane, with

The Ford of Kine.

fragrant tufts of hay, caught from passing wains, half hiding the thick leafage.

Past an old-world foot-bridge, with a ford below it, across which the kine, red, speckled, and milk-white, are loitering mistal-ward. The farmstead skirting the beck belonged once to a Religious House, and still carries records of its ancient dignity. Over the stile, and along the river-bank again, with the reek of hay and chatter of

farm folk piling the rounded ricks against the pale face
of the rising moon.   Into the highroad, and past the
" Brown Cow" tavern, and on by the river, leaving the
corn-mill and the town behind us.   And so to pleasant
Marley, a dying hamlet that has seen brave days.

The Hall is aloof from the world's way now, but once
the Saviles held it, and kept high revel here, and carved
their three owls so staunchly over the gateway-arch that
still the wise birds look out on us, saying nothing at all,
but blinking round eyes, doubtless, when the night grows
over-dark for us to see them, and saying one to another
that times have altered sadly for the worse.   They were a
branch of the Halifax Saviles, these lords of Marley, and
were connected by marriage with the Elands, who waged
as bloody a feud with the Beaumonts, the Quarmbys, and
the Lockwoods as ever the feud-hot shire of York has
seen.   Great folk they were, and laughter-loving ; yet
they are out of mind by this time, and it is their Fool—
one Sil o' Marley—who still walks shadowy through the
old folk's tales.   Fair treatment, too ; for the Fool was
doubtless the only one that gave a serious glance at life,
among all who tucked legs beneath the Marley board.

A five-gabled pile, the Hall, with poetry roofing every
gable.   A wilderness of shrub and weed usurps the
walled-in space where once the garden was, and of the
old-time furnishings that graced the house, but few are
left to us, save a carved door here and there, and a stair-
case—broad, oaken and antique—such as craves the

burden of fair ladies of the Savile household, late
released from embroidery to play Tantalus games with
hot young gallants gazing upward from the stair-foot—
Sil o' Marley hovering somewhere near the while, and
offering a history of love's illusions for their benefit.

Well, they are flicked into dust, maiden and Fool
and lover ; and the breeze that falters from the moon-

Bingley from the Druid's Altar.

tipped western hills recks little enough that Marley's day
is spent.

Up the rough track, and the moor is close above us,
a silvery slope of heath and bilberries, with farmstead
orchard-trees standing on the frontier line between the
barren and the sown. Up, and the bracken clings about
our feet, and cushats murmur from the ragged cleft that
splits the rough face of the heath asunder. Wild with
rock the place is, and leaf-sheltered from the moon's

intrusion; a lone stream tinkles far below us in the
hollow; a shaft of moonlight filters through upon the
bare face of the precipice yonder, from whose edge two
passion-driven youngsters, maid and lad, once leaped
outward to their death.

Up, and out on to the moor again, past the legendary
altar of the Druids, past the rustling hill-top firs at whose
further margin Protector Cromwell's warriors lie in their
peaty beds. The valleys are below us and beyond; the
breeze blows keener; and there in the moon-haze
Haworth leans dark against the darker shoulder of the
heath.

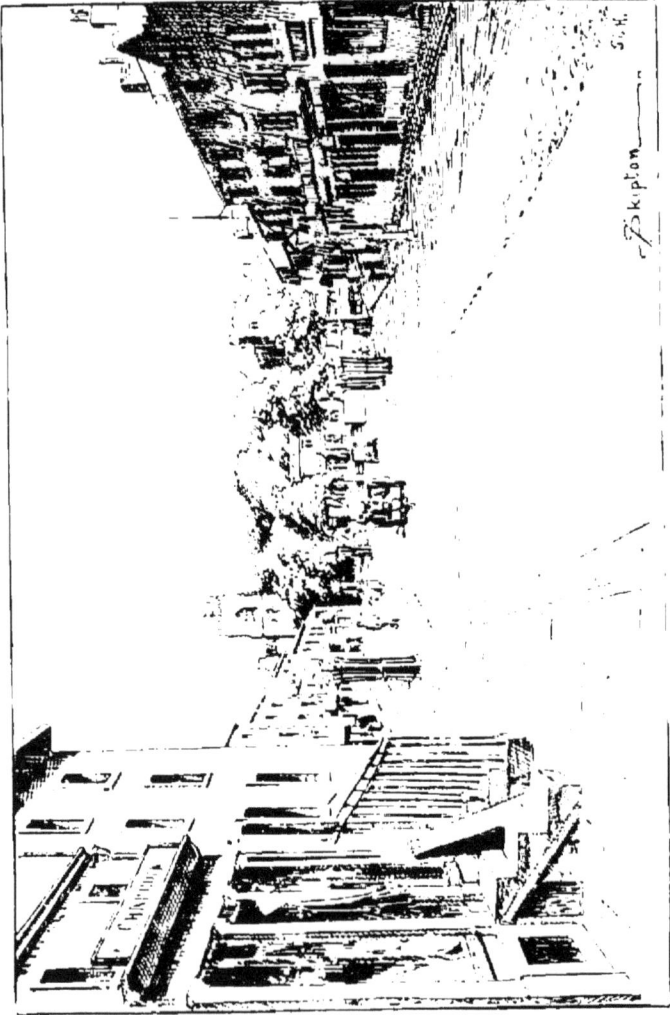

Skipton

CHAPTER X

SKIPTON, old Skipton, that was
the capital of Craven before the
Norman came, that is to all
intents its capital to-day.
What shall we say of the
pleasant market town which
is still a village in ancient
kindliness and honesty? It
lies but a dozen miles or so
from Haworth; yet its character is totally distinct, for
it marks, not the wilderness-edge, but the fringe of that
well-favoured land of fells and pastures which stretches,
untouched by commerce or by smoke, to the stream-
lapped dales of Wharfe and Ure and Wensley. A
market town of the old type, where straight-backed
yeomen, with faces brown as midsummer, move leisurely
and bring the flavour of the hayfield and the byre with
them.

There are fifty excuses for dawdling up the wide High
Street, with the cobbled spaces on either hand the road
that mark the site of the weekly cattle fair.   Taverns, old
and quaint, meet one at every other step.   Over yonder
was the barber's shop where Edward Sugden started life
with a brush in one hand and a lather-pot in the other ;
he finished his career as Lord St. Leonards and
Chancellor of England.   The harshest-tempered man
that ever sat the woolsack, this Sugden ; one of the
smartest lawyers of his day ; an uncompromising Tory.
From the lather-pot he went as clerk to a Skipton
attorney ; thence to town, where his father established
himself as a wig-maker ; and it was in London, while he
had no prospects beyond those of any other hard-work-
ing clerk, that he was frequently employed to carry com-
munications from his firm to a certain Mr. Duval, a
distinguished conveyancer of the time.   Duval chanced
to discuss a legal point one day with young Sugden, was
astounded at his insight into the law of the case, took
him as a pupil without asking any fee, and set him on
the road which was finally to lead to the Chancellorship
of England.   The barber's son, indeed, was not suffered
to forget the lather-pot ; his birth was no secret, and the
enemies whom his rough tongue daily earned him did
not scruple in return to ape his own ill manners.   Even
yet it is remembered how Sugden stood for Parliament,
and how a cartoon of the day showed him, in barber's
costume, touching up a wig ; underneath was the inscrip-

tion, " Whigs dressed here "—an allusion to the depth of
Tory bitterness for which Sugden was as famous as for
his knowledge of the law.

Over there, too, lived the little dressmaker, Miss
Rodwell, who had once been an actress in the same company as Edmund Kean ; and round the bend of the street
is the " Devonshire Arms," to the door of which the
Duchess of St. Albans drove once on a day in dashing
style—nor did the Duchess blush to remember that in
other and less prosperous times the landlady of this same
inn had, of her charity, given her a woollen petticoat as
protection against the keen northern winter. Her Grace
was growing elderly by this time, and none of the staring
townsfolk who wondered at her stateliness recognised the
quondam Harriet Mellon, who had played with Edmund
Kean and the little dressmaker when the Skipton theatre
stood in the Hole-in-the-Wall Yard. The dressmaker
called on the Duchess and was embraced with tears.
" God bless you, Rodwell ! If you want anything, do
write to me at Highgate," cried her Grace at parting, all
in the style of our great-grandmothers.

All being well, however, we shall fall in with the little
dressmaker again, with Kean and Harriet Mellon, so we'll
keep the rest of the story for our next meeting. It is
good to stand in Skipton High Street ; but it is better to
push on until we gain the Castle gateway upstanding
there among the trees that top the street. For Skipton
is the Castle, and the Castle is Skipton, just as much as

in the days when the town was no more than a
dependency of its over-lord, relying on him for employ-
ment and protection. The drawbridge is gone ; weeds
wave in place of pennons above the gateway ; the embra-
sures hide no wide-lipped ordnance ; my lord has ceased
to rattle over the bridge with hawk and hound and noisy
bustle of the chase ; beggars no longer air their sores this
side the gate, nor frightened villagers run to the shelter
of the walls when the cry, " The Scots !   The Scots ! "
rings down the street.   Yet, for all that, the Castle rules
Skipton still, and draws us to its gates by very force of
the brave tales that are hid behind its walls.

Fairest of all our Northern castles is Skipton, and fullest
of romance.   Nay, there's a story for every stone, and a
deed of high endeavour, or of dark passion, for every
battlement ; and the Clifford motto over the gateway-
arch stands solitary among the family devices of old time.
DESORMAIS, says Skipton Castle to the world ; you
can read it as you will, as a boast of immortality, or as a
grim hint of the welcome which foemen might anticipate.
It is cut out of the solid stone, this motto, and the unsubstantial sky, which fills the hollows of the letters, adds
force to its robustness.   There's truth in the device,
moreover ; for, though the Cliffords have crept into the
shadows, their name lives yet, clear in the memory as if
we had passed the time of day with each one of the line,
from Clifford of Armada fame to the Shepherd Lord,
from the Shepherd Lord to him who fell at Bannockburn.

Outside the Castle gate is the hum of busy folk ; but once it has opened and closed again behind us, we are aware of yesterday. Chivalry is no longer a half-hearted myth, nor battle a phantom dimly realised. To-day is the shadow now, and those who fought, those who loved and wrangled here, are flesh-and-blood, turning surprised glances on us and thinking us strangely unsubstantial.

The Castle resisted assault in the days when the sow and the crossbow were each in their turn new-fangled implements of war ; it was attacked when arquebusses were a novelty, and again when cannon were a scarce-understood development of the power of gunpowder ; it stood a three years' siege at Cromwell's hands, and learned that gunpowder, after all, was a foe to be reckoned with. Then it fell into the hands of the Parliamentary army, was partially destroyed, and was last of all built up again after the Civil War by the heiress of the Cliffords, who was careful to follow the old model in all particulars save one—and that was in the construction of the roof, which she filled with little turrets to the end that cannon might never again be mounted there. She was one of the few Cliffords, this last heiress of her line, who could ever have too much of war.

As a matter of fact, her task was simpler than has been supposed, for the joining of the new walls and the old is in some places scarce a dozen feet from the leads, and the oft-repeated contention that the Castle was rebuilt from the foundations upward does not hold. Nor need

we trouble about the matter ; substantially it is the Castle
of old time, and we can wander through the dusty
chambers, and up the curious stairs, and down to the
bed-rock of the dungeon, with a sure sense that our
Romilles and Cliffords, and all the titled guests who in
their day have shared the Skipton hospitality, will know
their way about when they return between owl-hoot and
cock-crow to the scenes of former revels.

It is more than a ruined fortress, this, and better than
one wholly occupied ; for the quiet, well-ordered air of
everything serves rather to give life and form to antiquity
than to disturb its memories. On one side, the inhabited
wing ; on the other, the stables, once the private chapel
of the Cliffords ; between the two, the older building,
roofed and weather-tight, indeed, but left to its cobwebs
and its ghosts. Add to these a strip of close-shaven lawn
which stretches to the outer wall, a hint of garden flowers
from one sequestered corner, and that is Skipton Castle
as seen from the gateway-arch.

The furnished wing, which is new only by contrast
with its hoary neighbour, holds many a relic saved from
the centuries' treasure-house. The Earl of Thanet's
weights are here—the weights which, scarce more than
five-score years ago, his bailiff used to carry down to the
butter-cross on market days. If the country folk chanced
to be selling honest pounds of cheese or butter, well and
good ; if not, the bailiff confiscated their whole supply
and gave it to the poor—a patriarchal style of justice, and

a simple, which was well calculated to make the Craven rustics a pattern to their fellows. Rare tapestries run round the walls of the octagon room upstairs—a chamber so spacious that two huge, four-post beds which have found their last resting-place here seem to do little more than fill an unconsidered corner. One of these tapestries, showing King Solomon and as many of his wives as space permits, is oddly conceived, and is worked out with a patience well-nigh incredible. Solomon is seated on his throne, with a far-away air of wisdom, and beneath him, rank after rank, the serried row of wives looks up and marvels at his greatness. Nor is the tale all told when the extreme border of the tapestry is reached ; there is a hint of other wives in the background ; and one realises, with a new sort of understanding, what were the realities of life in Jewish days.

And the ladies who worked this tapestry ? Come to the court that stands in the middle of the older wing— the court which is so shadowed by its yew tree that the branches tap the windows on each of the four sides. Climb the stairway that leads to the banqueting-hall, and pass down this chamber where mead, or wine, or nut-brown ale, was wont to warm the wits of Clifford and of Percy ; turn to the right, into the withdrawing-room, which, like the banquet-hall, looks out upon the yew-court. It was here, likely, that the tapestry of Solomon and his wives was wrought, while the men-folk were away at fight or hunt, while the ladies, weariful a little for their return, plied tongue and needle with equal speed—discussed this stripling's verses, or that knight's wooing, or wondered, like any modern dames, whether there was venison enough to furnish forth the evening meal.

The principal guest-chamber, too, is eloquent of an older day; for it could serve likewise as a prison if need chanced. In one corner is the recess and the raised slab for the bed, so common in Scottish and North-country dwellings; and half up the wall there is a separate little room, no bigger than a good-sized cupboard, connected by a stairway of its own with the outer passage—a convenient sentry-box for the night-guard when distinguished visitors needed looking after without any show of ostentation in the business. Henry the Eighth—a boon-comrade of one of the Lords of Skipton, as we shall see —is said to have slept here, and many another of the men and women whose humanity it is hard to realise under the mask of greatness with which our thoughts of them are cumbered.

Fair Rosamund's chamber lies on the south side of the yew-court, and tradition says, without doubt or hesitation, that she slept here; nay, more, they will point you out the very chair on which she sat, and proof can surely go no further. The frail victim of Queen Eleanor was certainly a Clifford, but they tell us nowadays that Rosamund died somewhere about 1176, while the Cliffords did not acquire the Honour of Skipton until more than a century later. It may be so—but we need her here at Skipton, the fairest and the frailest ghost that ever moved shadowy across the rose-strewn stage of romance; and, needing her, we cherish the legend of her chamber, and enjoy a lively faith that for some motive, of love or policy, the King saw fit to bring her up to Skipton, out of harm's way and his wife's.

What is it that has made us all feel lover-like toward Fair Rosamund ? Rose of the World she was to thick-thewed Henry the Second, and Rose of the World she is to-day, half-open still to the warm June air of poesy and profligate of summer fragrance. He built a maze about her, this Royal lover—but not so intricate a maze as we have woven round her name. Beautiful—yes ; and full of the resources which beauty is wont to lack—yes ; yet that is not enough to account for the place she has taken, and will always take, as the sweetest heroine of story. Mary of Scots has caught something of her glamour, something of her elusive, over-mastering charm ; bonnie Prince Charlie, too, in his own swift, impetuous way, has power to touch the self-same chord in us ; but none else. These three stand solitary upon the mountain-tops of story, large against the sky, yet shadowy behind the trailing hill-mists of fancy and romance.

Frail Rosamund starts us well on the road of the Clifford pomp ; for Skipton, though the Romilles held it once, and after them Piers Gaveston, only begins to tap its richest store of legend after the coming of Rosamund's family to its Castle. And with their coming the old battle begins—the battle between fact and fantasy, legend and proven truth. Tradition defends the walls, and history attacks; and the honours of war lie all with the sturdy garrison. Nay, legend has the better of it even on the count of truth, for it gives us real folk, moving flesh-and-blood through the fast-succeeding pictures of the centuries; while history—poor, frugal housewife, counting her pence and letting the yellow guineas lie unheeded—rarely gives us more than an empty puppet-show, pulled by the strings of policy and statecraft. Of what use is it, for instance, to tell us that the Pilgrimage of Grace—which, by the way, touched Skipton closely—was the result of widespread discontent, that forty thousand Yorkshiremen massed in arms, full of a conscious effort towards a settled goal? Is it the fact? Or did Tom join because his neighbour Bill joined, and Bill because his friend over the way—who chanced to be in need of a little excitement, or lacked the wherewithal to pay his tavern reckonings—had persuaded him to take a holiday? If we can once realise Tom's frame of mind, and Bill's, and Bill's neighbour's, we see those forty thousand men; they are alive; we approach the understanding that is fact. History without the romance of detail is the nut without the kernel, and the bold story of the Cliffords brooks no such niggard handling. Much is definitely known of them after their coming to Skipton; much is guessed; the gossip of the countryside has its own say in the matter; and the truest history of the Clifford pomp is compact of the three elements.

Let us keep the picture of the Castle in our minds—the banquet-hall where gallants gloried and drank deep—the withdrawing-room where their ladies wove the skeins of wool and scandal—the bed-chamber which even in the Cliffords' days was legendary of an ancestress of whom they were half-ashamed—the battlements above us there, from which they rained arrows, stones, and molten lead on the besiegers—the spacious gardens, lastly, where they took their ease and exchanged love-banter across the rose-beds and the heartsease-clumps. For these things are the setting of the Clifford pomp.

From the moment of their first coming to Skipton the Cliffords are singularly alive—alive, as their dusty compeers, pulled from out the sanctuary of muniment-rooms and family papers, are not wont to be. Century after century we find them still at Skipton ; and all down the long line of story we chance upon the vivid deeds and the magnificent self-assurance which have left them a little less than kingly, but more than noble. Their motto was their creed, and their one grim word *désormais* was brief and crisp as the blows they dealt in defence of family honour or in furtherance of family pride.

The first of them all at Skipton, Robert, Lord Clifford, was a mighty hunter of the Scotch, and a prime favourite with Edward the First, who had taught him alike the scholarship of peace and the scholarship of blows. At

nineteen we find him busily concerned with establishing
the English claims to the sovereignty of Scotland ; at
five-and-twenty he was made Governor of Carlisle, " to
repress the insolence of the Scots "—a task which before
this had proved so much to his liking that he had ridden
across the Border and had driven a matter of three
hundred Scotch into a marsh hard by the Kirk of Annan.
This was the beginning merely ; and the King liked his
taste for blows so well that he raised him from dignity
to dignity, and accorded him, amongst other privileges, the
doubtful one of retaining certain lands belonging to the
Maxwell and the Douglas. An Englishman might as
well have sought shelter in a hive of bees as have settled
among the free-lance Border men, and it is not surprising
that Clifford cast about him for a likelier home. It says
no little for his skill in courtiership that he kept the
new King's regard after the death of Edward the First,
for never surely were two sovereigns more opposite in
tastes ; but he succeeded in this, and when, shortly after
he had helped to teach Robert the Bruce a little-expected
lesson of defeat, he asked his royal master for the
Castle and Honour of Skipton, his request was granted
without demur. The site was a fair one, and not too far
from the Scotchmen whom he loved as men love the
fallow-deer they hunt ; and the latter consideration, we
gather, weighed more than the first with him in his
choice of Skipton as a residence.

Well, he fought, and loved, and feasted at Skipton here,

high in favour with the King, popular with the nobles
whom he overtopped ; and then he went once too often
to the well, and the Bruce wiped off old scores at Bannockburn. None of the Clifford line, it seems, was ever
in battle but he left his mark on the history of the fight,
and we find Robert of Skipton in the very fore-front of
that skirmish which in a measure predestined the issue of
Bannockburn. This was on the day before the fight,
when Edward the Second of England, advancing with
his army from Falkirk in the early morning, found the
Scottish army drawn up at little more than a league's
distance. The King at once ordered Clifford to take an
advance force of eight hundred horse, to outflank the
enemy, and to throw himself into Stirling Castle ; and
the manœuvre should have been successful, for Clifford
completely outwitted Randolph—Bruce's nephew—who
had been stationed between Stirling and the main army
of the Scotch to repel any such attempt. Bruce, however, seeing the intention of the English cavalry, so
whipped his nephew with his tongue that Randolph,
taking five hundred footmen with him, ran at top speed
to give battle to Clifford. The English turned as Randolph approached, and galloped, spears in rest, upon the
little band of infantry which they outnumbered by nearly
two to one ; but the Scotch, though on foot, had lighter
armour and longer spears than Clifford's cavalry, and,
massing in square, they let the English charge break
helplessly against their four-fold front. Again and again

Clifford galloped to the shock, striving to crush the stubborn adversary by sheer weight of onset; but neither courage nor pertinacity, not all his hard-won skill in battle, served Robert of Skipton to cope with this unlooked-for method of defence.

Our sympathies are all with Clifford, who fought to the last ounce of his strength; yet there is something that warms the heart in this spectacle of five hundred footmen, back to back, maintaining the long battle against overwhelming odds. We scarce regret—for the moment—to see the English give back, to watch the Scotchmen change from stubborn defence to swift attack, to mark our men waver, and make one last despairing effort, and break into hopeless flight. Inspiriting it is, too, to watch this Bannockburn in Little with the eyes of the Scottish army, who were noisy spectators of the tumult from their hill. For Bruce, thinking, doubtless, that the experience would be wholesome training for the lad, would not break his line in order to bring succour to his own nephew; and it was with the utmost difficulty that Douglas gained permission to advance to Randolph's aid. When he did so, he found the little square so nearly on the point of victory that, like a true knight of the type which hand-to-hand warfare was apt to breed, he held his men off, saying that it was in no wise seemly to step in after the heat and burden of the day and to share a victory which rightly belonged to Randolph. The words were scarce out of his mouth

when the English broke and fled, and Clifford, striving
to the last to rally them, was compelled to gallop back
to the main body of his army.

Robert the Bruce was not so accustomed to defeat, we
take it, that he had forgotten how once on a day this
same Lord Clifford had trounced him merrily at St.
John's Town ; and we are not surprised to read in

The Home of the Cliffords.

Barbour's chronicle of Bannockburn that Bruce laid
especial stress on the defeat of Clifford, telling his men
that they had vanquished the flower of the English
cavalry, and bidding them fight on the morrow with the
remembrance that already they had worsted Clifford, Lord
of Skipton.

The morrow came, and Randolph's battle of the

14

squares was repeated on a larger scale, and Clifford went down beneath a Scottish battle-axe, with more English nobles and English yeomen than we like to think of to bear him company. Bruce, generous to a fault, sent his old rival's body to the English King at Berwick, that it might be honourably interred; and Clifford is thought to lie at Bolton Abbey, just over the hill from Skipton.

It is a pleasant kirkyard, and a quiet, in which to lie. Yet sometimes, when the wind comes blaring his trumpet-note from over Beamsley Hill, does Clifford turn unrest-ful in his slumbers and mutter, "Bannockburn"? It may be so: for we who took no share in it remember - and should he forget, who fought to the vanward of that losing battle?

The Inner Court.

CHAPTER XI

THE SHEPHERD LORD

THE first Clifford had settled at Skipton because the town lay within convenient distance of Scotland ; but Bannockburn was fought and lost, and after that the Craven gentry, and the Craven shepherds, and the Craven womenfolk, learned that there were two sides to the argument which had determined my lord's choice of residence. If Skipton was no far journey from Scotland, Scotland likewise was within easy reach of

Skipton, and the Borderers had long memories for the insults they had taken time and time at Clifford's hands. One raid followed another, until a visit from the Scotch grew, throughout the Craven country, to be a looked-for incident of each season's work. It was a fat land, full of bleating ewes and dew-lapped kine and buxom lassies, and the Armstrongs, Bells, and Elliots took good cheer of it. Stalwart barbarians they were, with no finicking half-measures about them; at Ripon they beat the woods, whither the country folk had retreated with their herds, drove them out again into the open, slew the men, carried off the women and cattle, and so made forward to Skipton, where they burned the town; and thence they fared all up the length of Craven back to Scotland. Robert the Bruce himself was with the invaders, and thus a second time he avenged that not-to-be-forgotten combat in which Clifford had proved himself the better man. Yet there was little malice in the Bruce's temper, and his harsh treatment of the Skipton town and Skipton country, part only of a settled policy, was in no sense a reprisal, we take it, for the reverse which he had suffered at the dead lord's hands.

They came "in the month of Maie," these Borderers— a significant date, that calls up as sharp a contrast between peace and war as well could be. The season has been open, say; the land is in its prime of spring, and they are washing sheep in every pool from Skipton up to

Kilnsey, from Kilnsey out to Hubberholme ; lads are
sporting in the pastures with their sweethearts ; there
is slow talk of sheep and cattle, of corn crops and of hay
—and swift out of the blue there comes a shout, and
hard after the shout there strikes the glint of spears,
the glitter of two-handled swords—and the red trail blots
out the greenness of the land, blots out the youngsters
who wooed, and the elders who gossiped, and the
babes that had scarce learned to suck the milk of life.
Neither cattle nor sheep are left ; they and the women
are driven close-packed together over the white-hot fells,
under the molten sun : the washing-pools, the fields, the
homesteads, are over-mastered by a silence that is tense-
strung as a cry ; the dead farm-folk stare up with horrible
entreaty at the unanswering skies ; and here, too, the
word *Désormais* crowns the scene. And that is the
under-side to the picture of the Clifford pomp.

In one year alone four of the manors about Skipton
were burned level with the ground. The monks of
Bolton Priory, two leagues away, kept fleeing hither
and thither, to Skipton, Nostel, or further still afield ;
for at each visit to Craven the Scotch never failed to tap
the spoil that lay ready to their hands in this snug-lying
monastery of the Wharfe. Yet, for all these thefts of
plate and what not, one thinks that the holy fathers
would grudge most of all the fact that for a whole year
the Scotch debarred them from keeping the records of the
Priory. An offence this was against the housewifely care

with which they put down pence and half-pence, heads of
game and bottles of wine and other ecclesiastical business
—an offence so dire that they must have forgotten dread
and peril alike in their sorrow for that blank year in the
registers. Panic seems to have turned their heads a little
when they did contrive to keep the records; for in one of
these we find so strange and schoolboyish a mixture of
three languages that, even amid the recollection of the
blackest days that ever Craven saw, we are fain to laugh
outright. "Le prior & sez Homes fled ae Castle de
Skipton per Feare dez Scottes," runs the quaint sentence.
It would have cost half the trouble, surely, to have said
in plain English that the prior and his folk fled to
Skipton Castle for fear of the Scots ; but the nearness
of Border spear-points did not make for sober-wittedness.

The years went on, and the rapine went on. The
Cliffords did what they could ; they kept their Castle
against assault, and offered protection to any who laid
claim to it ; but the long carnage of the years that
followed Bannockburn is not good to think of, and it
fits our Yorkshire taste better to move on toward the
time when Craven asked her price of the folk beyond the
Border—and received the same in ruddy coin.

Yet in and between there is history and to spare
touching the lords of Skipton. Fighters always, they
turned to battle like kine to pasture-grass ; and when
there was a lull in Scottish matters, the discords that
were ruining their own country of England gave scope

enough for sword and cross-bow. One of the Cliffords
shared in the rebellion of the Barons against the Crown,
a rebellion which was embittered by the King's
infatuation for that very Piers Gaveston who was once
in possession of Skipton Castle ; another Clifford was
embroiled in the fiasco of Perkin Warbeck more than
a century and a half later ; but their feats of arms
stand out most clearly against the sombre background
of the Wars of the Roses, when Yorkist fought
Lancastrian and sowed the seeds of a race-hatred that
has slumbered on between the two counties almost to
our own day. The Cliffords were hot for Lancaster,
and the death of Thomas, eighth Lord of Skipton, at
the battle of St. Albans, laid the foundation of that story
of Black-faced Clifford which went deep into the minds
of old historians, and which touched the fancy of
Shakespeare himself.

Reared amid the hot victories and counter-victories
of the Roses, untameable by nature and readier to hate
than to love, this Black-faced Clifford, even before his
father was slain, had shown such zeal in arms against
the Yorkists that he had already earned the by-name
which his deeds and his swarthy features alike merited.
The death of his father gave him the lordship—gave
him, too, a savage lust for vengeance which outran
every impulse of humanity. It was he, if tradition
deals fairly by him, who tricked the Duke of York
into the bloody conflict at Wakefield, who slew young

Rutland, lad as he was and defenceless, who cut off
York's head, and brought it with a low obeisance to the
Queen, saying, " Madam, your war is done ; here bring I
your King's ransom." Truly, as Shakespeare interprets
his character, he sought his fame in cruelty, believing
that the most sacred blood-feud of all—the avenging of
a father's death—cried out for stroke on pitiless stroke,
cried with parched lips that blood alone could moisten.
For that day's work they crowned him with the laurels of
opprobrium he had coveted, for no man, Yorkist or
Lancastrian, was on the field but named him Butcher.
And in this there is an odd coincidence ; for Shakespeare, writing in an age when the Cliffords were, in fact,
Earls of Cumberland, gives Black-faced Clifford the title
of that county ; and the only other actor in our history
who fairly won the epithet of "The Butcher" was that
Duke of Cumberland, not kin to the Cliffords at all, who
fouled the English honour nearly three centuries later
on Culloden Field.

Not that blood-guiltiness, or any unsavoury nickname,
served yet awhile to check Clifford's passion for the
shambles. He was foremost at the second battle of St.
Albans, which all but assured the crown to Henry,
and it was in his tent that the King and Queen came
together after the victory was won. He was minded to
carry his oath of " no quarter " to Towton Field likewise,
the battle that was to end so disastrously for his party ;
but on the day preceding the fight, whilst retiring from a

preliminary skirmish with the enemy at Ferrybridge, he was struck in the throat by an arrow as he stooped to drink at a wayside stream. He was buried ignobly, so the family legend runs, among the common ruck of the slain; for neither his widow, nor any other of his people, dared make attempt to recover the body, now that the Yorkist turn had come and the Lancastrians were being driven to such places of concealment as they might chance upon.

Afterwards the Cliffords found occasion to build a memorial chapel near the spot where rumour said he had been slain. The chapel stands hard by the village of Towton to this day; and to this day they hold services there twice every year, in memory, not so much of Butcher Clifford, as of the thousand acres of fat land which were devoted to prayers for the warrior's soul. That is one of Time's ironies, and the Reformed Church, that still takes its tithes year by year from those thousand acres, seems never to hark back to the true history of the matter.

Solitary this chapel stands in the midst of a wide field; for six months of the year it is left to brood over old memories and to watch the filmy spider-webs write their "No entry" on the noiseless door; and when the night comes silent from the east, shrouding chapel and guardian field and noisy evensong of birds, it is easy to see Lord Clifford jingle, with armour and cross-hilted sword and silver spurs, up to the chantry door. His visor's up, and blood is streaked for ever down the hollow cheeks and under the relentless eyes ; he rattles his sword-hilt fever- ishly against the oak and prays to be let in; and when the creaking silence only answers him, the grey light of the damned spreads ashen in between the blood-streaks. The prayers of a thousand years were needful to wash the Black Lord's crimes away, and to give his soul the first foretaste of repose ; but no voice sounds from the deserted altar, and Clifford, cheated of his prayers, clanks wearily again to the darkness whence he came, friendless, un- prayed-for, and alone.

Full of quick turns and striking contrasts is the Clifford story ; for the Butcher had scarce bidden his wife fare- well as he rode to Towton, promising a quick return from the field that was to be his last, when she found herself a hard-pressed fugitive, compelled to shield the heir of Skipton, a lad of seven years, from the keen pursuit of the victorious party. The Yorkist blood was up ; they had cursed Butcher Clifford many a year for his pitiless slaughter of their kindred, and his treatment of young Rutland had given passion so loose a rein that had his heir been no more than a baby at the breast they would have riven him limb from limb.

Resourceful, possessed of the tireless bravery that comes of breeding, Clifford's widow, Margaret, sent the lad to her own property of Londesborough, had him placed with some trusty shepherds there, and contrived that he should adopt their own dress, learn their speech,

and in all respects be reared as a shepherd-lad of lowly
birth. The rumour got abroad that young Clifford was
in England; Margaret parried all questions, and then,
thinking that Londesborough was no longer a safe hiding-
place, and having in the meanwhile married a second
time, she sent the boy to her husband's estate of Threlkeld, in Cumberland. He grew to manhood there,
ignorant of his birth, unlettered, sharing the rough life of
his foster-parents to the last particular. Now and then
his mother would snatch a peep at him as he watched his
flock on the hillside, but she kept her own counsel; the
same forethought that had bidden her make him a shepherd in fact, not in disguise merely, the wisdom that had
denied him training in the least of the cultured arts, held
with her even in these moments when, seeing him so
straight-limbed and so comely, her heart must have
yearned over the lad and temptation knocked loud to
open the gateway of her confidences; for at such times,
apart altogether from her fear of eavesdroppers, she
would deem it unfair that this boy, who was happy in
the full belief that he was peasant-born, should be roused
to the disquietude of knowing that he was nobler than
his station.

They grow very real to the fancy, those stolen moments
of the mother's. Seeing her there, alone on the hill-tops
with him who was flesh of her flesh, we seem to read
straight into her heart; we understand the still, deep
power of endurance with which she met her life-tragedy

--the lady's eager revolt against this mean upbringing of
the heir to a stately name—the woman's shrinking from
the thought of real dangers past, of fanciful dangers that
might come from the woodland or the fell while the lad
followed his rough calling—the mother's steady resolve
to be patient, and to thank God that at least the boy was
growing safely into manhood.   For five-and twenty years
she bore it ; and her stubborn courage has come down
to us, the fairest star in all the Clifford blazonry of
pomp.

The seasons came and went. Young Clifford did not
feel the lack of books, for he taught himself to commune
with the stars, he learned the tongue of birds and of sleek,
dun-coated deer, he knew the hours when every flower
folded tired petals in sleep or opened them to the night-
dews or the sun.   He had a quiet dignity, inbred in him ;
he was more prone to meditation than his fellows ; for
the rest, he was a skilful shepherd, could follow the rustic
pleasures of his comrades, and had a pastoral eye, belike,
for the roundness of a milkmaid's cheeks or the sly peep
that was offered by kirtles raised a trifle over-high as the
lassies crossed the rime-wet meadows with their pails.

Then, in a moment, his whole sky was changed.
Bosworth field was lost and won, the red rose and the
white grew neighbourly again in the same garden, and
Margaret could open her heart once and for all to the son
whom she had guarded through five-and-twenty stormy
years.   The attainder passed against Black-faced Clifford

was reversed by Henry the Seventh, and the lad who tended sheep at Threlkeld came south as Lord of the Honour of Skipton. Men whose fathers had dubbed Black-faced Clifford the Butcher called his son the Shepherd Lord, and the halls whence the sire had gone out ravening received the gentlest of all the race as his successor.

The poetry of it still lived on, though it took a new phase ; for Clifford, modest, studious, distrusting his knowledge of the new world that had been forced upon him, went little into the society of his equals, and still more seldom to Court. When he did appear to do duty to his Sovereign, he bore himself with a certain honest dignity, bred of the star-spaces and the hills, which won him praise even among the courtly gallants, who, hearing his story, had awaited his advent in London as something of a jest—looking, doubtless, to see a lubberly swain who would hold his sword-hilt as if it were a shepherd's crook, and who would make obeisance to the King after the fashion of a farmer-lad bobbing to a country wench. And so, when they found that he was their equal in dignity, their better in guileless honesty, their lips uncurled, and their brows came down again, and they welcomed the Shepherd Lord among them as a rare and piquant curiosity, much as the London of to-day welcomes distinguished children of the backwoods.

Clifford, however, cared nothing for such shows. Country-bred, he could no more have settled down in

London than green corn could have grown along its
streets ; and so we find him living for the most part at
Barden, a lone and gloomy tower that lies over the northward hill from Skipton. It had been no more than a
hunting-lodge, this Barden ; but Clifford had it fitted
with all the astronomical instruments known to the
scientists of his day, and here, night after night, he would
study the mysteries of the stars, and live over again in
fancy those half-regretted hours when he had lain on the
Cumbrian pastures, obscure and free of care, and had
watched the Milky Way trail white across the dark
middle-arch of sky. To Barden, too, the monks from
Bolton Priory came day by day, to teach this man of
thirty what he had failed to learn at ten, to ground him
in reading, writing, and Latinity, and to wander with him
down those by-roads of philosophy which he loved to
tread. Nay, more ; the stars possessed a subtle magic of
their own in those days, and it is suspected that our
Shepherd Lord went deep into the forbidden lore of
astrology, and that he passed thence by natural stages to
that search for the Philosopher's Stone which still has its
charm for mystics of our own generation. Thoresby
has preserved an old French treatise on alchemy and
astronomy which was presented by a later Clifford to the
monks of Bolton ; few of the lords of Skipton before the
Shepherd's time had had leisure, and none had found
inclination, for such studious pursuits ; and it seems
certain that the recluse and his friendly fathers from the

Abbey thumbed its pages during those quiet years at Barden.

Then, on the sudden, while we are thinking that Clifford will end his days thus, and that the curtain of his life will be rung down upon a comedy of learned peace, the scene changes for him once again, with an abruptness that puts one all at fault. For thirty years the fat monks, on fatter palfreys, cross from their Priory to where Barden stands gaunt and naked above the sweet, tree-studded vale of Wharfe ; for thirty years the Lord of Skipton, a child at heart still, and eager still to learn, pursues his search into the Unknowable. The fare is a trifle over-simple at Barden, in keeping with its master's tastes ; but doubtless the monks see to that, and bring at their saddle-bows, along with treatises on alchemy, many a bottle of ripe vintage and many a savoury pie to garnish the feast of reason withal. All has become habit by this time—the morning ride, the spelling out of yellowed parchments, the reverend joy in feast ; there seems no reason why monks and Lord of Skipton should not grow thus into extreme old age together, and sleep their last sleep together beneath the stars they love.

And so they might have done, had not King Harry of England gone over-seas to France with an army, leaving his kingdom at the mercy of those same Scots who never could resist the temptation of a jaunt into our bonnie Northern counties. Henry's Queen was well-advised when she entrusted the defence of England to us Northern folk.

15

Old hatreds woke ; we counted the raids that had left our homesteads black, our women dishonoured, our pastures barren—tales which our fathers had told us from childhood, lest, when the good hour came, it should be found that we remembered not.

Ay, we reckoned the tally, drop by drop of blood, and we girded our loins, and we wanted no southerners to come between ourselves and Scotland.   Percy of Northumberland sent a horseman, hell-for-leather, to the Lord of Skipton, to bid him bring yeomen to the battle.   The messenger found Clifford, likely, deep in some recipe for manufacturing gold ; and the Shepherd Lord looked up, his eyes dim a little with long study, and did not understand at once ; and then the old blood stirred in him, and he knew that it was a better thing to spill Scots blood than to make the yellowest gold that ever sought the mint ; and he got him to horse, and rode at the gallop for Skipton Castle, and set his folk driving spurs into tortured flesh all up and down the Craven borders, from Bingley out to Langstrothdale.

It grips our hearts to-day, this tale of Flodden Field. Small wonder, then, that it so took hold of a Yorkshire poet of the sixteenth century, that he broke out into as full-flavoured fighting-stanzas as ever the sturdy literature of blows has seen.   The very tale of Clifford's preparations for the fight goes true, and swift, and staunch, as the battle-chargers that went thundering north to Flodden :- -

From Penigent to Pendle Hill,
  From Linton to Long Addingham,
And all that Craven coasts did till
  They with the lusty Clifford came.

All Staincliffe hundred went with him,
  With striplings strong from Whorledale,
And all that Hauton-hills did climb,
  With Longstroth eke and Litton Dale.

Whose milk-fed fellows fleshly bred,
  Well brown'd, with sounding bows upbend ;
All such as Horton fells had fed,
  On Clifford's banner did attend.

From Penigent to Pendle Hill they passed their greeting one to another, these thick-thewed Craven fellows ; and the greeting was " remember " ; and when they were marshalled under the Shepherd Lord, and saw how straight he sat him in the saddle for all his sixty years, they lifted a cheer that echoed backward from Pendle Hill to Penigent, up the quiet valleys where wives and sweethearts were whispering God-speeds in between their work at churn or distaff. And then it was north to Newcastle, with " remember " whistling down the wind ; and after that, north again toward Flodden Field, where they were soon to see the one sight that they hungered for—the Scotch drawn up, rank after rank, to square old reckonings once for all.

Wearisome it must have been to the blunt yeomen to have to wait until the courtesies of chivalry were over, until his Grace of Surrey had gravely sent a herald to offer battle to the Scotch, until King James had gravely sent back an acceptance of the challenge. Our Craven folk were spoiling for a fight, and they fretted on the curb. Then Surrey found that he had offered battle to a foe who was entrenched within the natural fortress of Flodden Field, and he complained bitterly to King Jamie that his behaviour was outside the rules of knightly conduct. Would the King come down and meet him fairly in the plain, asked Surrey, with the ingenuousness of a chivalric age. But Jamie would not, so Surrey led his army as if to cross into Scotland; and the Scotch grew fearful lest we should steal something, and came down the hill, setting their encampment afire, while the English wheeled about to meet them. The smoke came yellow down the slope of Flodden Hill, hiding the combatants each one from the other; and when it cleared we found that the longed-for moment had arrived, and the old enemy stood scarce a bow-shot from us.

And the fight began. Swift, stormy, desperate from the start; desperate to the last edge of nightfall, when there was scarce light enough to show the down-descending glint of sword or axe. Clifford and his Craven lads were in the van, the Lancashire men to rear-ward. Long-bows of yew they had; and they had likewise as fair a fighting-tool as man could want—those double-headed axes, spiked between, which carried six-foot poles of ash to give grip to the two hands and weight to the downward swing. No quarter was asked,

or given ; the bow-men rained in their arrows, and the
Scotch ran headlong to close quarters to escape the
shower, and it was toe to toe all up and down the width
of Flodden Field. The Craven men were in the thickest
of the moil, yielding inch by slow inch before the onset
of the Lowlanders ; but Lancashire swept forward in the
nick of time, and rained their arrows in afresh, and then
fell to with cut and thrust ; and Lancashire and Craven
fought each by the other's side, and hewed with the tire-
lessness that long acquaintance with sickle and with scythe
had taught them, and gasped "remember" as the red
sweat ran down the hollows of their cheeks. The field
grew boggy with the strife, and men kicked off their shoes
and fought in their homespun hose for better footing.
And still the sun crept lower to the sky-verge ; and still
the blood-lake deepened ; and Clifford, Lord of Skipton,
still led his gallants forward on to the wavering line of
Scots.

One last whirling mist of steel—a last sky-splintering
yell—and the Scots were down. And we were racing
forward, killing, always killing. Never a hint of quarter ;
never a thought of weariness. We washed out Bannockburn for ever, and cleansed the memory of old indignities, and let the battle-madness sweep us as it would
across the slippery gloaming of Flodden Field. The
King of Scotland, thirteen of her earls, gentry and lords
without number, lay upon the field—and of the common
soldiers ten thousand odd or so. And that was the

North Men's answer, slow-mellowed through the frets and indignities of ten-score years.

Our old ballad-maker moves through the fight as if he loved it dearly, with minute regard of detail, and yet with a steady, swinging breadth of poetry that sets our blood a-tingling. A schoolmaster he was, according to one legend—a village pedagogue, doomed to thrash ignorance into country lads when all the while his heart was hungering for the hiss of stricken steel, the sob of keen-barbed arrows, the crash of bills and pikes and leaden mells on splintering skulls.

> And some their boots left down below,
>   That toes might take the better hold ;
> Some from their feet the shoes did throw,
>   Of true men thus I have heard told.
>
> The sweat down from their bodies ran,
>   And hearts did hop in panting breast ;
> At last the mountain-top they wan,
>   In warlike wise ere Scotchmen wist.

The picture is there—limned in half-a-dozen clean-cut strokes. And then the poet is carried away by the rollick of it all, and he makes Lord Stanley cheer his men with the merry cry, " My Lancashire most lovely wights "—the lovely wights who brought aid to the vanward folk of Craven in the nick of time. And again :—

> Which when the Stanley stout did see,
>   Into the throng he thundering brast ;
> " My lovely Lancashire lads," quoth he,
>   " Down with the Scots ! The day we waste."

They carried all before them then, to the music of two-edged axes spiked between ; and our schoolmaster, who scraped a mean livelihood with the birchen rod, grows virile once again as he drives down the Scotchmen verse by thundering verse.

So the Shepherd Lord came home again to Skipton with ringing of joy-bells and shouts of a populace run wild—came home almost exactly two centuries after the same bells had tolled with muffled voices for the death of his ancestor at Bannockburn. Banners and plumes and sun-smitten caps of mail came glancing to the Castle gates. The beggars this side the drawbridge reaped their own harvest from the victory, and maidens strewed flowers before old Clifford's path—maidens who were one day to sit in the ingle-nook at eventide, telling their grandchildren how the good Clifford left his books to wield a sword-blade for the honour of his house and for the peace of all the countryside.

And not horsemen and footmen only rattled over the drawbridge that day, for three of the Seven Sisters came back with Clifford as part of his hard-won spoil. Fair they were, and until the rude chance of war gave them into alien hands they had been prime favourites with His Majesty of Scotland. And Lady Clifford ? Had she no stormy welcome ready for these fruits of victory who bade fair to ruin the good order of her household ? Why, no ; for the Seven Sisters were like to trouble no one's peace, unless a man approached their mouths too

nearly ; and then they were wont to give him kisses that
were something of the hardest, and fiery love-tokens that
rove him limb from limb.   Neither more nor less than
culverins of large size, these sisters, which had been so
christened by King James for the beauty of their shape,
their delicate moulding, their likeness one to the other.
Amongst all the ordnance that was captured after the
battle, Surrey marked out this bronze sisterhood as being
finer than any culverins the English King could show ;
and it speaks more eloquently than any other fact, perhaps, for Lord Clifford's valour in the battle that he
should be chosen as the recipient of so unique a gift.

Well, the tale of Flodden Field is old by this time, and
its rancour all forgotten.   It gladdens us Craven folk yet
to retrace step by step the splendour of a fight which, for
fierceness and for heat, is second to none in all tumultuous
history ; but, looking back with the changed passions of
to-day, we see that it was more like a civil war than a
combat between hostile nations.   The Lowland army,
apart from its borderers and gentlemen of quality, was
built up of tenant-farmers, yeomen, shepherd folk, speaking a kindred tongue to ours, possessing almost the same
characteristics.   It was fitter that we should be friends
than that the artificial boundary of Tweed and Solway
should put bad blood between us ; and so, when the edge
of the defeat at Flodden was blunted on the one side,
and on the other old memories of the raids were out of
mind, the first steps could be taken toward that amity

which comes after the shrewd give-and-take of blows. They thrashed our Yorkshire levies handsomely at Bannockburn ; we thrashed them just as handsomely at Flodden ; and to-day, may be, we like each other none the worse for it.

As for our Shepherd Lord, he lived a good ten years after his home-coming with the Three Sisters. The speedy change from homespun to hereditary silks and satins had shaken his balance not a whit ; he remained unshaken still after the bewildering suddenness with which he had exchanged a student's life for one of martial fame. Through all vicissitudes he stands the same courteous, modest, valiant gentleman, and he, who had had contact with the realities of humble life, lives yet to us as the ideal over-lord, jealous of his high traditions, but jealous also for the welfare of his people ; and the old Castle, when the night is kindly with its dreams, turns oft in sleep and smiles upon the memory of a master whom it counted dear.

A Corner of the Castle.

CHAPTER XII

HOW SKIPTON MOCKED THE RABBLE

THE ball of the Clifford pomp still rolls merrily on through the eighth Henry's reign. The star-loving Shepherd Lord, whose father had been wedded to the shambles, is followed in his turn by a son whose tastes are remote at once from study of the stars and from blood-thirstiness. A buck, a robber of abbots, a gipsy ne'er-do-weel, in his younger days, this eleventh Lord of Skipton. He was educated with Henry the Eighth when both were pleasure-loving youths ; and the

King's jovial friendship led him into revelries which, as the Shepherd Lord laments in one of the saddest letters ever a father penned, were little in keeping with the means of a poor baron's son.   Then our gallant, unable to keep up his expenditure in any other way, turned Robin Hood, gathered a band of like-minded youths about him, and kept the countryside awake.   Monasteries, fat villages, stray travellers—all was fish that came to their net.   But most of all they loved to hunt the fallow deer, and young Clifford's reputation as an archer was known as far as London town.

History is not slow to deny that Clifford was the hero of the ballad of the Nut-Brown Maid ; but tradition again proves stronger than its harsh step-mother, fact, and for all time we shall see the wild young heir of Skipton roaming the Percy's woods, bow in hand, in search of fat bucks that belonged to the Northumbrian Earl.   He found more than red deer, moreover, under the greenwood tree ; for all on a summer's morn, as he fitted an arrow to the string, friend Cupid did the like and brought a daughter of the Percys over the velvet sward.   And Clifford wooed her there, with vows, and poesy, and logic of a comely face mated with well-turned limbs and straight-poised body ; and Margaret Percy became all in good time Lady of the Castle of Skipton.

A dainty ballad, this of the Nut-Brown Maid, and one that touches a curious depth of faith in womanhood.

He and she—our gay, deer-hunting Lord of Skipton and
Margaret Percy—have verse and verse alternate ; and he,
after confessing his love, is urging her to let him go
" alone, a banished man." He tells her all the hardships
that attend an outlaw's life—she'll have no wine to drink,
no shetes clene to lye between ; she must crop her hair,
and shorten her gown to knee-height, and wield a bow
against the dun deer and against enemies. And to all the
Nut-Brown Maid replies that she will go with him, be the
running stream their wine-bin, the bracken their clean
sheets, men's scorn her wedding-portion. *For, in my
mynde, of all mankynde I love but you alone*, is the persistent burden of her answer. He still pleads against
her ; but she, who has been long in bending to his love,
will hear no logic once her troth is plighted. She is a
woman to the core, this Nut-Brown Maid, and when her
hand is to the plough she drives a clean furrow. *Therefore I wyll to the green wode go, alone, a banyshed man*,
says the outlaw for the seventh time. And what does she
answer, this daughter of the Percys ? What any cottage-
maid would have answered, had her tongue been bold
enough for truth.

> Yet am I sure
> Of one plesùre ;
>   And, shortely, it is this :
> That where ye be,
> Me seemeth, pardè,
>   I coude nat fare amysse.

Without more speche,
I you beseche
  That we were sone agone ;
For, in my mynde,
Of all mankynde
  I love but you alone.

So in the finish, after proving her with every device
that a lover's cunning could suggest, he tells her that he
is no squire of low degree at all, but of noble birth ; and
the Nut-Brown Maid, we fancy, honest to the last, would
not conceal her satisfaction that this banished man had
all the dignities with which her fancy had endowed him
—though, whether he were squire, or lord, or clown,
her love was of the self-same calibre, and she would in
truth have turned gipsy or aught else for sake of this
gallant archer. And the author of the ballad draws a
healthy moral from his tale—that women, namely, are
far more leal to true love than the world admits.

In vain they tell us it is doubtful if the Nut-Brown
Maid were a Percy, doubtful if the outlaw were
friend Clifford, for we heed them never a whit ;
and tradition heeds them never a whit ; and we
shall always be sure—ay, and our children's children
will be sure—that sweet Margaret of Skipton was
wooed beneath the greenwood trees of old Northumbria. One thing is certain—that Clifford did lay
successful siege to my lady Margaret at the time when he
was roystering up and down the Northern deer-forests,

after making the Craven country too warm to hold him. The Percys were ever hot for pride, accounting themselves the best-born nobles north of Humber; and were they like to welcome a merry stripling of Clifford's reputation as a good match for a daughter of their house? Nay, it was settled between the two of them, with the cushat and the doe for counsellors, and lawny fragrance of the forest glades for worldly argument; and they loved till their life's end therefore—a rare happening that is not wont to enter into the marriage calculations of the great.

Our outlaw reformed then, succeeded the Shepherd Lord at Skipton, and lived in such high state as became one who was a Clifford, the husband of a Percy, and the cherished friend of a right royal monarch. Curiously akin his story is to that other breezy tale of Hal the Fifth, who likewise brought anguish to his father by madcap pranks, who poached and drank and gambled with companions of lowlier birth, who, last of all, pulled up in time and proved that a lad's light-heartedness, neither more nor less, was in fault for what had gone before.

The Clifford household accounts read well at this stage of the family history. Priors and abbots are no longer called upon to fill his lordship's purse; but the money is there to be spent, and Margaret Percy, one guesses, brought more than a nut-brown face to Skipton town. Henry the Eighth is still partial to his old boon-comrade, and soon we find Clifford going up to town, with six-and-thirty horsemen and blare of trumpets, to be created Earl of Cumberland. He was invested with the title at those famous junketings which attended the raising of the King's son by Elizabeth Blount to a Dukedom ; and the record of his expenses bears testimony to the good company he kept. My lord's tailor, for instance, one Ridley, profited greatly, and there are wondrous tales of velvet, russet and crimson, of tawny satin, of silk and buckram and fur. The old Adam is hid under all this weight of clothing, though, for we find records of brede arrow-heads and Strand arrow-heads, bugle-horns and shooting-gloves, which were to go with him on many a hunt across the Craven fells. Lastly—lest the goodwife in the North should sour his home-coming—he spends two-pounds-ten upon a white frontlet for my lady, bordered and wrought with gold.

The days went by at Skipton, after this elaborate visit to town, with ever-increasing magnificence. Social ambition replaced the sturdier aims of the old stock, and Clifford touched the zenith of his hopes when he married his son and heir to Lady Eleanor Brandon, daughter of a Queen of France and granddaughter of Henry the Seventh of England. Yet he, too, had to take his share of martial exploit, and when an occasion offered that called all his nerve and hardihood into play, he was not wanting —nay, he stood alone among the Yorkshire castellans for the pluck with which he faced disheartening difficulties and kept his walls against the onset of the rabble.

This was during the Pilgrimage of Grace, which saw a

mob of forty thousand rogues break loose from end to
end of Yorkshire. Rustics for the most part, they yet
had with them such nobles as Lord Darcy of Temple-
hurst and the warrior-archbishop of York—who rode, all
in the olden style, with armour underneath his archiepis-
copal vestments and a sword by way of cross. They
demanded wholesale redress of grievances, these precious
rebels, but chiefly the restoration of the Religious Houses
and the punishment of the Protestant bishops; they
swarmed over town and country, lewd and unbridled in
their passions, tempestuous in their gluttony for spoil;
and Holy Church, who has rarely lacked a certain mellow
dignity peculiarly her own, had cause to blush for this
refuse of the kennels, which hid its love of riot underneath her mantle. Lest any stroke of irony should
be wanting, they marched under banners emblazoned with the symbols of their faith, they carried our
Lord's name on their sleeves, and they affixed the title
" holy " to all their rascal enterprises.

Their leader was one Lawyer Aske, a shrewd fellow who
overstepped himself in cunning, as the event proved; for he
had looked to gain both riches and honour from a movement in favour of a Church which knew how to dispense
honour and riches alike with a lavish hand. He seems to
have been the ne'er-do-weel of the family, for the Askes
were gently-born and kinsfolk of the Cliffords; and when
the lawyer's brothers, Christopher and John, heard what
was toward, they wished him unaffectedly to the deuce,

16

and swore that they would be hewn in gobbets before
they would stain their allegiance to the King.

Hull was taken, Pomfret, York. Manor houses were
attacked, and their owners compelled on pain of death to
join the sweaty throng. Yorkshire was powerless before
them ; like an unclean wave they passed from east to
west of the good county, and the labouring folk were
sucked resistless into the after-wash that marked their
passing. Skipton and Scarborough alone held out at last ;
and then Scarborough, too, went under the deep waters ;
and only bluff old Skipton, with its motto of *désormais*,
looked undismayed upon the rebels, and watched them
mass, a howling, jostling throng, without the Castle gates.

Clifford, to add to his peril, was deserted by the five
hundred gentlemen who made up his retinue ; but
Lawyer Aske's brothers, by rare good luck, had crossed
the fells from Cumberland, with forty followers, to bring
succour to their kinsman, and they and Clifford, desertion
or no desertion, peril or no peril, resolved to play the
game out to the end.

The rebels grow more and more infuriated, as time
goes on and still this handful of brave fellows declines
to follow the example which all the rest of Yorkshire
offers. The cries of the mob ring day-long from the
market-place that fronts the Castle gateway — raucous
cries, mingled with obscene threats of vengeance which
reach the strip of lawn where Clifford and his followers
are taking the after-dinner air. Young Clifford mutters,

"Thank God there are no ladies' ears to be polluted," and goes on to the battlements, Christopher Aske beside him, and taunts the mob below with dainty, nicely-cutting speech. They have no culverins, nor ordnance of any sort, the besiegers —only pikes and pick-axes and rusty hedging-bills. Clifford tells them lightly that his walls will stand the onset of five-score thousand such as they, with five-score thousand more to back them ; thanks them for courteous inquiries ; and assures them the Castle is victualled for many months to come. Christopher Aske, doubtless, has passages of wit with his lawyer-brother, and others of the garrison join gaily in, resolved to make a holiday of danger and to prick these rascals into fury as they would so many baited bulls.

There is a fine carelessness about it all ; the gentlemen of the garrison have taken a plain road, and they mean to follow it ; but all the while they under-stand that it is no child's play, this — that they stand alone in a wide country overrun by thousands such as these who bivouac in Skipton streets, that food must ultimately fail, that their weakened force may any moment tempt some one of the baser sort within the walls to treachery. No matter ; they will live gaily for as long as may be, and after that—they will meet death in disdainful sort, because it comes from hands unknightly.

Three days pass by in this idle fashion ; and then, in a

moment, their gaiety is lost, and they look one at the
other helplessly, and young Clifford takes back his
thanksgiving that there are no ladies' ears to be polluted
by the uproar. Lewd speech is no nice companion, indeed ; but it is pollution itself, pollution in its worst and
least endurable shape, that threatens Clifford's love and
the pride which is stronger still than love. For his wife,
with other ladies and their women, was at Bolton Priory
when first the Castle was besieged, and found herself
compelled to stay there in sanctuary ; and the Pilgrims of
Grace have learned as much ; and Clifford, when he goes
to the battlements on the third morning for his wonted
greeting, is assailed by ribaldry and threats. If the Castle
is not surrendered by the next day, he is told, his wife and
the ladies with her shall be brought under the very walls
and handed over to the worst that this holy mob, which
fought beneath the banner of Christ's wounds, can compass against their honour. A trim exploit, that was conceived, we take it, in the crafty brain of Aske the lawyer.

The garrison is dumbfounded. The elder Clifford is
held by such anguish as a man could scarce live through
twice. To foul his honour by giving up what is the
King's, or to stain his son's honour irretrievably by
defending what is the King's—the issue is hideous in its
blunt alternatives. The day wears through and finds him
still in doubt ; either way of shame seems over-bitter
to accept, yet one of the two he must take upon the
morrow.

And then, clear out of the mist of doubting and suspense, a plan suggests itself to young Christopher Aske. He takes the Vicar of Skipton with him—God rest the Cloth for this one service !—he takes a groom, a boy, and led-horses for the women-folk who lie over the hill at Bolton, innocent of the brewing trouble. They swim across the moat under cover of the darkness, Christopher and the vicar and the stable lads, leaving the Cliffords, father and son, to defend the walls against surprise ; they move up the wooded slope behind the Castle— fearful all the while lest their horses should whinny their lives away—and cross the loneliest by-tracks of the moor, and so gain Bolton Priory. They mount the ladies, after parrying their questions with such adroitness as haste permits, and set off again across the moor.

Six good miles to Skipton, and the penalty of capture too fearful to be lost sight of for the space of a single step. Young Christopher, reverent toward all women, is racked with the burden of their honour that rests upon his stripling shoulders. He has the good fame of all in charge ; and one of them is niece to His Majesty of England, delicately bred and proud as any of her kingly line. Under Skipton walls lie yonder greasy rogues, whose breath is profanation. God, God, they *must* win safely into Skipton !

At last ! Silently, like ghosts from the night that watches over the fells, they creep down the wooded slope. They cross the moat. And Christopher Aske,

By the Castle Moat.

whose name is writ fair for ever on our Northern scrolls, calls for a measure of sack, a deep measure and a wide, while he watches young Clifford play the hot lover all afresh to his hardly-rescued lady. And the vicar also calls for his wine—and leaves, we warrant, no heel-taps in the tankard.

Clifford is up on the battlements again with sunrise. He calls for Lawyer Aske, and he bids him go bring the spoil from Bolton ; and the brute clamour of the mob, when it knows itself outwitted, is sweet as a lute-song to his ear. Christopher Aske, his errand done, grows reckless for his own safety. He gets him into full armour, takes a half-dozen of his friends with him, has the draw-bridge lowered, and rides out, debonair and disdainful, to the market cross. The mob, cowed by the daring of the move, makes way before his horse's hoofs. Christopher cries " Oyez, oyez, oyez !" in a voice like a trumpet-call, and reads aloud His Majesty's proclamation, and affixes it to the market cross. And then he turns ; and the Pilgrims of Grace watch open-mouthed as he disappears within the Castle gateway.

The fate of Christopher's brother, the leader of the riot, is told with such quaint simplicity in Drake's "Eboracum" that for sake of the language it is worth preserving. After describing how this or that pilgrim was hanged and suspended in chains from a convenient eminence, our chronicler adds, " Robert Aske, who was the principal of them all, had the same suspension on a tower, I suppose

Clifford's tower, at York." Whether the phrase, " had the same suspension on a tower," is intended as a simple statement of fact, or whether the narrator aimed at the dry, contemptuous sarcasm which the words imply to us, one cannot say ; but, from Drake to Whitaker, we find among antiquaries a whole-hearted, stately contempt of all who took arms against the King, and the historian of York, we fancy, smiled grimly to himself as he penned this neat summing-up of Lawyer Aske's departure from the stage.

That is the tradition of Christopher Aske. And Skipton, who has more legends than she can well hold in her lap, rates none more highly than that which tells how the honour of the Lady Eleanor was in jeopardy, and how featly it was kept.

The Sailor Earl.

CHAPTER XIII

H E died at forty-nine, this eleventh Lord of Skipton, and was succeeded by his son—the Clifford whose wife was rescued from the mob by young Christopher Aske. The new lord, like his shepherd grandfather, was a great student, the owner of a library which was reckoned notable at that day, and an eager searcher after that bog-o'-lanthorn, the Philosopher's Stone. Apart from aiding Lord Scrope to make head against the gallant Northern gentlemen who rose on behalf of Mary of Scots, his life shows like a tranquil island set amid the sea of tumult that preceded, and the storm of daring deeds which followed, his reign at Skipton ; and he would be scarce remembered if it were not for his singular escape from a coffin that was already yawning for him.

This was after the death of his first wife, while he was living quietly at Skipton and rebuilding the fortune which his marriage with the granddaughter of a King had sadly impaired. In the midst of this frugal labour he fell sick of a disease that baffled all the physicians of the day, and he slipped away from life by quiet, scarce-perceptible degrees, until they thought him dead. He was washed for the burial and laid out in state, with all the cere-cloths and the trappings of the bier which the custom of the age demanded ; and his servants, whose attachment for him bordered upon adoration, drew near to whisper praises of the master above the master's quiet body. One, keener sighted than the rest, saw Clifford's eyelids quiver, and cried that he lived yet. They stripped him of his funeral garb, put him between warm blankets, and forced cordials down his throat until the life came back to him. Then, under the leech's orders, they sought for a healthy goodwife who had a baby at the breast ; and her milk was Clifford's only sustenance for many weeks to come. A hardy race, these Lords of Skipton, for we find our sick man, who had paid his passage to Ferryman Charon and had put one foot on board his boat of dole, marrying another wife, living with her for close on twenty years, and rearing five children of this second wedlock.

Then he, in his turn, gave place to George, his eldest
son, who was destined to add a new and dazzling lustre
to the Clifford pomp. Soldiers had lifted the family
honour high ; it had known a shepherd warrior, and
a Robin Hood ; but not until this thirteenth lord came
to reign at Skipton had it boasted a sailor among its
sons.

We need space, and a sense of free, salt air, before we
can weigh aright the glory and the vices of the Sailor
Earl. He was sworn fellow to such sea-riding blades
as Drake and Frobisher, Raleigh and Hawkins and
Howard. A horse-racer, a free lover, a gambler, a
courtier—nay, what was he not ? Singularly handsome,
of a fine and sturdy figure, he could break a lance or
forswear himself in the interests of his lady's eyebrows
with any courtier in England—qualities which secured
him, needless to say, the special favour of Elizabeth, the
Queen. For Elizabeth, with all her greed of power, her
liking for the intricacies and stir of statecraft, was by
instinct a passionate coquette ; no man of Clifford's
personal beauty need have gone hungering for her
glances—but when, in addition to the physical qualities
which were Elizabeth's first regard, he could tilt, and
fight, and match wit against elaborate wit, like the Sailor
Earl, his place in the royal affections was secure indeed.
Not that Clifford had patience or manlessness enough to
dance puppet to the caprice of any woman for long
together. The sea was the one mistress with whom he

could keep troth, and spindrift and the upward hiss
of wave-rain from the decks were the only sort of kisses
that he craved.   Even in his Cambridge days, which
he spent under Whitgift's care, he had no taste for any
learning except mathematics and its application to the
construction of ships ; but in his favourite subject he
was, *for a lord*, the most knowing and eminent man in
his time, as his daughter quaintly puts it.

As early as 1586 we find him fitting out a little fleet at
his own charge, with Sir Walter Raleigh in command
of one of the vessels.   They sailed toward the South
Seas with the object of annoying the Spaniards, captured
a few ships, and returned after a twelvemonth's con-
tinuous battle with wind, waves, and reckless odds.
They had effected little so far as actual gain went ; but
the next year, his ardour unabated, Clifford himself put
to sea, with the object of aiding the besieged town of
Sluce, which fell, however, before he could reach the
scene of action.

Then the Armada set sail in awful majesty—sailed
with pomp and prayer, with blessings of the Pope and
chant of priests, and over-little ammunition of the
practical, leaden sort.   Clifford had command of the
old *Elizabeth Bonaventure* in the engagement—a six
hundred ton vessel, which had weathered storm and shot
for eight-and-twenty years, and which was still, to
Admiral Howard's thinking, the strongest English ship
that rode the sea.   Throughout the battle Clifford bore

himself with unique and foolhardy valour, and touched the
highest point of gaiety that ever his roving life afforded
him. He saw the Spanish galleons bear down, Castilian
in their dignity and mulish in their slowness, upon the
little, quick-to-move vessels of the English ; he was with
our fleet when it ran in almost to speaking distance
of the Spaniards and let drive its broadsides into
their quivering timbers ; he saw the enemy's scuppers
running blood, saw heads and limbs fly thick amid the
smoke and cannon balls, saw, finally, the panic-stricken
race for safety, which was the end of all the prayers, the
ceremony, the vaingloriousness that had heralded the
approach of the Armada. Then the wind swooped out
of heaven to applaud this splendid battle of the few
against the many, the cockle-shells against the galleons ;
and the waves got up and licked at the scudding cloud-
wrack ; and the ships which had escaped mortal injury
from our fire went staggering up the wild North Sea—
staggering like maimed human things, and bleeding from
every cannon-opened artery.

Clifford put on full press of sail, once the storm had
hidden the remnants of the Armada ; and the old
Elizabeth Bonaventure, trim yet and water-tight, went
racing, fast as the wind could take her, home to
England ; and the Sailor Earl was first, as became his
valour, to carry the glad news to the camp at Tilbury.
The Queen was very gracious to him—as, sooth, she had
need to be ; for she, and England with her, would have

been well-nigh defenceless had it not been for the private enterprise and the public spirit of such subjects as Clifford, Lord of Skipton. It has grown habit now to credit the Maiden Queen with all the foresight and resource that went to the manning of our fleet ; but the fact is otherwise, and victory was won, as is usual in our annals, by happy-go-lucky disregard of the shiftings, the niggard craving for economy, the spinelessness, of those who were supposed to guide the helm of State. Clifford and Raleigh, Frobisher and Drake, whose motto at all seasons was *attack*—these are the men to whom we of to-day owe our overlordship of the seas ; and it is strange that Clifford's claims to honour should be so little recognised, when those who bore no greater share of the heat and burden of the day bulk large in every history of the period.

It was probably during Clifford's audience of the Queen, after the Armada had been shot-riddled into flight, that Elizabeth dropped her glove, and he, knightly fashion, handed it back to her on bended knee ; whereat Her Majesty smiled, and told the Sailor Earl to keep it in remembrance of his sincere well-wisher ; and Clifford had it set about with diamonds, and ever afterwards he wore it in his hat. The incident has been placed as much as ten years later than the sea-fight ; but the admirable painting of Clifford in our National Portrait Gallery, which shows Elizabeth's glove fixed jauntily in the sea-rover's hat, bears the date of the Armada.

Clifford had not satisfied his battle-hunger as yet. A few months after he had carried the good news to Tilbury, we find him off and away on another buccaneering expedition. He returned disappointed, but in no wise daunted ; and the next year he took the Queen's ship, the *Victory*, and three other vessels, all furnished at his own cost, and made a voyage to the West Indies which has left its mark on history, not only for the daring shown and the rich spoil captured, but by reason of the agonies, unparalleled almost in naval records, which the crews suffered on the homeward journey.

In all he captured eight-and-twenty of the enemy, carrying goods in their holds to the tune of twenty thousand pounds. Spanish vessels, or French, big ships or little, two against one, or whatever odds fate chose to send against him—it was all one to the Sailor Earl. He and his sailors, indeed, seem to have regarded battle as the stay-at-homes looked on sport, in the light of relaxation and an excuse for boisterous foolhardiness. In Fyal harbour, for instance, which was commanded by the guns of the castle, they spied seven magnificent vessels. Clifford at once gave the order to attack ; they ran in under an overwhelming fire from the castle, captured the whole seven ships, and looked one at the other in amazement that this mad escapade should have met with such instant and scarce-looked-for success.

Not a hint that they stopped at such times to remember how closely death shadowed every movement of the game ;

never a thought that one ship of the Navy and three small
pinnaces were scarce the sort of armament with which to
tilt against flotillas of the enemy.   At Fyal, indeed, they
were not content with the one enterprise, but landed
and stormed the town, and had serious thoughts of
holding it in behalf of Her Majesty of England ; but the
smallness of their force, and the vastness of their prizes,
compelled them to forego this entertaining project, and
they allowed the Fyal folk to ransom themselves at a cost
of two thousand ducats.

So far the frolic went ; but there was another side to
the expedition.   The *Victory*, which Clifford commanded
in person, fell in with a mighty Brazilian ship, and promptly
offered battle.   Clifford, in addition to being wounded
several times during the action, was all but blown to
shreds by gunpowder, and when he started at last for
England he was so scorched and riddled and cut that
a man of less spirit could never have survived.   Then,
not far from the Irish coast, they encountered stress of
weather ; and what followed, as told in the narrative of
one of the crew, is more nakedly awful than any picture
that fancy could draw unaided.

The wind, says our chronicler, came about to the east-
wards, so that they could not fetch any part of England.
The allowance of drink, scanty enough before, dwindled
from less to less, from half a pint at a meal to a quarter of
a pint, and at last to three or four spoonsful of vinegar
each day.   They tried to make the Irish coast, but were

driven persistently to the leeward ; and the water-famine began in earnest. They dared not eat much, for fear of the ensuing thirst ; their wounds cried ceaselessly ; and for fourteen days they did battle with the weather on this fighting-food of meagre flesh washed down with vinegar.

" Saving that now and then wee feasted for it in the mean time," the record runs ; "and that was when there fell any haile or raine : the hailstones wee gathered up and did eate them more pleasantly than if they had bene the sweetest comfits in the world. The raine-drops were so carefully saved that, so neere as we coulde, not one was lost in all our shippe." They hung up sheets, tied at the four corners and weighted in the middle, to catch the rain ; any napkin or dirty clout was reckoned a dear possession, for they held out all such to the rain till they were soaked, then sucked them dry again. The very water which washed away the garbage of the decks was not suffered to escape, but was lapped up greedily. " Some licked with their tongues, like dogges, the sides, railes, and mastes of the shippe : others that were more ingenious, fastened girdles or ropes about the mastes, dawbing tallow betwixt them and the maste, that the raine might not run down between, in such sort, that those ropes or girdles hanging lower on the one side than on the other, a spout of leather was fastened to the lowest part of them, that all the raine-drops that came running down the maste, might meet together at that place, and there be received.—Some also put bullets of lead into

their mouths to slake their thirst. Now in every corner
of the shippe were heard the lamentable cries of sicke and
wounded men sounding wofully in our eares, crying out
and pitifully complaining for want of drinke, being ready
to die—yea, many dying for lacke thereof, so as by reason
of this great extremitie we lost many more men than wee
had done all the voyage before."

And Clifford, the master of the enterprise ? Wounded,
scorched, he shared all in common with his men, the
vinegar, the wine-lees squeezed from out the bottoms of
the casks, the "sweet comfits" of hail and rain ; he
shared, too, his unconquerable gaiety of heart with them,
and not once through all that stormy fortnight did he
slacken in his efforts to keep up the spirits of his crew ;
and this courtier, the maker of verses and idle love-
pleasantries, showed, when the need came, as a man who
could strip the tinsel fearlessly.

Nine voyages he made altogether, with varying fortunes,
but with constant search after the dangers that were meat
and drink to him. Spain, defeated in the one great
conflict, still needed watching, and every blow struck at
her prestige or her commerce was so much gained for
England. There was something of the gambler's zest,
doubtless, in Clifford's love of buccaneering ; he staked
his money on sea-horses, and hoped to win his races as
any other sportsman would ; but he spent far more than
he gained, and knew that it must be so, and the commer-
cial aspect of his enterprises was no more than a detail

of the deep passion for adventure which pricked him on from one wild voyage to another. Illness did not spare him, but he disdained it ; once he rose from a sick bed to lead a handful of ships to the Azores; a twelvemonth later he built another ship, which the Queen herself christened the *Malice Scourge,* and which was destined to play a conspicuous part in the story of Elizabethan sea-fights. With this *Malice Scourge* and a fleet that numbered close upon a score vessels he prevented the Spanish carracks from sailing to the Indies, delayed the return of their Plate-fleet from America, and made himself in all ways possible as great a thorn in the side of the Dons as any of the sixteenth-century Vikings who sprang up about Elizabeth's person.

He does not neglect the duties of his rank meanwhile. The Court, if it cannot prison him in its narrow meshes, is pleased at all times to have him hovering near its throne. He is on pleasant, intimate terms with his Sovereign ; now we find him presenting her with " a jewell of gold like a sacrifice," and again with "one pettycote of white sarcenett, embrothered all over with Venyce silver plate, and some carnacon silke like columbines." The Queen, in return, gives him plate and what not. Again, it was the custom of the age to affect the older forms of chivalry, and Sir Henry Lee, when he grew too infirm to carry on his duties as Queen's Champion in the tilt-yard, was succeeded by our Lord of Skipton, who was invested with the honour, under circumstances of peculiar pomp, on the two-and-thirtieth anniversary of Elizabeth's coronation. At a later date, again, he presents a show on horseback before Her Majesty, at which, in the guise of a romantic knight, he delivers himself of an ode to Cynthia. It is not pleasant, in a way, to think of Clifford playing the rôles of Queen's Champion and of masking knight. When only the lion's skin was needed, it seemed a waste of good material that one of so sincere and stout a chivalry should be made a player in an idle show. My Lord of Leicester would have fitted the part admirably, had he been living, or many another subject-lover of the Queen's; but Clifford was of statelier mould.

It is hard, indeed, to follow him through the quick changes of his restless talent, and to realise that he is all the while as hard-hitting and strenuous a rover as ever set sail in search of Spanish galleons. If he is not at sea, or with the land forces, or at Court, he must needs run down to Cambridge to settle a free fight between some scholars and Lord North's retainers; or we find him superintending the building of a ship, each little item in the construction of which is known to him; or he is suppressing the rebellion of Essex and his friends against the Crown and sitting in judgment upon the conspirators.

Elizabeth dies, and a new monarch takes her place; but still our Sailor Earl stands near the throne. James the First, when he was no more than James the Sixth of Scotland, had already shown himself keenly wishful that

Clifford should attend the baptism of his son ; and afterwards, when he came south to be crowned, it was Clifford
who carried the sword of State before him at York—with
such an equipage of followers, we are told, that he
seemed rather a King than Earl of Cumberland. And
here again we see him in a new light, as one who, careless in many of the matters of life, is yet stubborn in
defence of family pride ; for the Lord-President of the
North presumed to claim the sword-bearer's privilege,
and Clifford would not yield his own right to the dignity
—a right which the King himself substantiated when the
matter in dispute was brought before him.

In all things, mock fighting in the lists, hard blows on
sea or land, rivalries of place, we find Clifford still the
kingly noble, sometimes impoverished, always in financial
straits, yet never grudging his last guinea or his last ounce
of blood. Behind every ebb and flow of fortune, however,
the sea is calling him ; the sob of salt winds, the creak of
cordage tightening to the gale, are music such as no
minstrel of the Court can give him. Like one of his
fellow-rovers—was it Raleigh or Howard ?—he could
laugh when his ship was pitching like a cork amid
the breakers, and could vow that never yet had he danced
to a merrier tune at masque or revel.

No man, perhaps, has offered more diverse faces to the
world, according to the outlook of his critics, than the
Sailor Earl of Skipton. Dr. Whitaker—a diligent searcher
after facts, but no good judge of character—gives him

scant credit for his pluck, his grace, his services to England at a time when private endeavour was a matter of stark necessity if our fleet were to repel invasion. All is overlaid by the fact that Clifford was a random lover, unfaithful to the wife who had been chosen for him before he was well breeked—the wife who, from the scanty hints that have been handed down to us, belonged to that class of patient, self-centred martyrs who are apt to drive men into the tavern or the madhouse.

Clifford went astray with a lady of quality at Court, says Whitaker; he founded many obscure branches of his family amongst the Craven yeomen's daughters; he plunged his estates into difficulties; and for these reasons, we are told, he was "a great but unamiable man, whose story admirably illustrates the difference between greatness and contentment, between fame and virtue." The worthy doctor certainly touches upon his naval exploits, but in a prefunctory, half-hearted way; there's no single moment when he glows with the memory of what such sailors as Clifford did, by suffering and by pluck, to make Elizabeth mistress of the seas—no moment when he forgets the pulpit and remembers by chance that even Whitaker is a man as well as a divine. *Clifford was not virtuous.*

Yes, but is this fair play? Let us lament his lack of private virtue, and have done with it; and after that we are free to give the Sailor Earl his full due of public merit. He spent his money, his health, the time that other men were giving to luxury, in sharing the hardships of his poorest sailors ; he fought the Spaniard, and harried the Spaniard, and destroyed the Spaniard's ships and treasure, at a time when England cried out for such bold services. The salt of the sea was in his blood, and the rover's heedlessness ; he might, indeed, have been a model husband, had he been fashioned on other lines— but England, in the day of the Armada, was not saved by model husbands.

None but Lodge, the Norroy King of Arms, has done our Lord of Skipton justice—none but he has weighed the worthier side of this complex character in so accurate and fine a balance. " He was by nature," says Lodge, " what the heroes of chivalry were from fashion, and stood alone, therefore, in a time to the manners of which he could not assimilate himself, like a being who, having slept for ages, had suddenly awaked himself amidst the distant posterity of his contemporaries." The whole trend of Clifford's life bears out this judgment, and it is not surprising that, wearied of the trickeries and mock-sentiment which minced through the Court of the Maiden Queen, he should so often kick over the traces, and put to sea, and search for the realities of life under robuster and less elegant conditions.

When we are told that Elizabeth, for all her personal liking toward him, would appoint Clifford to no weighty office of State because his politics were shifty, we can only marvel at the argument, knowing that it was not shiftiness, but honesty, which barred his way in this direction. Could he have shared the self-complacent ruthlessness of Cecil, or have followed the tortuous diplomacy that was in fashion with Randolph, Throck-morton and the rest, he would have risen high in office ; but the very downrightness of his character, his im-patience of any sort of trickery—whether in statecraft, or in his dealings with his neighbours—made it impossible that he should be entrusted with the larger matters of policy.

It has been often alleged, moreover, in connection with Clifford's political career, that he was one of those who sat in judgment on Mary Queen of Scots ; but the accusation rests on no sufficient authority, and until the charge is proven, we, who have spent many a pleasant hour with the Sailor Earl, and have learned the free, straightforward way of him, prefer to dissociate him altogether from that long-drawn drama of ill-usage which closed with the tragedy of Fotheringay.

He died at middle age, our Sailor Earl—died of that dread bloody flux which carried off so many of his companions in arms. His body, after being embalmed, was laid in the Parish Church of Skipton, on the south side of the chancel ; and Whitaker, whose judgment is dependable on a point of this kind, doubts whether any tomb in the country can show such a blaze of armorial bearings. Clifford and Russell, within the Garter, Clifford between Brandon and Dacre, Clifford and Veteripont, Clifford and Percy—there are seventeen shields in all, and the Sailor Earl, who did not live soft in his lifetime, can fitly sleep under blazonries which, covering lesser men, would be crass ostentation.

A singular story is connected with this tomb; for Dr. Whitaker, two centuries after Clifford had been laid to rest, obtained a faculty for opening the vault and examined it in presence of several other antiquarians. On raising the lid of Clifford's coffin, they found the body wrapped in ten folds of cere-cloth, of which they disencumbered it with painstaking care; and then they started back, for what lay under their eyes was life-like enough to raise a passing thrill of superstition. Clifford lay there, his features perfect, his hat and plume, his frill, and all the bravery of Elizabeth's day, fitting as trimly as when they buried him two hundred years before; and Whitaker—a point which would, we fancy, please him mightily—discovered that the extant portraits of the Earl were excellent, but that they lacked three warts plainly visible on the left cheek.

As they watched, the remains—in the words of those who stood round the tomb—began to shake like a jelly, and in a few seconds all gave way and collapsed into dust. This, however, was not the end of the adventure; for soon afterwards one of the antiquaries chanced to be at Chatsworth, where the housekeeper was showing him the picture gallery.

"That, sir, is the portrait of Admiral Lord Clifford," said she, pointing to one of the paintings.

The visitor glanced at the portrait, and then singled out another on the opposite wall. " I must correct you," he said, with exquisite gravity ; " *this* is the Admiral, for I saw him only yesterday."

What the housekeeper responded has not been left on record—nor what form her amazement took when inquiry proved that her visitor had spoken a true word as to the identity of the portrait. The situation, surely, is unique, in history or in fiction.

The pomp of the Cliffords ends with George, the Sailor Earl. His successor was noteworthy for nothing in especial except that he contrived, in an age of short-lived men, to die at eighty-one. Henry, the next of the line, was the last Earl of Cumberland ; as Governor of Newcastle, in 1638 and the year subsequent, he shared the disastrous expeditions against the Scotch, and so the last Lord of the Honour of Skipton ended the military history of his family where the first Lord began it - fighting the auld enemy.

An easy-going man, this last Earl, fond of the table and greatly addicted to gout. The Civil War which broke out in 1642 found him too infirm of body and too peaceful of habit to hold his castle for King Charles, and by his own request another Governor was appointed.

Once for the King, always for the King, seemed to be the interpretation which Skipton Castle put upon its motto of *Désormais.* Time after time it had shown a gallant front to the King's enemies, whether they came in the guise of Borderers or as a rabble wantoning under the banners of religion; and now again, with the outbreak of the Civil War, it held its own for three long years against the forces of the Parliament.

Sir John Mallory was the Governor of the Castle, Lambert the besieger—destined to be General Lambert, and a dangerous rival to Cromwell's deep, unalterable, self-deceiving ambition. Yorkshiremen both, they were, and Lambert a Craven man to boot; and, Yorkshire-like, they liked each other none the worse, we take it, because they breakfasted together daily on cannon balls and supped on skirmishes.

Rarely, perhaps, have the oddities of civil war been more clearly marked than during this siege of Skipton. Clifford himself was a boon friend of Sir Thomas Fairfax; Lambert was on terms of intimacy with all, or with most, of the gentlemen who helped to garrison the Castle. Fairfax was loath to see his old friend's property demolished; Lambert was not keenly anxious, until he accustomed himself to the idea, to send a greeting of the warmest to men who had once drunk his wine and eaten his saddles of mutton. It was natural that the siege should be loosely carried on during the first months, that its record should read more like the play of schoolboys than a sober struggle.

All that was changed, however. The Royalists within the Castle grew impatient of confinement; they lost no chance of sortie, and grew to be a sharper thorn in

Cromwell's side than the future Protector relished. We find them making a dash for Keighley, nine miles away, where the Parliamentarians had a camp; they came upon the enemy like a whirlwind, routed them utterly, took a quantity of prisoners and horses, stayed to plunder the town and to drink of the best they could find there, and set off again for Skipton in the gayest spirits. Unhappily, they fell in with Lambert on their homeward way, and after a hand-to-hand encounter were driven back behind their walls, with the loss of all their spoil except the wine that they had drunk. Before this they had joined the garrison of Knaresborough in a sortie which led them almost to the gates of York. Their enterprise was never-resting, and at last it roused their adversaries to a like activity.

The blockade was begun in earnest then; but still the old Castle gibed at all its enemies. Scarborough Castle fell, Sherborne, Sandal, until, for the second time in its history, Skipton alone of all the Yorkshire castles held out for the King's cause. The Clifford pomp had died from its walls like the sunset of a departed day, but the spirit of its ancient masters was strong yet upon the time-greyed fabric; and when at last it could hold out no longer, when every Royal stronghold—not in York-shire only, but throughout the North—had given way and left it solitary, when privation had reached its extreme limit and further hardship meant only the slow death of starvation—then the garrison surrendered, and hardy to the last, demanded that they should be allowed to leave the Castle with full honours of war. The condition was granted, and the grim gateway-front looked down upon the closing scene of all its glory—looked down and saw the tattered gentlemen of Craven, gay to the last and of a sturdy carriage, wind down the High Street and disappear along the road that took them to the south.

Lady Anne Clifford succeeded—student, pupil of the poet Daniel, philanthropist, and clear-headed business woman. Twice married, she confesses naïvely that she got little joy from either of her husbands, and she seems to have been well content when the death of the Earl of Pembroke left her free to live among her classical and household books at Skipton. Dr. Donne said of her that she knew well how to discourse upon all things from predestination to slea-silk, and we can well believe it, seeing that in early youth her favourite books were "Camden's Britannia," "Abraham Ortemus, his Maps of the World," "Cor. Agrippa of the Vanity of Scyences," and "The Feigned History of Don Quixote." She earned, too, the title of Repairer of the Breaches, by reason of her passion for rebuilding the many churches, towers, and castles which lay within her properties. A quiet, virtuous, peace-loving woman, a little vague in outline, it may be, yet full of the old Clifford spirit when any slight or wrong was put upon her ; a woman who claims our affection, if only for the work she did in handing down the history of her family.

A century after the three years' siege of the Castle came to a close, the cloud of war again rolled near to Skipton, but passed it by and left it open-mouthed with wonder that, in so late a Year of Grace as 1745, a second civil strife should gather to a head and break. Craven had grown to deem itself a peaceful land, and it was startled, as well it might be, when news came that an enemy was marching through its borders. From the old quarter, too ; for the men who followed Prince Charlie south were of that same Scots race which had harried Craven past endurance in the days before Flodden Field was fought. Did some echo from the far-off years return to the Skipton folk when they heard of the march of the Scotchmen ? Did they hear again that cry, " The Scots, the Scots ! " and cast a rapid glance behind them at the Castle which no longer offered them protection ?

It may be so, for their alarm was near to panic, and everywhere men ran about distractedly and asked their neighbours what was next to come. Messengers were scurrying in every direction—to Gisburn, to Clitheroe, and further still afield—to learn if Prince Charlie were minded to march through Skipton town. The constables' books are full of entries during the winter of 1745–6, concerning sums of money paid to the watch— for watching, but more especially for drinking ale. *Ale for the watch, ale for the watch*—the entry grows monotonous. And with it all they took but a single prisoner

—one luckless William Wright, whose shoes, poor rebel, were not fit to carry him to York. They spent a handsome sum on him—a sovereign for conveying him to York, eight shillings for a pair of shoes in which to make the journey, and so on—one-pound-ten in all, less sixpence. A sorry capture, truly; but one out-at-heels vagabond, it seemed, was better in their view than no rebel at all, and they were disposed to make the most of him.

Yet, all absurdities of detail apart, it is only by standing in the position of the Skipton folk of 1745, by viewing the matter eye to eye with them, that we can understand what this Rebellion really meant. News-sheets were few and far between; Prince Charlie's landing at Moidart, his subsequent movements in the Highlands, would be scarce known, and certainly not realised in Skipton. Then, like a thunderclap, came the news that he had left Carlisle with an army of the wildest hill-folk who ever set mouth to bagpipe or hand to the claymore-hilt. Prince Charlie ceased on the sudden to be an abstraction—he was a reality which loomed ever closer and more close to their own homesteads.

All through Cumberland and Westmorland they followed his march, and held their breath as he advanced more southward still. It was monstrous, a thing incredible, that the Scots should march on the old bloody trail at this late day—but, monstrous or no, it was a fact.

18

Would they come down the valley of the Aire, or would they strike through Lancashire ? Either road was likely, and for a long day and longer night the Craven folk watched breathless for the issue ; and then news came that they were safe, that the Prince had left them to the westward of his line of march ; and such a load of terror was lifted from their minds as we of to-day find hard to understand.

There are fifty ways of viewing any matter, and none is the true one save from its own standpoint. The Craven folk feared for their property, for their personal safety and that of their wives and bairns, and they wanted none of Prince Charlie ; the historians, again, eyeing the Rebellion from far-off considerations of policy and government, are convinced that England was the better in the long run for the defeat of the Stuarts at Culloden ; but in Skipton here, with the storied Castle close behind us, there's but one way of regarding the Jacobite Rebellion. It was the most magnificent forlorn hope that the world has ever seen ; and for this cause the ghosts of Clifford and of Percy—the ghosts of all the gallant gentlemen who fought behind the Percy or the Clifford —stand close ranged about that yellow-haired laddie who set the world on fire with his kingly laughter and his human tears. Born over-late was Charlie Stuart ; romance and courtesy, gay recklessness to tilt at over-powering odds, grim courage under hardship—these were the blood and the brain of him. He was the leader lacking only men to follow him; and our thoughts run back to Christopher Aske, who snatched a lady's honour from peril of the mob and afterwards rode out among them all to fix the King's declaration to the market cross. Cheek by jowl would bonnie Prince Charlie and young Christopher have fared to capture

The Castle Gateway.

London, for it was an adventure after the heart of both; and Aske would have dinned his shout of " Oyez, oyez, oyez !" right merrily into the ears of those ten thousand troops at Finchley who waited only for the first onset to break and flee back to the capital they guarded.

But the yellow-haired laddie sleeps in alien soil; and

Christopher Aske has crumbled long since into senseless dust; and Nature has lost the mould in which she framed such men. Yet Skipton's memory is long, and not till the Castle drops stone from stone, not till walls and gateway and *Désormais* motto are hidden under the heedless ground, will she forget what deeds she holds in keeping.

CHAPTER XIV

BY COACH ON A JUNE MORNING

FROM Skipton town to Buckden the coaches still ply
through a score miles of country as fair as any to
be found under shelter of the Northern fells; nor is the
bustle attending the to-and-froing of this highway-traffic
the least part of old Skipton's charm.

It is nine of a June morning as we go up the broad
High Street—scarce awakened yet to the business of the
day—and cross to the "Red Lion" tavern, and mount
to the box-seat of the Buckden coach. Ostlers are
vaguely busy about inn-fronts; market-women are setting
their wares in order; a couple of gossips dawdle to the
seat this side the churchyard gates and fall to confidential

talk. Instinctively the mind swings back from the world
of racket and unrest, and opens to the ampler breadth of
rustic life, slow-moving through a day which the country
folk find long enough for work, and long enough for
gossip, and, above all, long enough for much contempla-
tion, straw in mouth, of summer skies and cattle-dotted
fields.

There are few corners of England so aloof from the
fret and uproar of the rail as this fell-land which sweeps,
clean, wide and still, from Skipton through the old-time
hunting-grounds of Clifford and of Percy; and the flavour
of the coach-journey is the self-same flavour that our
grandfathers knew when they coached the Great North
Road in bottle-green coats and peg-top trousers.

The earlier coach—leaving Skipton at six of the clock—
has carried Her Majesty's mails, all in the olden way; the
one we have boarded at the " Red Lion " takes parcels of
all kinds—haunches of mutton, milliner's ware, a stray
basket of fruit—to the houses up the dale; the driver
knows everybody, knows the people who bring the
parcels, staying thereafter for an exchange of raillery,
and those for whom they are destined. They are a race
to themselves, these drivers of the Skipton coaches—well-
favoured fellows, with shrewd faces and tongues that wag
merrily upon occasion; they are in fellowship with their
horses, and get the most from them, but there is no
"springing" of cattle on the Buckden line, for they
scorn such dark traditions of the older roads.

The change of atmosphere is apparent soon as we start Northward-Ho, leaving the castle and the church behind us, and mount the first stiff mile of road. We have crossed the line between partial town and absolute country, and the world, for as far as the coach will take us, is innocent of any business save agriculture. The very guide-posts have names that touch old memories— so many miles to Rylstone, to Cracoe, or to Kendal. Over yonder, at the meeting-place of the old roads to Gargrave and to Rylstone, is the hill from which Cromwell's guns poured iron balls into Skipton Castle; this, and many such-like echoes of the past go with us on the road. The Duchess of St. Albans, too, and Edmund Kean, and the little dressmaker—we can all but see them get up beside us to revisit the scene of former triumphs in quiet Lintondale; and the journey speeds the faster for their company.

Half up the hill a red-faced shepherd is lying under shelter of the hedge, nod-nodding and opening a sleepy eye when our driver passes the time of day with him; at the top of the rise we come upon the shepherd's flock, which is wandering aimlessly along the road. Just as we near the bleating herd of ewes and half-grown lambs, the bell-wether at their head looks through a five-barred gate that opens on the roadway, sees a green stretch of pasture, and yields to the temptation; one by one the others hurry after—over the wall, and up the pasture, cropping as they go, and over the hill-top out of sight.

A backward glance shows us the shepherd still slumbering tranquilly beneath the hedge ; and we wonder how this modern Bo-peep will enjoy the comedy when he awakes to find that his flock has vanished into space.

That is the keynote of a careless holiday. One's neighbours on the coach are cheery ; the driver is full of rollick ; it is hail-fellow-well-met from Skipton up to Buckden, with the keen limestone breezes on the face, and the rhythmic swing of horses' flanks between the fell-spaces and the eye. And all the while we know that story and romance lie ambushed at every turning of the road ; and all the while we have the limestone hills with us, grey under the red-brown carpet of the heath, or white against the climbing pine-woods. The hedgerows change their fashion ; they are smoother, greener, and the flowers that grow in them—wild lilac and hedge-apple, cowslips saffron-belled, red-spotted oxlips and primroses shy of face—look all as if they had found good soil in which to thrive.

A land of fairies, this road to Rylstone. Close House stands over yonder, and all the countryside could have told you a generation since how once on a time this house was honoured by the protection of a fairy. The fairy was called Hob—a decent little fellow enough, who used to get in the hay and thresh the corn for the owner of Close House, until the latter rashly presented him with a red cap. No self-respecting fairy would tolerate such a gift, naturally, and Hob departed in a huff ; nor did he

ever return to his labours in cornfield and in meadow,
and the incautious farmer spent much in wages during
the succeeding harvests of hay and corn.

Did not Churn-milk Peg, too, inhabit Shore Lea Lane,
not far away ? A fearsome hag, whose only business in
life, apart from that of smoking a very dirty fairy-pipe,
was to scare children when they were bent on plucking
unripe fruit from out the hedgerows—a hobby to which
she owed her name, since churn-milk is the phrase in
Craven for the pulpy kernel of a hazel-nut before the
summer's sun has ripened it.

> Smoke ! smoke a wooden pipe !
> Getting nuts afore they're ripe !

was the burden of her song, and if the bairns were rash
enough to disregard the warning, Churn-milk Peg carried
them off forthwith to some dim abode where the sun
never shone and the stars never twinkled.

A useful scare-boggart for the mothers, this pipe-smok-
ing hag ; for just as in Haworth parish the phrase ran,
" Wilt 'a be gooid now, or dost 'a want Barguest to fetch
thee ? " so in Craven the children were awed into good
behaviour by threats of Peg the ruthless.

There was another fairy called Hob who wrought
strange deeds far up in Netherdale ; but he must wait, for
the coach is already swinging past None-Go-By, a trim-
built house and a roomy. It was an inn once on a day,

they tell us, and over the door the landlord scrawled a pleasing request for custom.

> Let none go by without a call,
> To taste my beer both strong and small,

the tempting offer ran.

The house is said to have taken its name from this couplet; but it is far likelier that the rhyme itself was founded on a strange usage which was in vogue long before the dwelling was a house of call. Why did so many brides leave None-Go-By the worse for lack of a left shoe? Because, tradition says, the owner of the house had the right to demand of every new-made bride who passed his door the sum of three-and-fourpence, or her left shoe in default thereof. The sum would be no light one even now for labouring folk, and in old days it was beyond the purse of any but the gently-born; and so there was many a maiden-wife went limping Skipton-wards, stocking to bare ground. The origin of the custom is lost; but there is little doubt that it harks back to an older usage still—that dread *Droit du Seigneur* which was once an integral part of all manorial rights.

Such tales—of fairy pipes and wedding fees—fit well the road to sweet old Rylstone; for we believe in the fairies yet, and romance is with us yet, if ever we walk alone among the little-trodden spots of earth; and the disused road yonder, grass-grown between its primrose banks and close-cropped pastures and bustling rabbit-warrens, is one of the few little-trodden corners that are left to us. It quits the highway at the old toll-house, and was once the chief road to Rylstone ; but the coaches take a different route nowadays, and one can go from end to end of this fell-sheltered road and meet never a comrade by the way, save still-staring sheep or kine that eye one solemnly between mouthfuls of lush grass.

When spring is eager with breaking bloom of hawthorn, when the dusk comes fragrant down this old-world lane and the day is ready for its bed—that is the fairies' hour, and willy-nilly they make you understand their presence and feel their strength, for mischief or for kindliness. The gnomes and goblins live to-day in the moorlands and in the mine-caverns of the fells ; but the Green Folk people the gentler valleys. And still, if you keep silence and tread the greensward lightly, you can hear the ripple of elfin-bells at this old roadside—can catch the glimpse of vapoury green between the moss-grown trunks—can find, with the dawn, the mushroom ring that was sown by the dancing feet of Queen Mab and her band.

The coach is waiting at the toll-house all this while, and the team is tugging at the bit, while we go loitering down unfrequented lanes. Forward again, and past Scale House, upstanding from among its pines. We stop here to deliver the butcher's basket, and a trim maid-servant comes to the gate.

" I have brought you a bit of mutton," says the driver, with a grave air of compassion.

" Very kind of you, I'm sure," answers the maid, saucy and debonair.

" Yes, it's all over Skipton that you haven't set tooth to meat at Scale House for a week past, and it like as it went to my heart—so here's the basket, and never say I haven't a soft side to me, to keep you all from starving at the cost of my own pocket."

A toss of the head from the maid, a merry laugh from the driver, a brisk interchange of wit between the two, and on we go again, with the road slipping white beneath us and the trees of Rylstone showing green ahead. Far up the fells old Norton Tower—the little that is left of it —stands gaunt and jagged on its spur of hill, guarding the brave traditions which have set the Nortons in the vanguard of those gentry of the sword who fought their way into a place in history. The Norton motto was "God us ayde," and the five wounds of Christ were on their coat-of-arms; yet, for all this piety, they were sad fellows in their time, and were never known to wield a blade in the interests of peace and order. Chivalrous gentlemen always, though, with a quick ear for the entreaties of the weak, and a quick eye for beauty in a Queen of Scots or in a nut-brown maid; roystering gentlemen, who could pull a bow or drain a flagon with the best, who took life at a canter, and never blinked when they reached the last grim fence of all.

Tree-hidden now and then, the Tower is never lost to sight for long, and it goes with us, a good companion, until we near the steep hill yonder that falls into a round and wooded hollow. The white road, roofed with trees, curves down to the low-walled pond that holds the centre of the village ; at the end of the vista is a garden gate, lilac-cumbered, and a strip of yellow gravel, and a brown door framed in clematis, with chestnut trees and beech, holly and flowering shrubs, hiding the well-ordered garden. A scrap of church tower here, and gently-smoking chimneys there, hint at rather than proclaim that there is a village nestling in this kindly dingle of the fells.

And this is Rylstone—the daintiest village in the Dales, and one that awakens wayward pulses, of fancy and of old romance, before the stranger is aware. Its intimates are wont to call it Bonnie Rylstone, and it is thrall to summer, and thrush pipes, and all the mellow peace that comes of storied centuries ; but the bonniest corner of it all is that strip of garden, sheltering the house with the brown door, which greeted us when first we turned the roadway-top above.

The house is home-like and at peace this morning, as if all were very well with it and with the world that shelters it ; but there is no figure leaning over the gate, to greet us as of yore. The kindly eyes, that were quick to notice the least stir of village life, are closed with grave-yard mould, and we who knew the old-world lady, the pivot about which the whole parish seemed to move, know also that we shall journey far before we meet her like

The House with the Brown Door.

again.   The garden is there, and the house is there, scarce
altered; yet the presence that gave subtle life to both is
wanting.   She was with us a twelvemonth ago, our Lady
of the Village, and we still look instinctively for the
familiar figure, standing with both hands on the gate
in expectation of the post.   The scene is no scene at all
without her; nay, the very lilac-bloom above the gateway
has lost a full half of its fragrance, and the chestnut-
blossom seems a shade less regal and less snowy than it
did in other years.

Small wonder that our Lady of the Village was
regarded in her neighbourhood—no narrow neighbourhood, indeed—as the best friend that man or woman
could have in time of stress.   Every one, gentle or
simple, took his troubles to her; she had a quick
sympathy to understand such troubles, and a ready wit
to meet them, and the experience which she had gathered
during her fourscore years—sad experience and bitter,
some of it—had left her undaunted still, not soured at all,
but with a clear eye for the border-line between what was
and what she would have had things be.   A rare and
accurately-balanced mixture of the romantic and the
common-sense distinguished her; she had known many
sorrows, and some joys; and her tales were instinct with
a curious simplicity—that charm of unstudied word-
painting which only the old possess when talking of
scenes long crystallised by the after-years of thought.
No one within a league of Rylstone was ever sorry that

our Lady of the Village had not forfeited the honourable
estate of spinsterhood ; for, had she married, how could
she have found leisure to play nurse, and mother, and
staunch friend in need to half the parish ?

A character unique, not to be touched by description ;
a character most admirably in keeping with the spirit of
this old-world corner of the hills, whose legends, thrice-
told tales to her, grew dearer at each repetition. The
coach is waiting at the hill-foot for us ; but once we
have started backward on that road of time which our
Lady of the Village loved to traverse, it is not easy to
return.

Strike up from the highway along the lane where
Barguest, the phantom dog, is said to wander at fall of
gloaming. Look up at the ragged cloud-line ; see how
the rock-jaws snatch at the sky. Like a trim lassie at a
giant's knee is Rylstone village, and the large gravity of
the fells uptowering round about it seems to relax, to
soften into indulgent kindliness, at sight of the winsome
garden-places in the hollow. The church tower stands
off from its neighbours a little, on a round slope of the
hill, and there was a chapel here when Harold fought
the tanner's son on Senlac field.

That was in the days when the Rillestons were folk of
prime consequence in Craven, and lived in the Hall
beyond this private chapel. The Hall has vanished, but
still the banks of the old fish-ponds can be traced, and it
is not long since flowers of strange species—among them

a rare variety of lily, scarce known at the present day--
bloomed every summer on the site of the forgotten
gardens. Stately gardens they once were, framed on the
Spenserian model of Queen Elizabeth's time ; but the
Rillestons were old before Elizabeth's day, and one of
them was a boon-comrade of the sixth Lord of Skipton
in many a madcap revel while Richard the Second was
mis-ruling merry England. Deer roamed wild on the
fells, and the property, in wood and warren, was a fair
prize enough when one Miles Radcliffe secured it by
marriage with the Rilleston heiress. The Radcliffes
passed in less than a century, and a Norton, marrying
the last daughter of the line, succeeded to this Hall of
many memories—himself to give to it the most lasting
memory of all.

History is confused when it touches the Nortons.
Tradition has much to say. Yet one thing is sure—that
their name, as it has come down to us among the folk-
tales of the fells, stands out from the past with a boldness
and a glamour that is all its own.

Rebels always, no matter against what, they waged war
perpetual with the Cliffords of Skipton Castle touching
their right to take the fleet, dun deer. The Nortons
hunted as they listed, and the Castle folk, after making
vain protest, took measures to keep their deer as much as
possible from straying on to the Rylstone lands. Old
Richard Norton retaliated by building a deer-trap on the
fells, the remains of which have only lately disappeared ;

19

and the Cliffords countered by coming out to Rylstone and killing every deer which they could find within its borders. Appeals to Queen Elizabeth were frequent, and blows not less so, until larger matters came to draw away the Nortons' light-hearted energy from snaring deer to fighting on behalf of captive Royalty.

Richard, the head of the family at this time, was a stalwart fellow who had reared nine big sons—eleven, some say—and eight daughters who were bonnie as the village that had given them birth. He had taken part, thirty years before, in the disastrous Pilgrimage of Grace; but that rising was short-lived, and so he killed lazy time as best he might by these perpetual quarrels with the Cliffords—by these, and also, one suspects, by following their bent for the cattle-lifting which was so popular a means of livelihood across the Border. It was Richard, we are told, who built the watch-tower up there above the Hall—the tower which seemed to follow us half through the drive from Skipton up to Rylstone—and the four corners of it, fighting the weather still in their nakedness, bear testimony to its old-time strength. It was to further their feud with the Cliffords of Skipton Castle that the tower was built, say the historians; but its situation and proportions alike suggest a wider scope. Three storeys high originally, with four-foot walls surrounding the one square room on each floor, it was clearly a model of the old Border peel; it had a far outlook across the northward hills, and its spur of fell was just wide enough to hold a stockade for borrowed cattle. Such spots are not chosen lightly, and it is almost certain that the tower was built in the first instance as a raider's peel.

The Borderers, as we know, used to be over-busy in the Rylstone neighbourhood, and nothing seems likelier than that the Nortons, whose genius lay all in the direction of unlawful frolic, should take a leaf out of the Scotchmen's book and should wage a war of reprisal, or make a casual journey now and then to the fat pastures which lay within the Vale of York. Yorkshire has lacked its poets to hand down to us the old tales of rapine; but a peel stands to this day much further down the Vale of Aire than Rylstone, and if all were known that dead men have carried churlishly undersod with them, we should have as rollicking tales of cattle-lifting, women-lifting, and the theft of insight-gear, as ever the Scottish Lowlands boast—tales that would bear out the old York abbot's accusation when he wagged his beard upon the doings in the North and railed on "the tumultuous gentlemen of Yorkshire."

Moss-trooping, however, in the days of Queen Elizabeth, was not what it had been aforetime, and the Nortons, hale-hearted vagabonds though they were, would be more and more compelled as the years went on to crush their love for this kind of enterprise; and it was then that Mary of Scots was brought a prisoner to Bolton Castle—a prisoner, because Elizabeth suspected her of being a traitor to the realm, and because Elizabeth was sure that her rival possessed a fairer face and sweeter manner than herself.

It was setting spark to tinder to bring the hapless Stuart Queen so near to the Norton men-folk. Her cause lacked no single quality that was calculated to appeal to their reckless, large-hearted sense of chivalry. Her beauty, her wit and tender grace, were known to all men by repute ; to these, now that she was a prisoner in the hands of jealous foes, were added helplessness, and that suggestion of suffering which gives a new persua-siveness to beauty. Small wonder that Mary was scarce housed in Bolton Castle before Christopher, old Richard's youngest-born, was up and across the fells, with a vow that before the moon was old he would pluck the Scotch Queen from her prison. There would seem to have been magic in that name of Christopher, for again we call young Aske to mind, who followed an adventure which, for wildness and for gallantry, was twin-brother to this ride of blithe Kit Norton.

He rode boldly up to the gates of Bolton Castle, our hot knight-errant, secured admission under pretext of loyalty to Elizabeth, and was given a post as one of the guard in immediate attendance upon the Queen of Scots. He made summer-love to the Queen's ladies, and played the peacock for Lord Scrope's benefit, and hoodwinked the good man completely. The lad's courage and re-source were indomitable ; after biding his time with what patience he could muster, he contrived to bring a led-horse under Mary's window ; her favourite maid of honour helped to lower her by a rope ; and in the sequel young Norton succeeded in getting clear away into the woods with the royal captive.

The local gentry were all for Mary—as good York-shiremen were like to be, with their love of beauty and fair play—and a party of these was waiting at the edge of the woods when Christopher Norton reached it with his Royal comrade. The garrison of Bolton, however, had taken the alarm by this time, and had turned out pell-' mell in pursuit. Their horses were the better, and they overtook Norton and those with him at an open forest-glade, thereafter known as Queen's Gap, and fought a bloody fray there, two to one, and carried Mary back in triumph to the Castle.

Christopher Norton, so far as can be gathered, escaped with his life ; nor had his enemies leisure during the stormy months that followed to seek him out in his retreat at Rylstone here.

And so the time wagged until the Earls of Northum-berland and Westmorland, hot-headed gallants both, called the whole North to arms on behalf of Mary and the faith of Rome. Northumberland sent a messenger all in haste to Rylstone, bidding Richard Norton join him, and the story bulks large among Percy's old-time ballads of love and dering-do. Richard, according to the ballad, had a young heart for all his grey hairs ; he was keen as any lad for the enterprise, and no sooner had Northumberland's little foot-page delivered his message than old Norton summoned his nine sons into his presence, and cannily asked his youngest-born's advice upon the point. Christopher, with what had chanced two years before at Queen's Gap in his mind, was naturally all agog at once, as his father had known he would be, and the greybeard clapped him gleefully on the back.

> " Gramercy, Christopher, my sonne,
> Thy counsell well it liketh mee,
> And if we speed and scape with life,
> Well advanced shalt thou be,"

he cries. Seven of the other sons agree to follow him, and only the eldest, Francis, holds back. Not a likeable young man at all, this Francis ; he protests that Elizabeth is all that a Queen should be—hints that they, the Nortons, are snugly housed at Rylstone—adds, by way of salting his mean love of comfort, a pinch of pious protest against the evils of warfare in general and of this quarrel in particular, and finally asserts that although he will pay deference to his father's wishes, he will go unarmed and naked, to show the little sympathy he has with such as take up arms against the Crown. Old Richard, as any honest father would, resents the late-found piety of Francis, and expresses his opinion of him tersely ; and then, gathering his sons about him, he starts

on that disastrous expedition which is to blot out every
man-child of his family.

Again history is vague as to the number of the Nortons
who perished ; but local tradition gives us as clear a
finish as need be—a satisfactory finish, moreover, in that
Francis gets his deserts right royally. For Francis,
despite his fine resolve to go unarmed and naked, is
said to have kept out of the broil altogether, claiming
his Protestant convictions as excuse for taking no part
in a Romish movement; and the story goes that he
crossed the fells on a certain day and rode to York for
the singular purpose of seeing his father and his eight
brothers publicly beheaded.

He witnessed the executions, dined and slept at
York, and set off home again on the day following.
What his thoughts were, we can only guess; but doubtless, as he rode over Barden Moor and saw the well-
known landmarks come in sight, he thought less of the
nine headless trunks behind him than of his own well-
judged security ; and as he was in the midst of such-like
musings, with Barden's gaunt pile melting into the backward gloom, he was met by a mob of Protestants. The
hunt was up from Wharfe to Tyne, by express command
of Queen Elizabeth, against all who had taken part in
the late rebellion, and gangs of fellows from such in-
dustrial towns as Halifax and Leeds—the country folk
were too loyal to the Northern Queen to join in any such
poor chase—infested every highway and moorway of

Yorkshire. It was such a band that met Francis Norton this afternoon on Barden Moor ; and no sooner did they espy him than they raised a shout.

"Here comes one of those accursed Nortons !" they yelled, and leaped upon him headlong.

In vain Francis avowed his Protestant convictions ; his family had achieved too notable a fame for its gallantry on behalf of the older religion, and the rabble paid no heed to his avowals. They slew him then and there, this cautious eldest-born, and a shepherd, passing by on the next day, carried the body over his horse's back to Rylstone, whence it was taken in due course to the graveyard of Bolton Priory ; and only a grassy mound was left to show the fruits of policy.

Whether the old ballad handed down by Percy has coloured the Craven estimate of Francis Norton, or whether the dalesfolk have a sturdy dislike of their own to any man who holds himself aloof from blows, one somehow feels that tradition has always looked askance at him. Perhaps he has been wronged, after all, for certainly his sister Emily loved him better than any of the eight brothers who died honourably upon the block. Francis, not long before his death, had caught a white doe on the fells during one of the Norton raids upon the Castle deer, had brought it home alive, and had given it to his sister for a household pet ; and Emily Norton, beggared of all her male kin in the one day, seems to have lavished her passionate tenderness for Francis on his last gift of his.

None ever saw the two apart. By hill and dale they raced the wind together, Emily and her doe, for it seemed as if the maid could find no shelter from remembrance save in these wild scampers under the storm-skies or the stars.

Francis lay in the quiet kirkyard at Bolton, and for years after his death Emily Norton was wont to ride across the fells on palfrey-back—the milk-white doe stepping sedately by her side—and to sit by her brother's grave while the folk were worshipping in the Priory hard by. She shunned companionship nowadays, and soon as the worshippers streamed out into the graveyard she would get to horse again and take the Rylstone track, the doe still footing it softly in time to her palfrey's paces.

Then Emily, outworn by the effort to forget, followed the father and brothers who had left her with such appalling suddenness; but the white doe, once every Sabbath, still made its pilgrimage to Bolton Priory, lay over Francis Norton's grave until matins were ended, and then, with slow step and sleek head downcast, returned across the hills.

A fine theme for the poet, truly—but one needing large handling and a sense of space. The white doe suggests inevitably a pastoral; yet to make it the keynote of a graceful ballad is to mistake its true significance. The doe was not the chief actor in the Norton drama, but the one soft touch that heightened tenfold the gloom of a majestic tragedy, a tragedy played out in bitter loneliness

by one frail, passion-driven actor. We must have the
sweep of the fells, the desolation and ruggedness and
lonely voices of the heath that went to the tryst each
Sabbath morn with Emily Norton ; we must feel the
throb of that harsh misery which shared bed and board
with her, which blackened every mile of the mourner's
track that lay between Rylstone and the Priory. You
can take the same road to-day ; it passes near the
spot where the mob raised their cry of " Here comes
one of those accursed Nortons," and the ravelled
threads of legend grow knit together as we look from
this place of dole toward where green Bolton lies on
the one hand, and on the other peaceful Rylstone
sleeps, fell-hidden, among its whispering trees. Yet
peace there is none up here ; only the plover and the
curlew keep one company, and they are mourning still
for what chanced three centuries and more agone on
Barden Moor.

The White Doe did not cease its pilgrimage until long
after its bones must have lain whitening among the
upland heather. The country folk have it that the slim-
footed beast was to be seen a century later than Emily
Norton's time, and superstitions gathered thick about it.
It was the spirit of the Norton warriors, the gossips said,
doomed to wander, forlorn and homeless, till time ended,
for sorrow that the old house had no heir to carry on the
name ; or, again, they said that Emily's soul had taken
this shape after death in proof that not the grave itself

had served to bring forgetfulness ; yet, oddly enough, none ever attributed ill-luck to this phantom deer, though grief of every sort is wont to attend on white hares, white rabbits, and all white creatures of the fields.

It was fitting that our Lady of the Village—she who lived at Rylstone here, in the house across the pond —should have had a white doe for comrade. A part of the romance of the place she was always, and his sense of this, no less than personal regard for her, prompted a bygone Duke of Devonshire, who at that date reigned at Bolton, to bid his keepers hunt far and near until they found a white doe and captured it alive. The doe was secured after much trouble, and sent as a present to our Lady ; and for years it wandered about Rylstone, tame as any other village pet and friends with all. It was shot by a mischance at last, and the culprit came to make his confession to the doe's mistress, with a face as white as if manslaughter were on his conscience ; and the villagers, too, moved heavily abroad, and murmured that they could well have spared another in place of their white doe of Rylstone.

We have missed the coach, meanwhile, that was to take us up to Buckden. The driver has delivered his messages, the ancients of the village have gathered round and passed slow greeting—all the wonted formalities have been gone through while we were pursuing the Norton legends up the Lane of the Ghostly Dog, and the team is already a league away on its northward road. Perhaps we wished it to be so, for no man who once finds himself in bonnie Rylstone is less than loath to part from it.

The house with the brown door invites us, and we pass through the gate and under the dropping lilac spray that shades the drive. Time, it may be, will move back for us this once, and we shall find our Lady of the Village sitting on the garden-seat just under the parlour window, or feeding the birds which grew so fat upon her bounty the long year through that they are said to have lost the art of fending for themselves. There was a feud, of course, between mistress and gardener touching these same songsters.

" The gardener wonders how he is to grow peas, when I entice every bird in the parish into the garden," she would say. " I really don't know, but the birds were here before the garden was, and surely they have first claim to what we grow in it."

And so the gardener watched with a gloomy eye while his rows of Sharp's Queen, Duke of Albany, and what not, grew fat and ripe to fill the thievish bills of mavis, wren, or merle.

The birds, however, have been fed this morning, and our Lady is sitting in the shadowed sunlight, her hands in her lap and her eyes looking far into the past. It is a privilege—nay, it is a distinction—to be welcomed as she welcomes one, with the simple warmth which has yet a certain stateliness behind it. The talk drifts back to other days, for the modern world slips past our hostess, unreal a little among the sharply-defined episodes of thirty, sixty years ago. Tale follows tale, tears and laughter chasing each other through her stories ; but those that have a sly jest or a quaint turn of humour in them she likes best of all.

Then there is the old-time morning walk to be taken through the kitchen-garden behind the house, a garden that grows fine roses, pink, white, and duskiest red, amongst its peas and beans, its strawberries and lettuces and celery. Our Lady disdains the help of a stick, though one favoured visitor was time and time allowed to lend her one. It is absurd, she tells you, that a lady of eighty odd years should grow into the habit of needing a third limb whenever she moves abroad ; walking-sticks, and late rising, and loss of memory, are seemly enough in old people, but for her part she counts herself a young woman yet. And even when that certain favoured visitor has persuaded her to use his stick this morning, it is droll to see her look askance at it, as though she could not quite forgive it for the part it plays.

We are, in a sense, trespassers in this kitchen-garden ; for, although the mistress's will is law among the hollyhocks and lavender, yet here the gardener reigns supreme. This gardener has seen long service with his mistress, as coachman, groom, man-of-all-work ; he is a downright honest fellow, and a monarch by divine right in stable and in garden. So we walk delicately among the vegetables this morning, with a sense of wrong-doing almost, as if we were robbing a neighbour's orchard or fishing his favourite stream. As we reach the marrow-frame, our hostess gives a cautious backward glance.

"Do you see Richard anywhere?" she asks, half smiling, half in earnest.

Richard is out of sight, as it chances, so we pull down the glass a few inches, with a breathless and a fearful glee.

"Ah, that is better!" says our Lady of the Village. "Richard is a good gardener, but he never lets the marrows have air enough. I wish I could persuade him to admit that he does not give them air enough."

By and by, after we have gone, the gardener will discover our wrong-doing, and will adjust the frame to the exact position it had before; and each morning the two feuds, the feud of the birds and the feud of the marrows, go merrily on, as if each scene in them had not been acted as often as the summer months held days.

Kindly remembrances, these—the kindlier for their littleness—and they are part of a life well worth remembering. And, after all, what is it that makes for worthiness in memoirs? Politics, battle, passion—the melodrama of kingship or the tragi-comedies of a Cleopatra—what are they but the struggle between one human unit pulling down the marrow-frames and another human unit pushing them up again?

We must not forget the Major, who lived just across

the village pond ; our hostess and he were friends of
ancient standing, and the fact that they favoured the
same special brand of cheese gave rise to a story which
has been oft repeated in this Rylstone garden.

" My brother was alive then," our Lady used to begin
the tale. " It was in August, and we were expecting
friends for the shooting. So was the Major ; and the
two of them went into Skipton to buy a cheese. They
could only find one really good piece of Wensleydale,
and this was too small to divide ; so they agreed to keep
it intact and to join at it. Of course, the Major lived
so very near, and it was easy to send it backwards and
forwards between the houses."

She stoops to pull down the glass of the marrow-frame
another surreptitious inch, and glances behind her again
to make sure that Richard is still out of sight.

"Well, the Major had a dinner-party not long afterwards," she goes on, "and the cheese was much appre-
ciated. The next evening we returned the compliment,
and the Major and his party dined with us. He had
sent the cheese across earlier in the day, and, oddly
enough, my neighbour turned to me soon after we had
sat down. 'I don't know how it is you have such
admirable cheese in Yorkshire,' he said. 'I never taste
any in London like that the Major gave us yesterday.'
' Perhaps you will taste some like it again,' I answered,
and saw the Major smiling at me across the table. At
the end of dinner *my* cheese was brought round, and,

'Yes,' said my neighbour, 'it is just as good. I could have vowed it was cut from the same piece.' And then the Major laughed ; and I laughed, too—I could not help it—so much that I was obliged to confess. ' It *was* cut from the same piece,' I said ; 'we share that cheese between us.' 'Ah,' said my neighbour, 'they don't do these things anywhere but in Rylstone.' And—I think that I see Richard coming "—instinctively standing so as to cover the marrow-frame—" shall we go into the front garden for a little ? "

The gardener is eyeing the marrow-frame, so we beat as hasty a retreat as dignity will permit, through the cool hall, with its half-circle of shelves filled full of curious china, and out again into the shadows of the chestnut tree. Our hostess goes with us to the gate, courteous to the last ; and, full to the last of old-fashioned lore, she keeps us, the gate half-open in our hands, for the length of one more story. It is of Hetton this time, the village that lies on the hill-slope a mile or so away. A dowager lived there, solitary save for the companionship of a favourite maid. Once every day, after her mistress had grown too old to leave her room, the maid went out into the village ; and once every day she returned from her expedition, and took up her sewing to the old dame's chamber, and sat in silence by the window, waiting for the daily question.

" Where hast been, child ? " the question would come, after the customary interval.

"Please 'm, I've bin down town." Town was a handful of cottages and a house or two.

"Didn't I tell thee I wouldn't have thee going down town ?"

"Please 'm, I saw a little coffin at Michael Brown's, the joiner's."

The old dame grows all alert. "Thou'rt a sad gossip, child. Who was the coffin for ?"

"Please 'm, I didn't ask."

"Then get away back with thee at once, and find out!"

The gate is wide-open now, and we have said our last good-bye to the Lady of the Village. *Our last.* Turning, we see her still in the old attitude that always suggested waiting for the post—both hands on the gate, and about her lips a smile which it has taken four-score years of kindliness to form ; and the thought of her mingles with remembrance of Bonnie Rylstone as we pass up the road and along the dusty track that our coach has followed two hours or so ago.

For whom was that little coffin at Michael Brown's, the joiner ? The thought of it is haunting.

CHAPTER XV

THROUGH LINTON TO THE LAND OF DEER

FOR whom was that little coffin? We have not answered the question yet, though we have left Rylstone well behind us and are already on the outskirts of Cracoe village—Cracoe, whose charm can neither be disputed nor explained. Substantial houses front the roadway—dwellings fashioned after the old model, with laithes and other farm-buildings abutting on the house-walls, and in front a round of velvet turf stretching from the white door to the highway. "Statesmen's" houses, they are—the word still preserves its ancient dignity in Craven—and they show sturdy as their masters and grey as the traditions of those who have lived here down the

long generations. There's many a village on this road to
Buckden, but Cracoe is individual—too grey for bonnie-
ness, a little over-stern for any softer sort of sentiment,
yet instinct with a peculiar charm. When the roar of life
sweeps by one in the crowded ways of men, when one
pauses, stepping back from the bustle, for a breath of
country air, trim Cracoe village steals into the mind, and
stays there restfully, side by side with bonnie Rylstone
and that House of Ponden which lies far off beneath the
shelter of the moors. And Cracoe's stories, which give
a human aspect and a warmth to its square-standing
walls, go with us like familiar friends each time we pass
along its road. ·

Through the village, and on to the dividing of the
ways where the Thorp road bids farewell to the main
thoroughfare and pursues its lone, scarce-trodden route.
To stand here at noontide of a day in spring is to
realise the silence of the fell-land. Only the sheep—
ewes and growing lambs—give voice ; from north to
south, from east to sky-blue west, there is no sound save
their ceaseless, loud-complaining bleat ; the land is all
a-throb with it ; and yet it does not break the stillness,
but interprets it. Instinctively that drama played long
ago in Palestine returns to one—and the prophet
Samuel's words, " What meaneth then this bleating of
the sheep in mine ears ?"—and Saul's dismay as he hears
just such another sound as this, insistent, not to be gain-
said. Nay, the very look of the lean pasture-fields must

have been much the same, there as here, and it seems
but a step from the primitive shepherd life of Hebrew
times to the primitive shepherd life of the Craven of
to-day.

Down the long drop of the highway and past the
"Catch-All" tavern. The road on the left leads on to
Threshfield, a pastoral village and a sweet, which seems
still to be dozing over a yesterday of peace. The village-
green here has been fashioned into a little garden, where
all the world of Threshfield meets to discuss the crops
and weather, the in-gathering of hay, the cutting of rush
and bracken bedding for the cattle; where the wind
blows softer than its wont; where a man can lie back
and be aware of green things and the sun.

The way to Threshfield, however, is not our way this
morning, and it is time we put our best foot forward
along the right-hand road that leads to Linton, where a
lunch of oatcake and cheese is waiting for us at the
"Fountayne Arms." The Fountaynes were folk of consequence here aforetime; but they are brushed aside,
and none knows whither they are gone, nor what they
did in Linton village, save build the hospital across the
stream yonder which still gives shelter to the aged poor
of the parish. We know more, indeed, of one Giles
Dakyn, a prosperous hemp-grower of the Sixth Henry's
reign who gave to heraldry the strangest motto that ever
graced a coat-of-arms.

Hemp-growing was once on a time the staple industry

of Linton, and Yeoman Dakyn grew so rich upon the produce of his fields that his descendants thought better of their pedigree and furbished up a crest and family motto. *Stryke, Dakyn, for the devil is in the hempe*, was the chosen motto, and, if they sought to arrest attention, they succeeded to the full, for to-day we are still trying to read the riddle which the Linton Dakyns set us four hundred years ago.

Tradition veils the story of its origin ; but it concerns a moss-trooping gipsy named Johnnie Faa, and a gang of thieves, and a mysterious message sent by Gipsy Faa to Dakyn, to the effect that upon a certain night the devil would be hidden in his hemp. Dakyn takes the hint, has all the villagers in readiness long after time for candle-snuffing, and waits quietly in his house until the leader of the thieves comes out of his hiding-place among the hemp and tries to force a way in through the parlour window. Dakyn deals the culprit a heavy blow with a cudgel, gives a shrill call to his friends without, and the thieves, who are waiting hard by until their leader has effected an entry, are surrounded by the villagers.

The loose tradition takes a new development here ; for a black-headed stranger rides into the midst of the chattering throng just as they are discussing what were best to be done with their prisoners. The stranger talks of Jedburgh Law, whose guiding principle is to hang first and try afterwards ; he takes command of the proceedings, in an off-handed way that proclaims him no

An Oft-told Tale.

less a personage than the redoubtable Johnnie Faa himself; the leader of the rogues is swung high on the
nearest tree, and his accomplices are tarred and wooled
—a variation of the wonted punishment which was due
to the fact that Linton village, as it chanced, was richer
in wool than in feathers.

The tale is lost in all its more convincing details; it is
nebulous as mist upon the fells, and as full of alluring
dream-shapes, now seen in part, now hidden by the
scurrying vapours of the centuries. Yet the motto has
come down to us, and in itself it betters any legend we
could chance upon. *Stryke, Dakyn, for the devil is in the
hempe.*—Good hap! we've half a hundred tales for fancy
to make light with.

Over Linton bridge, with the brown stream whispering,
"Stryke, Dakyn, stryke!" as it glides through the village.
We cannot rid ourselves of the conceits which the old
phrase conjures up. The waters vary the call; now it is
a fevered appeal that Dakyn should strike before it is too
late; and now again the stream moves with a full-
throated, bubbling cry of "Stryke!" as if Yeoman
Dakyn had just knocked up an enemy's sword-blade
and needed but the one home-stroke to make his vengeance sure. Vengeance for what? The stage grows
ampler; we are not content with a mean, workaday
robber crouched among the hemp; there's a maid now
in the story, and the clash of arms, and Yeoman Dakyn
fighting for his life and for the maid's honour. *Stryke,*

Dakyn, stryke! The cry pursues us up the road till the
village is out of sight among the trees behind us; and
Linton, for as long as it lies beside its pleasant stream,
will be one with him who found, or lost, the devil in his
hemp four centuries and more gone by.

They were famous play-actors in their time, the Linton

Linton Bridge.

folk, and one wonders if no rustic genius turned Dakyn's
story into a drama, with *Stryke* for the keynote and the
climax; it would be as fine a cry as the " My horse, my
horse! My kingdom for a horse!" which was declaimed
more than once or twice from the rustic boards of Linton
and of Grassington. For we are on historic ground here,
and Shakespeare was known as well as the price of a

horse or cow by many a tough farm-fellow who trod this remote highway of the Dales.

The Grassington coach comes swinging past, carrying the evening letters, and we clamber up to the vacant place beside the driver. He flicks his whip—we murmur, *Stryke, Dakyn, stryke*—and the team plunges forward. And we remember—not too late, may be—that Yeoman Dakyn has put out of mind another romance as vague and nebulous as his own.

A romance of to-day, it is, and it concerns the deserted mill behind us yonder, with its queer, obtrusive ghostliness. Ruined mills we know, with their bare, unwindowed fronts, and the scowl with which they look out on the waterway that once did all their work for them; but this of Linton is trim-kept still, and the machinery within— out of date long since, and useless—is bright as oil and cloths can make it. What purpose does it serve? Who gives the necessary toil to keep in order piston-rods and valves and levers whose working life is past? We do not ask; it is enough to stand among the machinery, to wonder, and to let the spirit of the place steal over us.

Nothing is lacking; a touch of driving-power, and this silent mill would wake again to full life and energy. All is ready for the hum and fret and rattle of yester-year; yet the machinery lies idle the twelvemonth through, waiting the call to action. There is a story under the silence; and poetry, which fights against all odds, moves in and out among these hushed disciples of unpoetic toil,

while fancy culls her flowers from an unlikely garden.
Like the sleeping beauty is Linton Mill ; where is the
prince, we wonder, whose coming shall complete the fairy
tale ?

We are rattling into Grassington now, and the village,
as we stand in its street this evening, and watch the to-
and-froing of its people, gives us no hint that tragedy

once flourished here, that comedy produced rehearsed
effects—and unrehearsed—in barns, in tavern tap-rooms,
wherever rustic Othellos and shepherd Desdemonas could
find a place in which to furnish forth their stage.
The younger folk forget, and the elders must be old
indeed to remember, how full of passion for the drama
was the life of other years. It seemed as if a wave
of poetry passed over these Craven uplands, engulfing

those who had heretofore moved well-content through the long days of tillage and milking of the kine.

The leader of them all was Thomas Airey. Old Airey, who died at three score and eleven—what gossip hangs about his name, and what a kindly, wholesome flavour his memory recalls. To think of him is to catch again the scent from full-loaded wains as they bring home the hay, and to move through scenes of Arcady. He could play Richard the Second—and play him well, so Edmund Kean thought—or he could don a farm-wife's gown and take my Lady Randolph's part " in a monstrous little voice " —or he could make the audience look to their eyes, while acting some disastrous scene, as well as ever his Athenian brother, bully Bottom, claimed to do.

Our Lady of Rylstone knew Airey well—as she knew every one, indeed, from Linton to Long Addingham—and there was one tale that she never wearied of repeating. Something had gone wrong one night with Airey's company ; a leading character had failed to get his farm-work done in time, or there was some hitch with the scenery— whatever the cause might be, the audience was clamorous for the curtain to go up, and the actors were not ready to meet the demand. So Airey, nothing daunted, robed himself in a blanket and a paper crown, advanced to the front, and declaimed, in a tragic voice that lent dignity and a measure of coherence to his gag—

" Here come I, Kikero, King of the Africans, much fatti-gued with my journey."

He paused, in order to let his personality sink well into the minds of his audience, and then he went on like the brook for a full quarter of an hour, extemporising gaily until a whisper from the rear told him that the actors were ready to proceed with the business of the evening. Then he made his bow, donned fresh attire, and went forward with the evening's tragedy, serenely unregardful of the nonsense which had gone before.

Kean and Harriet Mellon, too, came into Airey's life, first as stars of unwonted brilliancy shining on the grimy boards of the Skipton theatre, then later as fellow-actors with him. Do you remember the little dressmaker whom we met in Skipton not long since, as she went to visit the Duchess of St. Albans at the old "Devonshire Arms"? Her Grace, however, was plain Harriet Mellon in those days, treading rustic boards in a borrowed petticoat ; neither had she a house in Highgate, for she could scarce find means to pay for one scantily-furnished room in the little capital of Craven. Nay, it was lucky for the Duchess that the petticoat afore-named was of wool, since coals in winter were beyond her slender purse.

Nor was Edmund Kean—whom the Skipton folk knew as Edmund Carey -in better case. London was worshipping another star at the moment, and he shone with clouded lustre at the theatre in the Hole-in-the-Wall Yard. He did not lack critics, however, and discerning ones, at Skipton ; for the Craven playgoers of that day, who knew their Shakespeare, and who could act him at

a pinch, were wont to give the lie to the usual estimate
of a provincial audience.

Let us stay for awhile and piece together the details of
this old-time life. Skipton was the metropolis for
Rylstone, Linton, Grassington, and many another village
of the Dales ; a journey thither, by coach or afoot, was
a jaunt to town, and a Saturday night at the theatre an
epoch in the round of sheep-shearing and hay-making,
ploughing and seed-sowing. Peasant-folk and farmers,
with a sprinkling of craftsmen from the town, made up
the audience which foregathered in the little theatre.
Imagine a stuffy pit, cramped and redolent of country
boots—an ill-fitted stage, lighted with noisome oil lamps
—Kean acting his best, not caring whether his hearers
were many or few, gentle or simple, so long as he caught
something of the ideal rendering of his part—and every
now and then a slow nod from one farmer to another,
and a muttered "He frames weel, does t' lad—ay, he
frames weel."

Why, the scene's plain before us, as if we had sat in
the pit of that old Skipton theatre and had seen it all—
seen Harriet Mellon play in frolic the titled part she was
to play in earnest one day—seen little Rodwell act the ill-
used heroine—seen Goldsmith, the versatile manager of
the enterprise, strut up and down declaiming heroics or
gagging farce as egregious as Airey's " Kikero, King of
the Africans."

Yet Goldsmith, for all his energy, did not prosper as he

deserved. The Skipton season ended, and he was persuaded — by Airey himself, one fancies — to take his
company to Grassington ; and the curtain rises on
another of the shifting scenes of Edmund Kean's life-
story, on another of the vicissitudes which the future
Duchess was to endure. The Skipton theatre had been
small, but at Grassington they acted in the attic of a
tavern ; the Skipton receipts had been none too heavy,
but here the very smallness of the attic lessened the
numbers of the audience. Yet still Edmund Kean pursued his ideal, and acted for these village folk with the
same earnestness which afterwards he showed on wider
stages—nay, with greater earnestness, perhaps. And still
the future dressmaker played beauty in distress. And
still the Duchess in the chrysalis was time and time a very
great lady indeed, when her borrowed petticoat was hidden
by the tinsel supplied by manager Goldsmith.

The venture, however, came to an abrupt end. The
sordid claims of cheese-and-bread waged never-ceasing
war against these happy-go-lucky devotees of art, until last
of all Goldsmith was compelled to disband his company
and to sell the properties for whatever they would fetch.
Airey stepped into the breach with his wonted readiness
and confidence, bought up Goldsmith's effects, lock, stock,
and barrel, engaged the chrysalis Duchess and Miss Rodwell, and gaily entered on the thorny path of managership.

He prospered, too, as the boy with a bent pin will
hook a fish when the seasoned angler fails. A sympathetic

landowner in the village lent him a roomy laithe, and the days of the tavern taproom grew small indeed. Kean was off on fresh wanderings, but Linton village, Hetton, Cracoe, rallied to the standard, and helped to increase Airey's company to greater proportions than its needs demanded. A crier went abroad on the afternoon preceding each performance, telling the Dalesfolk and the quiet grey fells that this play or that would be acted at seven of the clock. It was Arcady run wild with frolic —and, strange to say, it paid.

Then enters jealousy, the villain of this rustic drama. For Airey's right-hand man, one Thomas Garrs, grows over-eager for comedy, and he resists Airey's tragic bent at every turn. The dispute waxes wordy and more wordy until Bottom the weaver, Flute the bellows-mender, wrangle and discuss again for us in this upland village, the self-same fellows who met by moonlight in the Athenian forest. Ay, and Puck, we fancy, comes down the fells at times, and listens, and holds his puny sides for laughter ; and it is Puck, likewise, who whispers in the ear of Thomas Garrs that he had better resist friend Airey's love for tragedy. Garrs follows the mad counsel, sets up a rival theatre, and comes to grief ; but Airey, shrewd, keen, and light of heart, goes featly forward with his undertaking, until on-coming years bid him betake himself to a more tranquil occupation.

All gone ! The street is here along which our Arcadians walked, along which the bellman sauntered, crying their

plays ; but none have come to take the place of the
Duchess and the dressmaker, Airey and Kean and Garrs.
We're getting old, may be, and play-acting and Morris
dances, jigs and wassail at the harvest-home, are wending
all together toward oblivion ; yet now and then a touch
of the old Adam peeps out upon the uplands here, in
keeping with the coaches that still ply their trade with
cheery disregard of steam and rail.

With disregard ?　Ay, and if, after passing the night
in Grassington here, you'll take the morning coach to
Buckden, you will come to places where a railway is not
disregarded merely, but scarce conceived, where steam is
a myth and fifteen miles an hour a dangerous rate of progress. There's a pleasant bustle up and down the little
street as the horses are backed into the shafts ; gossips
gather round the coach to see who is bound further up
the dale and to speculate as to the business which takes
them thither ; a cherry-cheeked dame hands up a box of
garden plants to be delivered on the way.

We are off at last, and the June sunshine lies hot upon
the horses' flanks and spangled on the dewy meadow-
grass to right and left. Over yonder lies Grass Wood,
which those curious vagabonds, the Potters, made
their especial haunt in days gone by. They were not
gipsies in the strict sense of the word, these Potters who
sold tinware, pots, and pans in the intervals of fortune-
telling ; but they had many of the traits attaching to their
cousins — they kept certain family names peculiar to

themselves, they were banded together under rough-and-ready laws of their own, and they offered to the intrusive stranger a combined and solid front of enmity. It is significant that the Dalesfolk believed them to be descendants of the Border moss-troopers, and the legend of Johnnie Faa, which met us not long ago in Linton village, goes to show that the same belief existed as far back as the fifteenth century. Johnnie, indeed, was dubbed "the gipsy moss-trooper"; and both he and the Linton folk who passed the legend on knew well what Jedburgh law implied. So did one Richard Norton of Rylstone, if we mistake not, and many another; nor has due weight yet been given to the long intimacy that has held between Craven and the Scots. Bannockburn began it; Flodden checked it; and at a later date the moss-troopers, driven from their Border haunts, resumed the old acquaintance on a new footing, and, in place of cattle and the like, took good Yorkshire money, by other methods than the sword. It explains much, this intimacy, and it is worth dwelling on; it explains, amongst other matters, why we share so many words in common with the Scotch, and why the Border Ballads ring true and understandable to us as if their minstrels had sprung from Craven soil.

The road is skimming past us all this while. Netherside Hall, sheer on its wooded cliff, peeps out between green leaves at us as we go by. Away to the right yonder lies another house, from which a maid and a man once wedded each other by that Gretna law which was

21

as powerful as the Jedburgh code. It is amongst the
stories one knows and may not tell ; and it concerns a
chaise and a garden gate, a tiring-maid and a mistress
much perplexed, haste and a marriage that brought no
leisurely repentance.

Trot and canter on to Coniston, a namesake of Cold
Coniston across the fells yonder, near where the folk of
Gargrave went out to fight the Scots and perished to a
man.

Rising dust, a flick of the whip, and we're over Kilnsey
Bridge. They are washing sheep in the pool below ;
dogs are barking, ewes are raising shrill protest ; a wide-
shouldered fellow, up to his thighs in the water, is calling
to his comrades on the bank, and fast as they push a
sheep towards him he dips it under, rubs hard awhile,
and despatches it to swim, cleaner and disconsolate, to the
further bank, where its dripping sisters are looking each
at the other as if to ask the meaning of it all. Time was
when the monks of Fountains sent their sheep by tens of
scores to be sheared at Kilnsey here, and they washed
them, likely, in this very pool before they robbed them of
their wool.

A halt at the Kilnsey inn, for gossip and a change
of driver. A leech once on a time went to his death
from the sister-tavern which stands a stone's-throw distant. The leech, it seems, had been called in to plaster
up a gallows-bird of the district who, after having been
roughly handled in attempting a robbery, had contrived

to escape in the darkness without leaving proof of his
identity. The doctor knew too much about the matter,
and traded on his knowledge, moreover, to rescue the
landlady of the Kilnsey tavern from the attentions of
the ne'er-do-weel ; and the stirrup-cup was his last which
he drained at the inn door that night.

Past Kilnsey Crag, where the jackdaws nest and the
limestone whitens the blue face of the sky. A tale or so
from the driver, and then trot and canter into Kettlewell.
It is all like the beginning of the century. The Buckden
coach, and its early morning forerunner, the mail, are
the features of the day in Kettlewell, and again the gossips
gather in narrow circles round about us. In the foreground, restful folk with hands in pockets and tongues
that wag full lazily ; in the middle-distance, farmer boys
moving scarce less restfully, trundling a cart-wheel or
carrying a broken spade to the mending ; in the background, comely houses and a sense of sunlight. That is
Kettlewell.

"Here's a trifle for you, mistress," says the driver,
taking the box of garden plants from under the seat
as a fresh arrival joins the loiterers.

"An' thankee. Twopence to pay—well, they're worth
a twopence or two. From Mrs. Calter, of Grassington, I
reckon?"

"Yes. I told her it was queer to go sending plants on
a dry day like this—and the soil as parched as parched.
They'll never thrive, I doubt."

"Well, ye can niver tell till ye try, as Tom o' Hebden said when he blew two fingers off wi' a rusty blunder-buss. An' how's Mrs. Calter? Better nor like?"

"Yes, she's middling. Up, lads! Off ye go."

Forward to Starbotton. Behind there on the fell, two hundred years ago, the waters burst at flood-time, ran upward in a liquid pillar, and fell with a crash that wrecked the village. It is Starbotton's only history—and it would have been happier for the lack of it.

Buckden now, and the end of the coach-journey. The deer that gave the village its name browse yet in lessening numbers on the hill-slopes, and this still, sleepy corner of the Dales has heard the horns of Clifford and of Percy on many a long-dead hunting day. But Percy sleeps, and Clifford sleeps, and the fells that knew them have forgotten.

Out of the world's way, you would say, this Village of the Deer; yet leave it behind you, and pass up the narrow streamway to Hubberholme, a world's-end hamlet that has no counter-type. If Buckden seems remote, Hubberholme is almost eerie in its solitariness. Beyond it are the hills, and beyond them—why, yawning space, one thinks.

Two possessions the village has for which a passing traveller would scarce think to look about him. One is a rood-screen, emblazoned with the Percy arms, which lies hidden by the squat roof and unpretentious walls of the little church; the other is an inn which likewise has the odour of sanctity about it, for it was once in the far-away past the dwelling of Hubberholme's parish priest. It makes but scant parade, this tavern with its back toward the roadway and its signboard well-nigh hidden ; yet, dropped by the wayside as it is with seeming heedlessness, it has the best custom, so folk say, from Hawes to Skipton town.

Life is quiet at Hubberholme, very quiet. It is told

Hubberholme Church.

how a certain vicar, who lived and died here, took to rabbit-shooting, despite the fact that he was a poor shot even when his prey was sitting, and how at last the sport grew to be a daily jest between himself and his parishioners.

"Killing rabbits, vicar ?" a farmer would say, as he met the pastor carrying his gun through the fields.

" I don't kill many rabbits," the vicar would always answer mildly—" but I kill a great deal of time."

There are folk here, as we said, who have never seen a railway, folk to whom the power of steam is a sort of fairy-legend, not half so faith-worthy nor so pleasant as stories of the gnomes and fairies. Nay, some of them have scarce been further afield than Buckden or Kettle-well, and the lonely hills, massed rampart-like behind the hamlet, have watched every incident of their lives—each going to bed and getting up, each hour of labour or repose.

Yet even here ambition plies the spur at times. The vicar can tell of farmer-lads who come on long winter's evenings to learn Greek and Latin ; and these in due course go out beyond the charmed circle that was their fathers' borderland, and find the world less than they dreamed of, or more, according to their disposition. They whom they forsake, however, catch no contagion from these more restless spirits, and Hubberholme sleeps on, untroubled save by wind and weather.

We came up here on a June day ; but our return shall be in late October. The long drive down to Skipton changes its fashion altogether soon as dusk has fallen and the night comes heavy-hearted down the fells. The villages are points of lights upon the blackness ; the coach-lamp throws strange gleams and fluttering shadows on road and limestone walls ; far on the hillside yonder the light from a farm-kitchen shows ghostly as

the candles lit by bog-sprites on the moors for men's undoing. Where the road is bare, one can catch a vague, grey gleam of it by looking far ahead ; where trees stand guard, the darkness is like a wall of fate, black, ruthless, and impenetrable. The harness jingles, and the beat of hoofs strikes friendly ; but for all that it is lonesome on this road to Skipton, with the fret of the underworld about us, and the echo of strange voices from the fells. When we overtake a traveller on the road, he has to shout to tell us he is there ; the coach-light flickers on him for a moment as we pass, and he is gone again, scarce more substantial than the cry he gave.

A mile of darkness, and then a light shows at the roadside, swinging to and fro as if in answer to our own. The driver pulls up ; out of the misty circle of brightness steps the figure of a farm-lass, with a grease-smudged lanthorn in one hand and a letter in the other ; there's scarce a word spoken, save the driver's good-night as he puts the letter in his pocket and whistles to his team. It is no more than a letter-posting, this ; yet there's a sense of mystery about it, as if a cloaked figure had come to give a secret message from the King, or my Lady's woman were sending an assignation from her mistress to some trim gallant of the town.

Forward again, past the toll-bar and the house of None-Go-By. Down the steep hill. And Skipton street is all alight to welcome us.

CHAPTER XVI

COBBLERS' LAND

WE are standing again at the corner of the road from Cracoe out to Linton, the corner where we halted on a day of spring and heard the bleating of the sheep rise skyward, the one living sound that broke the stillness of the fells. It is late September now ; the grass hangs ragged in the pastures, and overhead a reckless autumn wind is driving, with light rain to vanward of it, and brown, wet leaves of sycamore and ash fast hurrying in its wake. A sad day and a weird, such as stirs the tragedies of other days, and sets one thinking of the past that has clean gone for ever from **Rylstone** and from Cracoe. A farm-man is shouting to his kine in Cracoe village ; a robin sings on the thorn-bush over yonder ; from some distant orchard-fire there comes the bitter-sweet reek of smoke—a reek that touches a subtle chord of pathos, in harmony with falling leaf and dripping pasture grass.

The ways divide here. Along the one road the Grass-ington coach is swinging down between the low, white walls ; the other track, scarce disturbed the year through save by a farmer's wain or the hoofs of some yeo-man's horse, leads to a village that is solitary beyond imagining.

It is a track that takes us nowhere, so it seems ; a track with bare green hills on either hand ; a track which craves no footfall to break its loneliness, which rather frowns upon intrusion. Bonnie Rylstone, with its trees and garden-places, is scarce left behind us ; yet gardens there are none here, and such trees as break the grey monotony look as if, strangers in a far land, they had wandered here by mischance, and had stayed rooted by the spell of silence that overhangs the fells.

Lonely as the moors of Haworth, this fell-land has a character which is different altogether from the wildness of dark heath and darker bog. The moor is well-nigh flat by reason of its vastness, and the sky's edge is far ; but each few acres here is a world in itself, bounded by grass-smooth hillocks that seem to bring the clouds to

the earth's level. Nay, the very roundness of the landscape adds the last touch of lone severity to this forsaken
road.   It is smooth, yet without hint of tenderness ; it is
friendly, but with the friendliness of winter and north
winds.   Heather breaks the foreground of a moorscape,
bracken bends to the wind and is alive ; but here the
pasture grass, hugging the lean ground, lies still and has
no speech.

Clean, rounded, and severe are the fells that stretch
from Cracoe up to Thorp ; and the folk who snatch a
living here and there from the hard breasts of the soil are
like the land that mothers them.   Rarely has a people
mirrored more faithfully the outlines of surrounding
nature, and to limn the country is to draw, feature for
feature, the characteristics of its children.   Clean-cut in
every line of face and figure, grudging of tenderness,
tranquil, stubborn and severe—these are the men and
women you find far off from the beaten tracks of Craven.
They do not fear storm, for it cradled them.   They look
twice at the hills, when the sun is kindly with their
slopes and the blue, fair-weather mist hangs light about
their summits, before muttering their quiet, " It might be
worse " ; for sunshine, to these dwellers on the treeless
uplands, is like a young maid's promises, quick given and
forgotten, and the grey chariness that sits most often on
the fields, if its promises are meagre, carries at the least a
grown man's trustiness.

Fells and people of the fells—they meet each other and

are one as we stand on this forgotten road, leading to a forgotten village, and let the thoughts range from the hills about us to the folk who lived and hated, loved and passed away, among the grandeur and the barrenness, under the shrouded skies whose clouds, like an old man's tears, are wont to gather long before they fall. Haworth bred such ; yet between the men of Haworth and of Craven there are differences clearly marked, as if they were brothers with a family likeness. Here, as there, a giant would spring up time and time in Heathcliff's image, would revel, and ride with rough-shod hoofs through life, and go his ways again ; and his passions would be joyless, crude and splendid as a storm-wind spurring from the belly of the thunder-wrack.

Yet the tales are not all of tempest and of grey, unhappy rain. Thorp had dealings, too, with the softer valley-villages, and the rustling of silks, the clack of pattens, mingled with the grimmer farm-life and the everlasting tapping of the cobblers' hammers. This road from Cracoe up to Thorp—what memories it holds ! Scarce trodden, hid by the round shoulders of the hills, it keeps its secrets well ; and only those who have known it long, and known it well, and known it lovingly, can wake the old dreams back to life. Along it the gentlefolk of Rylstone and Cracoe and Linton used to come, on foot, on horseback, in rumbling vehicles ; and they dined, or took a dish of tea—it was always a dish of tea in those days—with the yeomanry of Thorp ; and they returned again through moonlit dust or mud that clambered to the axle-wheels.

A trivial round ?   Nay, if you please ; for Rylstone is poetry itself, and Thorp is the mellowest prose ; and the folk who passed along this road have left us memories that are personal, real, and gracious as the courtliness with which they met the world.   Our Lady of Rylstone used to cross to Thorp this way, the white doe footing it by her side—used to cross, in the dress of sixty years ago, to visit yeomen whose manners and whose hospitality were centuries old.   There is little to tell of these gatherings ; yet they stir among the rosemary of memory, and speak to us, and make us understand the things of old.   Nay, we can see the very set of the tea-table—the silver urn, the wafer pink-and-whiteness of the ham—the yellow butter rounded into little pats—the yeoman at the head of his table, despising the new-fangled fashion of dining at an hour when all his honest forefathers had tea'd--the good-wife opposite to him, with grave, proud kindliness and a quick eye to see if any guest ate less than the old custom of the house demanded.   Then afterwards there would be cribbage and gossip for the elders, games of hunt-the-slipper and the like for the younger sort ; and after that there followed the jolt and rattle homeward through the mystic stillness of the night, with the fell-stars overhead and the wet breeze sobbing in the hollows.

And Thorp itself ?   Where is this hamlet of the fells ? Behind us the hills sweep downward—curve and lesser curve, descending to the far-off valleys. To right of us, one rounded hill stands clear out above the rest. Yet sign of habitation there is none ; the road, it seems, will wander till it loses itself among the grey-green acres. A farm building comes in sight, perched on the shoulder of the fell ; the road dips downward on the sudden ; and there in the hollow a bunch of chimney-stacks peeps out and almost smiles at our surprise. And that is Thorp— Thorp, where dead cobblers once plied their trade and yeomen long since buried played cribbage with their women-folk on winter's evenings—Thorp, which lies so deep in its hollow that every road to it drops downward at a break-neck speed.

Thorp's day is done. Its work and play, its jealousies and hopes and fever-fret of passion, are clean gone by ; and, like a greybeard who sits with chin in hands and counts his well-spent days afresh, Thorp has its pathos and its dignity. It seems that the ghosts have right of way here, and that men walk up and down its road by sufferance only.

Again the cobblers wake to toil and ply their bradawls featly. Fifty and two of them lived here once on a time, in the cottages that have crumbled into dust ; their handiwork was famed from Langstrothdale to Foun- tains, and half Craven walked on leather that had known the shoemakers of Thorp. Again the apprentices walk their twenty miles and back in a day, to carry the one pair of shoes from mending. Again, as we stand in the dying village and let the mind go down the past, we see a master-cobbler stride out with well-filled pack upon his shoulders, and return with straighter gait and pockets heavier for the journey. Again the busy knot of workers foregather when the day is spent, and crack rough jests, while ruddy firelight glints from the cottage-hearth upon their froth-topped mugs.

Ay, and again there sounds the far-off echo of that shout, " The Scots, the Scots," which six hundred years and more ago was wont to rouse the Craven valleys to despair. And over the road from Cracoe come grave-faced yeomen with their women-folk, their cattle and their sheep—come in silence, with terror sitting beside them on the saddle—come with backward glances and a half-expectation that they will see the Bruce and all his lusty Scots fast-riding in pursuit. For Thorp, tradition says, was the refuge of the country folk against the Scotch, and it has guarded many a woman's honour in its time.

We can believe tradition, and name it sure, as we look up from this deep hollow and note how jealously the green hills guard it round about. A Borderer had a keen eye for trace of plunder ; yet even he might well start out on the road to Thorp, and turn him back again, thinking the land to be as barren as its face. So fathers brought their daughters, husbands their wives, to this snug-lying village ; and Thorp kept both inviolate.

The cobblers have taken their cottages with them ; but the more substantial houses stand yet beside the roadway.

A lone homestead, this at the far end of the village, with its blank, uncomely front and its drear double line of shrubs from the gateway to the door ; a tragic house, from behind whose walls a man might look out sourly on his neighbours and grudge the knock that claimed his hospitality. Then, further down the street a little, are two more comely dwellings, where our cribbage-parties could muster at their ease and feel the warmth of welcome ; each is precise in its own way, with the distinction between an old maid's primness and the ordered gravity of a bachelor hardened in his celibacy. Yes, it must be that a spinster and a bachelor lived hard by each other here, and exchanged a glance or so, may be, when they met, and wondered how far the roses hid the thorns on that path of wedlock which each had failed to tread.

And so past the Manor House, and up the road to Burnsall, with a halt at the hill-top for a farewell look at Thorp. The wind is dreary in among the branches ; rain patters on the drift-leaves that lie underneath the wall ; the grey mists roll and curl along the fading line of fells. A low growl creeps from out the belly of the hills—it may be thunder, or it may be the muttering of the Brown Folk underground. And Thorp is not less grey, less sorrowful, than the hills that shut it in and the ghosts that move about its street.

Tap-tap, tap-tap. It is the last sound that we hear in this forsaken village—the beat of the cobblers' hammers as they work for bread.

CHAPTER XVII

THE RESTFUL VILLAGE

TO every place its fitting season. Wet autumn winds, with sorrow underlying all their bluster, fit well the eerie Land of Cobblers; but Burnsall village, though it lies scarce more than half-a-league away, craves no such atmosphere. There should be a June sun in middle-heaven as we swing down the road, and the land should be hard-set to choose between the spring that is scarce over and the summer that is yet to come. The air is clean as a river-bath and full of tangled scents; the meadows are bethinking them of haytime; farm folk are leaning over walls, and are passing the gossip of the day one with another until they can determine what task they shall next undertake.

The house on our right there as we bend round toward the village—a house that is half farm and half a gentleman's substantial dwelling, with more carved oak in it than the four walls can well hold—gives us a sober welcome to old Burnsall, and on the left a grey church and a tranquil looks out at us across its restful graves. There are few church-yards like Burnsall's acre of the dead, few with the same deep undernote of stillness and repose. The lych-gate itself, with its lichen-softened stones, speaks less of the dead whom it has sheltered from the rain on their last journey than of the quiet to which the dead have gone. The grass creeps soft and thick about the headstones, and from the gardens of the village the fragrance of old-fashioned flowers steals up and whispers its tender "It is well" to those whose fret is overpast.

A little further, and we are in Burnsall street, with its river and wide bridge, its village-green, its cosy tavern lying almost at the water's edge. Above are the pine-woods and the rolling fells ; below, square-set in their sheltered gardens, lies a nest of houses, with clematis and roses half hiding the trim doors, and all the windows open to the freshness of the day. And we are aware of a peace that is beyond our understanding—a peace which, like the wild-flowers in the hedgerows, springs from the soil without leave asked or granted. It is a haven for tired feet, this pleasant Burnsall, and none who cares to set his steps this way needs lack a friend.

Before breakfast is Burnsall's happiest hour. The sun comes early through your window and will not let you lie abed. A plunge into water that has come, crisp, cold, and clear, straight from the windy uplands—a peep into the "Red Lion" kitchen, to make sure that the rashers are beginning to curl before the fire—and then you stroll up the village street to see how the world is wagging on this morn of June. For Burnsall, in some odd fashion, grows personal to one almost at first acquaintance; your business is everybody's, and everybody's business most certainly is yours. Very white the village looks, very clean, as if it, too, had had its morning dip. The folk are all astir—country-lads, strangers who have taken refuge here from the dusty outer-world, maids in summer frocks, all meeting on the one ground of cheeriness and unstudied sociability; for the little state of Burnsall is, pure and simple, a democracy.

There are many pleasant houses here; but pleasantest of all, to our thinking, is that trim dwelling—the one with the white door—which looks down the street. A yeoman's dwelling, this, with the pride of long centuries writ plain upon its face, and hospitality hidden behind the staidness of its front. Then, too, there is the house hard by, where the postmaster keeps shop for all the village. Who does

not drift into the little shop at least a dozen times a day ?
For you can get postage-stamps there, and cricket-bats ;
you can get tobacco, and old china, and gossip that is
hall-marked with the willow-pattern. A busy man, the
postmaster, as popular folk are wont to be ; yet he never
grumbles, however often one comes to lean against his
counter ; and what he cannot tell you of Burnsall and of
Burnsall ways, present and long past, is not worth the
knowing.

Then, after you have had your morning gossip, have
discussed the weather and talked sagely of the effects of
early drought and of May rain upon the hay-harvest, you
wander up the street to see how the peas are flowering in
the garden round the bend, and to learn whether the
lettuces are fattening as aforetime. You retrace your steps
at last, and cross the village green to see how the trout are
rising ; and then, finding that the boys are playing cricket
on the green, you needs must try your hand at bowling.
A youngster of ten or thereabouts cracks your first ball
across the river, and the next into an adjacent garden ;
and then you remember that breakfast is waiting for you
all this while. It is no hardship in Burnsall to have your
finest deliveries knocked about the village, and the ten-
year youngster is your sworn friend so long as you and
he live neighbours.

After breakfast—which has already been waiting half-
an-hour or so—one of two things you will surely do.
You will either set off across the fells, and cover from

sixteen to a score miles before your next meal ; or you will be drawn on to the seat that overlooks the village green, and no persuasion will serve to move you for the remainder of a long morning. It is of little moment either way ; for there is one thing you cannot escape in Burn- sall, and, whether you walk or whether you idle, you will bring the same untroubled appetite to meat.

Country-folk are moving about the village as you cross the " Red Lion " threshold—picturesque fellows, with broad shoulders and wide-brimmed hats and breeches reaching half down their well-turned calves to meet their homespun stockings. No one is busy, whatever work they have to do ; labour is almost leisure in Burnsall village, and life a roundelay.

Why, indeed, should one walk twenty miles, or even half-a-league ? The seat on the green yonder has a cool, persuasive look about it, and one's steps move toward it by a kind of instinct. The sun is hot in a sky of gauzy blue ; but the village, with its white road and whiter houses, still looks as fresh as when the dawn was on it, and the overmastering fells are cool to the eye as lime- stone and the grey, fair-weather mists can make them. From the " Red Lion " stables comes the whistling of an ostler as he harnesses the new-bought pony—a bonnie roan of twelve hands or so—into the gig. A red-cheeked wench moves up the road, carrying a wheaten loaf which she has borrowed from a neighbour.

A lazy curiosity is in the Burnsall air, and one wants to

learn why this country maid, just disappearing with her
loaf, needs come a-borrowing.   Have friends taken her at
unawares and dropped in to breakfast ?   Or did the persistence of some rustic swain delay her baking yesterday ?
The question goes unanswered, however, for a tramp
comes loafing towards us along the river's bank—a
genuine tramp, with the slouch that is born in a man, like
any other form of genius.   He has a sleepy eye, which
hides its alertness craftily—a sad but uncomplaining face
—trousers' pockets that gape a little at the seams through
perpetual friction of his hands.   To look at him, you
would suspect some unforgotten tragedy which has killed
his hopes, yet left him brave to live out the drear remainder of his life.

He approaches the seat by a zigzag, devious way, and
holds out a dirty palm.   A dirty halfpenny lies snugly in
the palm, and I stare at him in wonderment.

" Mebbe you couldn't sell me a ha'porth o' baccy ? " he
says gloomily.

" Sell you——," I begin.

" Ay," he goes on, not heeding the interruption ; " it's
all th' brass I've getten, an' they willun't sell me no less
nor a half-ounce at t' public yonder.   Now, don't be hard,
master, for I'm itching for a smoke !   I met a chap i' t'
road just now, an' he says to me, ' It's a day i' a hundred,'
says he.   ' Mebbe,' says I, ' for them as hes loving friends
an' a pipe o' baccy.' "

He never varies his even flow of voice, and the

halfpenny still looks at me from his extended palm. It is masterly, and I hand him my pouch without a protest.

" Pocket your halfpenny, and fill up," I mutter.

He is an artist. He shows no haste in restoring the coin to the pocket with the gaping seams ; nay, he even presses me to accept the money, and withdraws it at last with a regretful air.

A silence follows, and he looks up from filling his pipe to find me smiling broadly at him. I think he sees in me the touch of nature that makes us kin, for he, too, lets the half of a smile wrinkle his mouth-corners.

" I'll give you a shilling if you'll tell me something," I hazard.

" A shilling's a lot o' brass. What is 't, master ? "

" I want to know how often that halfpenny has filled your pipe for you. Fairly, now—how often ? "

" Well—twenty times since yesterday, so far as I can reckon up. But, master," he adds, leaning confidentially towards me as the shilling changes hands, " if iver ye think o' trying that game, keep clear o' Lancashire. I once tried it on a chap fro' Lancashire, an' I lost my ha'penny."

And so the morning wags—peacefully, with such un-spoiled, Arcadian vagabonds to keep one company. My friend leaves me by and by, but a couple of village elders come to take his place.

" Warm," says the first, guardedly.

"Ay, warm," puts in his fellow, taking the vacant place on my right.

The one is full-fleshed, broad, and ruddy ; the other is thin as a rake, with a fitful glance that never wanders far from his companion's face. And soon, as their tongues loosen, one notices that they are Oracle and Chorus.

" Rare weather for hay harvest," says the Oracle.

"Ay, rare—rare weather for hay harvest," echoes the other.

" They're thrang already wi' hay-making."

"Ay, thrang, for sure."

"School broke up yesterneet, maister ; that's allus a sign they're cutting t' grass, for t' childer is all wanted for work i' t' fields then, an' it's time to stop their laking wi' printed books."

"Ay, laking wi' printed books—it's time to stop, I reckon," answers thin-voiced Echo.

Time is not fleeting in Burnsall village, and talk is slow. The sun has taken a lengthy stride from the line where blue sky touches grey-white fells before our gossips have reached the tales of other days. They were keen musicians once in Burnsall, and keener bell-ringers, the full-fleshed ancient tells us ; and the rake-lean greybeard, nodding his head upon his stick, makes the fact sure by repetition. And then on the sudden the Oracle falls to laughter—the inward, gently-shaking laughter of the old. And his comrade laughs with him, secure in his trust and content to await the explanation of the jest.

" Nay, I war thinking of how they once rang t' owd
year out," says the first, soon as his merriment is
quenched.

" Ay, sure—how they rang t' owd year out an' t' new
year in."

" They'd as soon hev lacked their dinner-ale i' them
days as let t' owd year die wanting th' sound o' church
bells i' his ears.   But times is different-like fro' what they
war."

" Varry different—different as chalk fro' cheese."

" I can't rightly recall how far back it war, but I mind
as weel as if 'twar yesterday how I went wi' Bob Sharp
to tak a bottle o' gin an' one o' Scotch whisky to t' ringers
i' t' belfry tower.   T' new year war nobbut a kittling then,
an' they'd rung it in that hard they war all i' a fine muck
sweat, an' hed stopped to rest 'em a bit."

" Ay, for sure," murmurs Echo, " stopped to rest 'em a
bit."

" Well, Bob got 'em going wi' t' gin, an' then he gives
a look at t' bell-ropes, hanging wi' their ends tied into a
loop.   He war allus one for a joke, war Bob Sharp, an'
he knew, weel as onybody could tell him, that t' bells
needed no more nor a touch to set 'em going."

" No more nor a touch," his comrade sighs, shaking his
head afresh upon his stick.

" So what does Bob Sharp do but run round fro' rope
to rope, while t' ringers' backs war turned—gives ivery
rope a pull—an' down t' bells come all i' a fitter, as if 'twar

Judgment Day. He-he! I mind it yet. Th' tenor bell broke its stays ; t' ropes went louping like wild things all across t' belfry, first rapping t' floor, then knocking agen t' ceiling beams ; t' bells war ringing all together, an' making a flaysome din."

"A flaysome din!" puts in Echo, with a shadowy laugh.

"Well, t' ringers turned 'em round an' about fro' their drinking, an' gaped an' gaped, wi' a whisky-bottle shaking i' one hand, an' rubbing their een wi' t' other fist to mak sure if they war waking. For Bob Sharp, ye mind, hed ta'en me by t' arm sooin as he'd set t' bells going, an' war off down th' tower stairway ; an' when t' ringers turned 'em about they could see nowt but them there bell-ropes louping up an' down without a hand to touch 'em. Eh, but it war rare! They just stopped for a two-three minutes, did t' ringers, staring gaumless-like at t' ropes ; an' then they scuttered fit to break their necks, down t' stairs an' out into t' graveyard. It war more like Bedlam nor owt they'd iver looked to see, an' they thowt owd Nick war here at last, an' proper."

" Ay, sure," murmurs Echo, " they thowt owd Nick war here."

"An' Bob Sharp an' me war waiting i' t' graveyard ; an' we set up a barking, an' a screaming, an' what all, an' pinched their legs as they ran under t' owd lych-gate. An' if ye'd offered 'em t' weight o' Burnsall Brigg i' gold, they wodn't hev gone back to yond belfry-tower that neet. Well, well, there's no sich rollicks now. Nay, we lig that quiet ye mud think we war asleep i' Burnsall t' long year through."

It seems my pouch is not to rest idle this morning, for the first gossip, at the finish of the tale, brings out his pipe and falls to searching his pockets fruitlessly. I hand my tobacco to him, and notice as I do so that my friend the tramp has taken a very liberal halfpenny-worth.

"Nay, tha wodn't leave him no baccy for hisseln ? " says Echo, anxiously. It is the first statement he has ventured on his own initiative.

The other goes stolidly forward until he has rammed home the last shred of tobacco remaining in my pouch ; and then he eyes me soberly.

"When I find middling, I taks middling," he says darkly—"an' when I find little, I taks t' lot."

The lean Echo, who has brought out his own pipe in faithful imitation of his comrade, sighs faintly as he looks at the empty pouch and puts his own clay back again ; and I can see him suck his empty cheeks in melancholy make-believe.

And so the day wears on, tranquil as the stream that laps old Burnsall Bridge ; and it seems part and parcel of a lazy afternoon that by and by one should move up the street and cross to a certain secluded corner, this side the church, which shelters Burnsall School—the quaintest school, surely, that ever saw youngsters wrestle

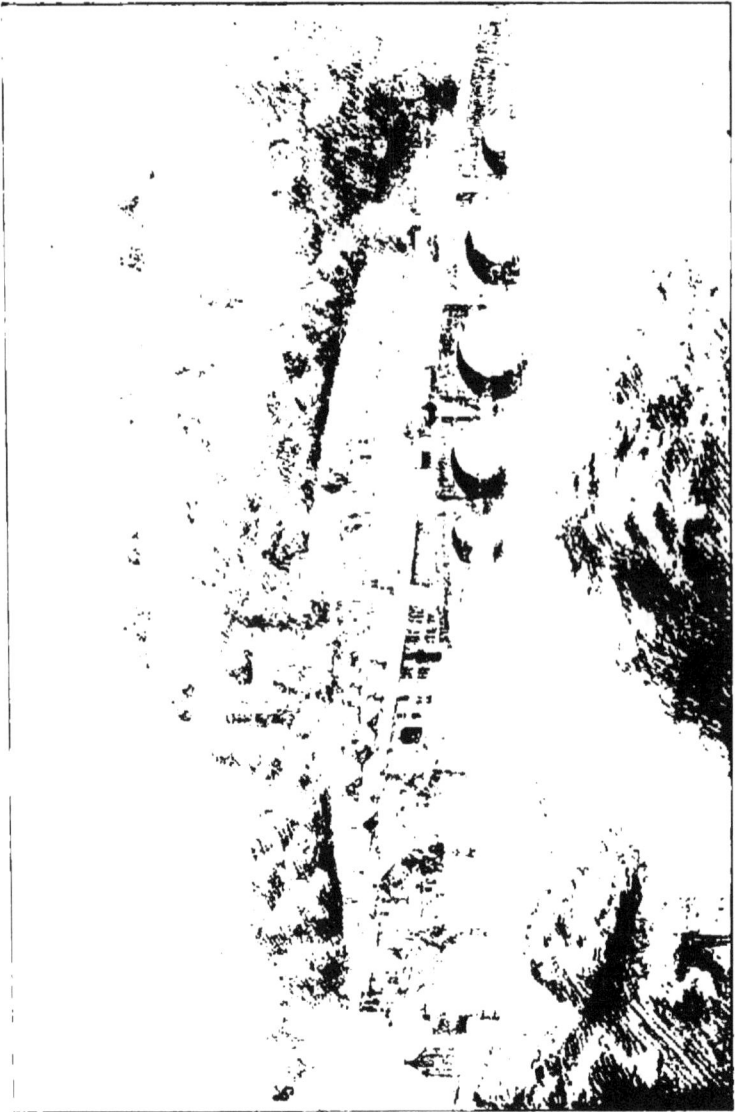

with the Rule of Three. The architecture is pure Elizabethan, and the white look of the limestone fits well the graceful severity of its style. In front is a garden, with the playground set in the midst of peonies and roses ; on the left the school-house stands, quiet, orderly, and self-contained.

The door is open this morning ; the children are away at haymaking, as our friendly gossips told us, and we are free to wander as we will among the ink-stained desks. Sunlight and shadow flicker underneath the latticed window-panes, and from without there comes the breath of nodding flowers, the singing of birds, the sleepy hum of bees. The world is far off from Burnsall village ; but it is remote indeed when once we step inside this school of other days. They are just boys who come here to be taught—boys who fight, and play marbles, and milk the village cows by stealth, according to the healthy fashion of their kind ; yet to-day, with the musty silence over-hanging books and slates and master's desk, it seems that here, if anywhere, a rarer generation should be trained, a generation of poets, strong to dream and to fulfil their dreams.

It has its history, this other-worldly school. Eugène Aram, the shadowy actor in a tragedy which has taken hold of all men's minds, was once an usher here. His very name wakens elusive thought. Romance hangs round him, though we scarce know his history. We see him—tall, sad-eyed and lean—move ghost-like once again through the drowsy hubbub of school-hours, watching his boys with the scholar's kindly and abstracted glance. His heart is with the books which are wife and comrade both to him ; his thoughts are high, centred in the middle-blue ; he dreams his way through life's uglier issues, and the taint of fact has no power to brush the dawn-dew from his fancies.

Then, on the sudden, the man in him is touched—at Burnsall School, it may be, on such another God-sent day of June as this. Dreams grow shadowy, and his humanity, late-found, is conscious of a want, an emptiness, an ache. It is the devil's holiday, they tell us, when the dreamers first realise their manhood ; and into this lean scholar's heart there creeps a madness, subtle, slow, and very sure. *Gold,* says a voice at his ear ; and he does not understand—save that the sound of it is sweet. Little by little it grows to be an eager cry, that first faint whisper, grows until it masters the student's brain, the student's child-like, unresisting heart. *He must have gold.* Every sunbeam that comes yellow through the latticed panes is an ingot of the precious metal. Gold, yellow gold—the tinkle of it rings day-long in his ears, whether he teaches boys to add their two and two together, or sits with dimmed eyes and strives to read the printed page that now has lost its meaning for him.

To what end ? He does not know. Gold is power— it can buy men's lives, their faith and good repute. Is it power he hungers for, he who has scarce been able to maintain his rule over a score village lads ? He does not know, nor care. *He must have gold.*

A madman now ; he has touched fact for the first time in his slow-moving life, and reality is wildness in his blood. And so he goes out from Burnsall School, haunted and accursed ; he seeks a refuge from himself at Knaresborough, and finds that the world can give him no such sanctuary ; and the sordid tragedy is worked out at last, and Eugène Aram stands dazed above the body of the man he slew for gold, and wonders, and is sore afraid.

Does Burnsall School remember ? It could scarce forget, one thinks ; and Aram's scholarly sadness is stamped indelibly on each subtle under-line of its grey and latticed front.

Well, we have dozed and dreamed here ; and the world has been exceeding quiet ; what if time has slipped by us with theftuous foot, setting the season later by a clear two months ? June was merry with lanes and fields when we came under the spell of Burnsall School ; but now it is mid-August, let us say, and the village mind is set on junketings. Caravans and swing-boats stand this side the green, and straight-set farmer-fellows are vieing one with another in accuracy of aim as they throw down cocoa-nuts with wooden balls. A hum of laughter, a buzz of jest and slow rejoinder, drift up the street ; and we know that peaceful Burnsall has awakened for its yearly spell of frolic, which runs the swifter for the twelvemonth's sobriety that has gone before.

"Come, play up at 'em," rings a stentorian voice at ordered intervals, "all the juicy cocoa-nuts—come, play up at 'em, play up at 'em, and a penny buys a ball."

There are folk from Grassington here, from Hebden, and from Aptrick—all the fell-world, surely, has gathered to the green. Snod lassies have left their churns and milking-stools to come to Burnsall Fair, and their swains look sideways at them, awe-struck a little, and sheepishly well-pleased to see Nancy's face so much rounder and merrier than its wont, or to find sedate Jobina ruffling it with the best in trim, short-skirted gown and roguish head-gear. The fells look down upon it all, grey, sombre, and surprised, and seem to wonder what madness has fallen on the little world below. The western breeze pilfers a faint odour from the pine-woods standing guard behind the green. Burnsall Bridge still brings fresh knots of folk across the peat-stained stream of Wharfe. And far up the sunlit pastures a peewit wheels and calls.

There is a stir by and by among the revellers; they look at the sun, wearing already to late afternoon, and the whisper goes abroad that it is time the runners came to toe the line. For the old fell-race is still kept up, year by year, in this white village by the Wharfe, and it braces slackened muscles to watch the staunch sport forward.

The competitors come in sight presently—five of them, deep of chest and thick of thew. The crowd flocks round the starting-point, the runners turn in expectation of the signal, then off they set, hell-for-leather up the slope—up and further up toward where a man's figure stands clear against the fell-top sky.

Steeper and steeper grows the hill, with slippery foothold for the runners ; here and there the climb is so sheer that they clutch the heather as they run, and their faces, set toward the still figure on the fell, all but touch the ground they clamber up. One of the five is down, but he struggles up and on again until a second heavy fall leaves him over-breathless to win forward ; another gives in at a score yards from the top ; and the three who have won the summit, breathing like smithy-bellows, swirl round the rustic who stands for turning-post and begin their break-neck journey down. Run, slip, scramble, they reach the bottom somehow ; the straight run home is reached, and neck for neck they thunder to the goal.

There's a fine, free air about it, a lustiness that brings echoes of old Homer to the mind. Even so they raced in Greece before white Burnsall village was built or thought of ; even so, fate willing, they will race in Burnsall for many a year to come, and that stiff clamber up the fells will teach generations yet to come the first requisites of every virtue—endurance, and the power to master difficulties.

23

The scene shifts again, as cornet and trombone send out a happy-go-lucky bidding to the dance ; and one must be a little less than man or more than human to resist the bidding that is given to all alike. The couples sort themselves. The cornet wails most tenderly ; the trombones move sturdily into the rhythm of quadrille or polka ; and then one pair of dancers, less diffident than the rest, moves down the green, and all the others follow.

Above, the fells are softening in the gathering dusk ; below, the feet glance ceaselessly over the velvet sward. Cornet and trombone quicken, but the dancers never lose the sedate and serious air which marks their revelry. Their polkas are grave, their quadrilles are faultless and serene ; they bring back a bygone atmosphere, of the times when our grandmothers danced gracefully into the hearts of our grandfathers. The cornet may wanton as it will, the trombones may call for boisterousness ; but no step of the quadrille is lost, no couple merges the polka-step into a gallop.

The moon rides white above the gloaming, and the fells are fugitive behind their mists. A grave delight is on the faces of the revellers. There is neither laughter, nor any fret of voices—only the pulse of feet upon the velvet turf. The charm of woven paces is on them, one and all, and speech would break it. Wind from the west, and moony fragrance of garden-flowers and firs. Live while ye may—and *dance.*

Again the scene changes; for there is a roomy chamber over the stables of Fell House above us there, and all the village turns its steps up the winding road. A new building with an old welcome, this Fell House; its host is Burnsall-born, and none knows better than he how to keep the ball of gaiety a-rolling. A concertina, nimbly played, replaces cornet and trombone, and soon they are moving, earnestly as ever, through polka or quadrille or the Ninepins Dance which is peculiar to the district. Lang syne is back again to-night; and, as we watch it all, it is borne in on us how at home here Will Shakespeare would have found himself. For it is testimony to the antiquity of Craven manners that all our rustics might just as easily be dancing through a comedy of Will's as keeping step to the measure of a latter-day concertina.

Faster a little now, as the night wears later, though still the paces of the measure are trimly kept. The farm-lad's eyes are tenderer, may be, with the milkmaid, and now and then a low laugh breaks from among the intertwining figures. Swirl of the music, and *thump* on the sounding boards. Jack has his Jill to-night in Burnsall village, and all is well beside Brown Wharfe.

Out into the moonlight, where the fell-quietness and the dying echoes of the dance wrestle together on the edge of silence. The dew falls heavy, sharpening the pine-fragrance. The wind sobs down the valley, and under Burnsall Bridge the water ripples soberly.

Still, white and lovesome is our village by the Wharfe, close-nestling under the strong arm of the hills.

It is night in Burnsall village. And magic walks its street.

.

.

CHAPTER XVIII

HOMEWARD BOUND

OVER Burnsall Bridge and between the limestone walls to Appletreewick. The barn on the left of the roadway there, unpretentious as it looks, has no light weight of history resting on its lichened roof, and the inscription chiselled above its doorway sums up many a year of storm and sun in the space of the one brief couplet :—

> 1512. Cabin Thatched.   House Slated. 1755
> Next for Cattle 1881 Was translated.

1512 ! A far way back, and the year before Flodden

Field was fought. Who knows but that the builder of the cabin, as he put the last touch to his thatch of straw, did not ask himself, with a slow shake of the head, if it were good to set such inflammable stuff in the way of marauding Scots. And little he guessed that the next year was to see his own over-lord of Skipton ride out with all the strength of Craven to put a wholesome check on these same Borderers.

Well, the cabin was reared, with pride, doubtless, and the satisfaction that comes of trim-done handiwork; and on its site a house was built, with yet greater pride, ten years or so after bonnie Prince Charlie, another roving Scot, came marching south; and now the house has gone the way of all pride, and cattle feed where once men ate and drank.

Not far beyond the barn, with its humble front and fancy-moving couplet, stands Appletreewick hamlet. Its familiars call it Aptrick, and it has an atmosphere that is all its own. A little hard it is, as befits its situation on the naked uplands which rise and rise until they win to sky-girt Simon's Seat; yet it does not lack softness altogether, as befits a village which lies scarce half-a-league from restful Burnsall.

Aptrick is unresponsive in full daylight, and wears something of the air of a deserted village; but that is the shell only, and its kernel is compact of old-world story. There are two Halls, important places once, within its boundaries, and in one of these a fair minstrel gallery stands over above the dining-chamber—a chamber which in its time has seen some worthy junketings. Sir John Yorke lived at this older Hall when the Cliffords lorded it at Skipton, and many a hot dispute there was, as with the Nortons, touching his right of free chase and of warren. Ay, and there was a gallant fight once on a day between Sir John's followers and my lord's ; for the knight had a fair at Aptrick, and certain shepherds of the Cliffords, carrying the pride of their betters under lowlier manners, sought to drive away a herd of sheep, which they had purchased at this fair, without paying toll for the same. The case came to trial afterwards, and it reads for all the world like a squabble of latter-day shepherd folk who come to blows at fair-time ; for the story ran, as it was told with many a contradiction in the courts, that one of Sir John's men seized a sheep by the head, while a follower of Clifford's grasped it by the tail, and that each pulled vigorously for awhile until, their patience exhausted, they dropped their bleating victim and ran in at one another with their fists. At any rate, a free fight followed, and the house of Yorke, as if another battle of Towton were in progress, right soundly trounced the followers of Lancastrian Clifford and drove them limping back to Skipton. Yorke's men, at the trial, denied that they attacked the Skipton fellows—just as to-day the victors in such a struggle are apt to fold quiet arms upon the matter and affirm that "they niver meant no harm, not they, but if folk's heads are that brittle— why, what can a man do ? "

Nor were such meetings infrequent. The right of fair at Aptrick was a minor question, and controversy raged hottest as to Sir John's claims to take such deer as he could shoot upon his manor. There was many a merry bout at fisticuffs and staves by moonlight in the forest glades, and Sir John, we fancy, filled brimming bumpers when his folk came back with tales of how they had thrashed the Skipton foresters and had brought the deer home in despite of Lord Clifford and his merry men.

That is the lighter side of Aptrick's history; but it holds, too, a quieter and more noteworthy romance of other days, for it is the birthplace of one William Craven, a peasant and the son of peasants who were over-poor to maintain him. The parish, taking pity on his friendlessness, apprenticed him to a mercer in London, paid his fare by carrier's cart, and despatched him on his long and tedious journey to town. He reached his new master in due course, much shaken, doubtless, by the journey, and bewildered by the noise and bustle of the city. We can see him, plain as if we had met him yesterday on the road, sitting in the bottom of the cart as it jolts and rumbles through Barnet village and on toward the City—a raw-cheeked country lad, in little homespun suit and thick-bottomed shoes that the cobblers of Thorp had wrought in their secluded hamlet. From time to time his head drops forward heavily, for he is wearied out; but now the cart is lumbering, past thatched cottages and country hedgerows, into the heart of London town, and the boy wakes up, rubbing two grimy knuckles into his eyes and wondering at the turmoil.

The cart stops presently at his master's door, and the lad gets down. Tears lie very close behind the blue-grey eyes; his mouth is twitching; he stands, the loneliest waif in Christendom, with the lean-faced, raucous hucksters about him, the precise, unsmiling merchants in their broadcloth, the women fighting in the kennels. The door on which the carrier has rapped is long in opening; what welcome waits behind its unresponsive face? The city folk begin to notice the lad's homespun and bewildered air, and after their kind they stop to ply him with their rapier-tongues. What chance has this rude Craven peasant among them all? For he is friendless altogether, now that the door has opened at last, now that the unknown master bids him enter, now that the Aptrick carrier has given him a last rough embrace and gone his ways with a muttered " God keep the ladkin, for he'll fret, I warrant."

No chance, it seems. Yet there was never a Whittington who turned so fruitful an ear as he toward the Bells of Bow. He attunes himself somehow to the uncleanly Babel of the city; he works with a man's will behind his laddish home-sickness; he shows himself painstaking, constant, accurate of judgment. His master trusts him, first with little, then with more. He makes forward as his own Craven folk move across the uplands, with a steady swing that is at once unfaltering and unhurried.

The bells of Bow, however, have no charmed music
for his ears; it is the Burnsall bells, soft echoing up the
vale of Wharfe, that sound for ever in his ears. There is
no temptation for him in the City life; its wiles are
noisome to him, its wickedness is mirthless and unkempt.
His eyes are turned homeward, to the cleanly, wind-
swept fells; and when the day is over, and sleep comes
to give him liberty—lo, he moves beside brown Wharfe,
and watches the fish flick lazy fins in shadowed pools,
and sees the farm folk cut lush meadow-grass in dropping
swathes. And when he wakes again to the uproar and
the fret, he is no longer solitary, but comes with new
eagerness to the work which one day is to set him free.

He could scarce fail to prosper, being what he is. He
passes from apprentice to trusted assistant, and then in
his turn he becomes a master; and wherever he touches
commerce he prospers, until the tale of his riches is
noised abroad among the great ones of the City. It makes
no difference, either to his energy or to his yearning for
the bells of Burnsall. Every day that passes finds him
but the richer, until at last the Aptrick lad, who was delivered like a bale of goods at his master's door, becomes
Sir William Craven and Lord Mayor of London town.

It makes no difference. Wharfe runs no browner for
his honours, London shows no fairer. He has earned
his liberty, and the call of *Northward* grows loud,
insistent. As cattle go to watering, this peasant-knight
returns to his own folk—the folk who paid his carriage

up to London. No trait, perhaps, is more in keeping with the Craven character than this ; there's no mock pride to bid him fight shy of those who knew him in his pauper days ; he returns, with a simplicity that is good-breeding in itself, to thank the villagers who once befriended him and to repay his debt.

The witchery and the gladness of that home-coming ! Nay, there are no words for it. Only the North-born man who has lacked his native hills knows how keen the thrill is of return ; and the glamour of it, that is half a pain, leaves him too awed for speech. We cannot set the music of such thoughts to words ; but we can move side by side with William Craven as he crosses the Barden Fells, as he notes the well-remembered landmarks, and swings up and down, down and up, the road that leads him home ; we can stand at his elbow when the first glimpse of Aptrick lies waiting for him at the turning of the way, and we can watch the man's steadfast face grow soft as a little child's. The breeze falls light toward the sunset that is dying crimson-gold all down the happy valley ; overhead the peewits give shrill welcome—the peewits, whose voice speaks more to him of home than any note of thrush or lark could do ; far off, the Burnsall bell rings curfew over gently-reeking chimneys and farm-steads greying in the sleepy twilight. We steal another glance at the wanderer's face—and we know that this one moment is worth all the fret and hardship of his London years.

From Aptrick up to Simon's Seat.

Fate has no after-sting in keeping for him. He is spared to live many a day yet among the folk he loves, under shadow of the hills that have been a watchword and a beacon to his industry. Restless only in his search after new channels for alms-giving, he travels a peaceful road to age. He rebuilds the bridge over brown Wharfe ; he endows the school to which Eugène Aram is afterwards to come as usher ; he fashions the very highway by which we fared from Burnsall up to Aptrick. He does more with his wealth, this peasant-knight, than any man in Craven, and when he dies, with the sound of Burnsall bells soft-ringing in his ears, there is but one judgment goes with him to burial—that it will be long before Aptrick village finds another friend so true as he.

The tale does not end here, with kirkyard-grasses rustling peacefully above an honoured grave. It takes instead a strange new turn, and blare of trumpets ousts the sound of Burnsall bells. Another William Craven, son of the peasant-knight, takes on the name ; he has his father's grit and honesty, but in all else he is his opposite in character. While the father was slow-moving, sure, the son is impetuous to folly ; while the father sought honour in the quiet paths of commerce, the son sees glory only in the forefront of battle. It is as if some fairy godmother had touched the mercer's yard-measure and turned it to a sword Excalibur. Before he is well out of his teens, young Craven is fighting under the Prince of

Orange in Germany and in the Netherlands, and for his services is knighted and dubbed Lord Craven in rapid sequence. Five years pass, during which the son of our Aptrick peasant is playing his part at the court of Charles the First, and playing it with grace and dignity. Then Gustavus Adolphus, whose name is in itself a trumpet-call, breaks lances with the German Emperor, and Lord Craven goes out to serve beneath the standard of the Swede. The youngster has earned his spurs already, but his valour on the field, his recklessness and devilry, rouse even the hardened Gustavus to give him caution and applause.

Love steps rosy-footed now into the tale, and a romance as strange and tender as story could invent crosses the ladlord's zest for battle. For Gustavus is fighting on behalf of the titular King of Bohemia ; and the King's consort—who is sister to Charles the First of England—is known through Europe as the Queen of Hearts, by reason of her beauty and her charm. A knot of eager youngsters gathers round her ; they fight no longer for her husband, but for the Queen of Hearts ; and any one of them would liefer lose his sword-arm than think less of his allegiance than honour bids or chivalry demands. Foremost of all the band is young Lord Craven ; the Queen looks kindly on him ; his regard for her stands out from the clash of arms, the squalor of intrigue, as something Bayard-like, something that is fashioned after the old heroic mould.

The King of Bohemia dies, but Lord Craven still fights on for his son's cause and his widow's—fights until he is driven to the wall and further struggle is but madness. The Queen of Hearts finds refuge in Holland, and Craven follows her. Sister to His Majesty of England she may be ; but she is penniless, lonely, and an exile. Lord Craven never falters in devotion ; his purse—well-filled by the pauper-lad of Aptrick—is at her command ; his help is always sought in difficulties ; chivalrous regard goes the old way of love, and an intimacy springs up between them whose meaning none can doubt. All the world looks on, and there are those who needs must whisper scandal ; but rumour, whose tongue is none of the chastest in any age, deals fairly in the main with the honour of this romantic couple, and credits them with a marriage which of necessity was kept a secret.

They live on in Holland, the Queen of Hearts and Lord Craven, through the years that see Charles the First tried and condemned by his own subjects ; and when, in consequence, Charles the Second and his Court become wanderers over the face of Europe, Craven does not stint them the last penny of his revenue. His estates are confiscated by the Commonwealth Parliament, so fervid and pronounced his zeal is for the Stuarts ; but still he maintains the loyalty and uncomplaining sacrifice of self whose roots are deep-planted in his passion for the Queen. At the Restoration, he and the Queen of Hearts

return to London ; he is one of the few whom merry
Charles the Second does not forget ; he has an earldom
bestowed on him, an estate, and many another honour
which the Crown has at its disposal. And the end of
this tale, too, is peace ; for the father who moved along
the quiet road of commerce, and the son who fought
hot-headed in the front of every fray that offered,
ran out life to its last tether and found quiet graves
at last.

The story of the Cravens moves over-bravely to be
left unquestioned. There is to-day a sort of itch for
doing old legends up afresh, and we are not surprised to
find yeoman-descent claimed on behalf of the founder of
the family. Since proof is lacking that the earlier Cravens
carried arms, the next best thing, it would seem, is to
assume that they were yeomen, and we are told how
unseemly and improbable it is that a knight, and the
father of an earl, should begin life in a lowly peasant
cradle—logic which rests upon the solitary fact that one
of Earl Craven's brothers was a knight, another a baron.
How, we are asked, should the three brothers have
reached such eminence, had their father sprung in good
truth from peasant loins ? Yet we know that Earl Craven,
for his part, won his honours by his own good sword, his
own grace of person and of courtesy. We know that
William Craven, the Lord Mayor, gained wealth enough
to set his other sons out fairly on the road of life, and
their chances of distinction would not have been bettered

by a hair's-breadth had their father been yeoman-born instead of peasant-bred. And so we decline to read modern theories into a story that rings true by merit of its very simpleness; the tale has stood for close upon two centuries, unspoiled and unadorned as when the Aptrick villagers told their children what William Craven found in London town; and we need sober proof—the proof of literal fact—before we throw to the winds a tradition as crisp and fair as any that graces Craven Fells. Are the Craven family losers by the tradition? They are the gainers—as we are whose hearts go out to the courage and the forcefulness of William Craven, peasant, knight, and very upright gentleman.

The night is fair for old-world stories in Aptrick village here. It is late September, let us say, just as it was when we came through Cobblers' Land; but the wind is quiet to-night, and a late-born second summer is tender with the fell-encircled valley. The moon rides high, and up from Wharfe river the white mists steal and wander. Appletreewick is quaint as its name to-night, and full as tender; the touch of harshness that marks its daytime mood has vanished, and its face is like a maid's who sleeps—quiet, with the dreams lying soft upon light-falling eyelids. The vale is mystic, white, moon-ridden. Not a light shows from the house-fronts; not a step disturbs the silence of grey walls and lichen-yellow roofs; only a farm-dog, far up behind us on the fell, barks fitfully.

24

It is a night for such a tale as Earl Craven's. The Queen of Hearts comes ghost-like through the mists— ghost-like, with her Stuart beauty and her Stuart hapless- ness. She turns as if expectant, and by and by another shape takes form beside her, as the courtliest gentleman in Europe returns side by side with her to the village whence his father went fortune-wards upon the bare boards of a carrier's cart. His eyes are constant with her, and she leans against his shadowy suit of mail as women rest when they have forgotten to be Queens. And she is the Queen of Hearts ; and he is no less than Bayard, with a man's hold on passion and a man's arm to prove himself loveworthy. And whenever we stand in Aptrick village, whenever we see the white mists gather from the stream, that strange romance, of love and the clash of arms, will wake again and float, faint and sweet as the music of our boyhood's dreams, across the pastures that are fed by old Wharfe river.

Well-a-day, but it's worth the while to know these lang- syne stories ! They give shape to a countryside, and people the bare stones of its houses with friendly voices. Glamour of hills and valley-lands is touched with a breath more fervid ; and the dead who add this greater glory to fell and vale take in their turn an added dignity from rolling hills and mellow, moonlit meads. And we, when we have gone—shall we leave the streets and highways that have known us the richer for our passing ? Nay, my masters ; for the age wags palsied, and the musicians

are few to-day who can catch the note to which the old
romance was tuned. Nobler than ourselves, and worthier,
we shall show when we are gone, because time in the
retrospect is apt to soften all ; but even at that there'll be
a glamour wanting, and those who hunger for the true
note of romance will pass us by and turn again to such
folk as the Cravens, who gave old Aptrick hamlet the
stories which it loves the best.

On past the farmsteads and along the road to Barden.
The way is full of hills and slacks, and sharp, precipitous
curves ; and at every turn the white mist lies in ambush.
Up yonder, fronting us, Simon's Seat uprears itself from
the bold outline of the fell. Its story—its legend, rather
—wears a humbler guise than Bayard Craven's, and
shepherd folk have given it a certain rough-spun aspect
of its own. For they say that once on a time a shepherd,
going to the fells at break of day to look after the lambing
ewes, found a starveling babe, wrapped in a woollen plaid,
on Simon's Seat. The shepherd was old with much
serving of those hard taskmasters, wind and weather ; he
had had children of his own, had reared them, and had
looked to have done with such matters for the remainder
of his days. He was puzzled. To take the child was to
begin the old round of dividing into three parts the food
that scarce sufficed for two ; there would be teething and
the like to be gone through, and wakeful nights in consequence ; it seemed a drear undertaking to one who had
served a long apprenticeship to fatherhood. Yet to leave

the bairn was scarce short of murder; its helplessness, moreover, touched a soft chord in him, and after much scratching of his scanty poll he picked up the bundle, took it down to his goodwife with a laugh that was half-ashamed and altogether foolish, and told her that they must care for the child as well as might be.

Times, however, grew harder for the shepherd. His limbs were stiffening, and he could not earn the wage he had done. Struggle as they would, the wife and he were unable to provide meat and drink wherewith to rear the foundling. So at the last he called his shepherd-brethren to a council, stated his case, and asked what should be done; and they answered one and all that they would contribute each his share and "rear t' little 'un amang 'em." And they did; and the child was named Simon Amangham in consequence; and the Amanghams live even to this day in Craven.

Moonlight and mist, and Wharfe river slipping softly over its rounded pebbles as we cross Barden Bridge. The old hunting-tower of the Cliffords creeps shadowy from the haze as we make up the hill; and now, as we draw nearer, each ruined window on this side the tower shows in the moonlight like a deep-set eye. It was here that the Shepherd Lord was wont to sit far into the night, watching the stars that were his friends, or searching among crucibles and mortars for the stone which was to turn all metals into gold. It was here, perchance, that the call to Flodden reached him, and he passed along

this road when returning from great slaughter of the
Scots. The moon is brighter now upon the battered
walls, and ghostlier on the wastes of fell. Come up the
road with us, old lord of Skipton! for the way is
lonesome, and we need such stalwart company as
yours.

Out upon the moor, with valley-lands and nestling
villages below us, and before us the drear space of silence
that stretches out and over to old Skipton. The dead folk
press round about us still, foregathering from the night.
It was on Barden Moor here that Francis Norton,
returning from the execution of his kinsfolk, was met
by the rabble and killed out of hand. There's a whisper,
surely, from across the moor ? *Here comes one of those
accursed Nortons*—it is the echo, softened by the centuries,
of that raucous cry which was young Norton's death-
warrant. A little further, and Emily Norton meets us by
the way ; her path from Rylstone Fell to Bolton has
crossed our own, and for a moment she halts spell-bound,
as if that old, unhappy cry had reached her, too. Her
head is turned, as if in expectation, toward Barden, and
in her eyes there is the seal of tragedy deep-set for ever.
And she, in her turn, passes out across the moor, with
the white doe footing it through the whiter moon-rays
and the echo of her brother's death-cry still floating down
the westward breeze.

Did not the first lord of Skipton, too, cross by this
moorland road to his last resting-place ? Still and quiet

he lay, heedless of the sad faces of his followers, untroubled by the jolting of the bier as the bearers stumbled
up the uneven road. His work was over, and he had
no longer any care to know if Bannockburn were lost or
won.

Moonlight and mist and throbbing waste of moor.
And all the way to Skipton, voices of the dead, and tumult
of the past which never dies.

Skipton sleeps brokenly to-night, and murmurs now and
then amid her dreams. Let us bid her a farewell from the
Castle leads, under the full moon that is riding white across
the cloud-flecked blue, with fell and moor and valley wide-
stretched beneath her rays. The mighty dead still keep
us company, sons of this land which wanders dream-like
into the mists of eld. Clapham and Mauleverer, Lambert
and Craven, Yorke and Radcliffe and roystering Rylstone
Nortons, come through the Castle gateway. The Shepherd
Lord has kept us company over Barden Fell, and joins
those at revel in the banquet-hall below us ; the Sailor
Earl is there, and Butcher Clifford, and Christopher Aske,
whose fame is white as the lady's honour which he
plucked from jeopardy. In among them, as they put lips
to wine, glides Fair Rosamund, frail as a dream and
sweet as the lingering after-scent of rosemary and rue ;
and she it is who claims their toast ; and Clifford, Aske
and Norton lift high their goblets and murmur " Rose of
the World," as they drain them to the dregs.

And that scene passes. The romantic dead return soft-

footed each to his own place. The moonlight and the
mist still lie on moor and fell; but they are the moors and
fells of our own day, and it is the folk that people them
who claim our fancy now. The yeomen of the Dales,
the farmer folk of Haworth parish, have ousted Clifford
and Mauleverer; yesterday is gone, but not our pride in
these straight-dealing, clean-limbed fellows of the uplands.
It is idle to praise such men, for their blunt honesty will
none of it; but to have known them—to have sat beside
them on the lang-settle o' nights and heard the old stories
cream and bubble in the cup of memory—to have felt the
touch of their courage, their keenness, their willing labour
in the face of northern wind and northern weather—that
is to learn life from a master who keeps no school beyond
the boundaries of Haworth and the Dales. However far
afield we wander, there is naught matters except home—
and our steps bend northward, always northward—and we
return, and look into the steady, blue-grey Craven eyes,
and know that it is well.

Haworth and Skipton! When the world is old beyond
belief and tired of all things, men will hear legends of the
stalwart folk who lived about Skipton and old Haworth;
and they will wonder; and it will be as though a wind
from the north-west had blown across the tattered
wreckage of the ages, bringing a clean taste to distem-
pered mouths, a strength and an uplifting to hearts outworn. And the men of Craven, when progress has filled
their places all amiss, will turn in honoured graves, and

wake, and live far down the centuries to a race that knew them not.

It is moonlight on the leads of Skipton Castle. And over yonder lie the mighty spaces of the moor. And the moor folk—God be with them—rest under shelter of the hills whose motto is

UNWIN BROTHERS, THE GRESHAM PRESS, WOKING AND LONDON.

9 780342 380732